ALIEN CONTACT

ALIEN CONTACT

EDITED BY
MARTY HALPERN

NIGHT SHADE BOOKS
SAN FRANCISCO

First Edition

ISBN: 978-1-59780-281-9

Night Shade Books
Please visit us on the web at
www.nightshadebooks.com

For Diane
whose unwavering patience with me
must be inspired by the gods.

CONTENTS

INTRODUCTION: BEGINNINGS...

MARTY HALPERN

cience fiction has always had a love affair with aliens, as far back as the early days of the pulps, with their BEM[1] covers and stories such as John W. Campbell's "Who Goes There?"[2] (written as by Don A. Stuart in *Astounding Science Fiction,* August 1938) and Murray Leinster's "First Contact" (in *Astounding Science Fiction,* May 1945).

I don't recall my age at the time, but I had the misfortune to be home alone on a Saturday afternoon when *Invaders from Mars* was the featured matinee movie on television. And to tell you the truth, I've not watched the movie again since! I'm going strictly by memory here, so bear with me if all the details in this brief recap aren't completely accurate (though I did look up the characters names on the Internet Movie Database).

As I recall, ten-year-old David MacLean wakes up one morning to a

---

1 BEM = Bug-Eyed Monster.

2 The story "Who Goes There?" has been adapted three times on the big screen: *The Thing from Another World* (1951), John Carpenter's *The Thing* (1982), and a prequel to the 1982 film, also entitled *The Thing,* which was released in October. The story is available online in its entirety: http://www.scaryforkids.com/who-goes-there-by-john-w-campbell/.

1

loud noise and bright lights outside. He rushes to his bedroom window in time to see a flying saucer land in the sand dunes just beyond the fence. He tells his father, who goes outside to investigate, but his father doesn't return home until the following day—and when he does, he behaves differently: moody, sullen, quick to anger. And, David spots an unusual, albeit small, scar on the back of his father's neck. Soon, the same personality change (and scar) affects his mother, the police chief, and other townspeople. David finally turns to, and confides in, a local doctor, Pat Blake, and she, in turn, confides in a local astronomer, Stuart Kelston. Together, they convince the Army of the danger, and the Army intercedes. The good doctor is captured by the aliens, but she is rescued just before the mind-controlling device is inserted in the back of her neck. At the climax of the film, the Army endeavors to blow up the UFO bunker, as the UFO itself attempts to lift-off. David, Doctor Pat, and others are racing down the hill, away from the UFO and the pending explosion—while the recent events pass before David's mind's eye—and then...

David awakes as from a dream, to a loud noise and bright lights outside. He rushes to his bedroom window in time to see a flying saucer land in the sand dunes just beyond the fence.

Whew! That was a creepy ending. Dream becomes reality?—not something I had ever seen in a movie, at least at that point in my young life. I can't say I had actual nightmares of that movie, but certain images were burned in my mind for many years, particularly the evil-looking alien head with the wriggling tentacles, encased in a large glass bubble, carried by two Martians: green, seven-foot-tall, primitive-looking creatures with insect like eyes. As I said, I haven't seen *Invaders from Mars* probably since I was around David's age, but the images, and feelings, still remain. (I will also admit that I haven't seen the movie *Alien*, either, since its original theater run—and a midnight showing at that; but I'll never shake the image of the alien bursting out of Kane's [John Hurt] chest.)

For me personally, it's a love/hate relationship with alien tales: they can freak the bejesus out of me—particularly movies—but I keep coming back for more. Something about the unknown, and the unknown possibilities—and the hope that, just maybe, there really is an ET out there somewhere.

This is why, in 2007, after Nick Gevers and I decided to work together on an original anthology project, I jumped at the prospect of doing Fermi Paradox-themed *Is Anybody Out There?*[3]—even though Nick presented me with a number of excellent anthology ideas.

And this is also why, on August 27, 2008, when I visited the house of Night Shade in San Francisco, and met with Jeremy Lassen, Editor-in-Chief, to discuss ongoing and future projects, I proposed an anthology of previously published "alien contact" stories. In the course of contacting authors for *Is Anybody Out There?* a few had expressed to me the fact that they had already written their Fermi Paradox story, or their first contact story, and thus weren't particularly interested in writing yet another such story. This got me to thinking: Classic Golden Age stories like Leinster's "First Contact" and Campbell's "Who Goes There?" have been collected in numerous anthologies [I strongly recommend *The Science Fiction Hall of Fame* anthology series], but not so these "contemporary classics" from, say, the past thirty years or so. Periodicals are ephemeral, and online 'zines even more so (if SCI FICTION[4] is any example). So, it falls on editors and anthologists to ensure these stories are collected for present as well as future readers.

Author James Gunn, professor emeritus of English, and director of the Center for the Study of Science Fiction, both at the University of Kansas, postulates that "humanity/the individual and the alien" is one of the fourteen Basic SF Plot Elements. Right up there with time travel, AIs, dystopian SF, space travel, etc.—though Gunn has a far more elegant way of stating these in his list.[5]

My goal with anthology *Alien Contact* is to present readers not only with an outstanding selection of fiction from the past thirty-plus years, but also to showcase just a sampling of the myriad ways writers tackle

---

3 *Is Anybody Out There?* was published by Daw Books in June 2010. A number of the stories in that anthology would have been a perfect fit for inclusion in *Alien Contact,* but I wanted to give voice to other stories. My blog has a dedicated *IAOT?* page, which includes links to the full text of six of the stories: http://martyhalpern.blogspot.com/p/is-anybody-out-there_17.html.

4 SCI FICTION, edited by Ellen Datlow, was an online magazine of sorts that published original and classic short fiction; after five and a half years, the sponsor, the SciFi Channel (now Syfy), eliminated the site because it did not generate revenue. Some online archives may still be available.

5 James Gunn's list of fourteen Basic SF Plot Elements (courtesy of author Kij Johnson): 1. far traveling; 2. the wonders of science; 3. humanity/the individual and the machine; 4. progress; 5. the individual and society; 6. humanity/the individual and the future; 7. war; 8. cataclysm; 9. humanity/the individual and their environment; 10. superpowers; 11. superman/superwoman; 12. humanity/the individual and the alien; 13. humanity/the individual and religion/spirituality; 14. miscellaneous glimpses of the future and past.

this basic plot element. When I read through these stories I just shake my head in utter awe, thinking: *How did she/he do that?* When everything comes together, just so, in a story it can simply be mind-boggling.

Though I had a number of stories in mind already, I posted a request for additional story suggestions on newsgroup rec.arts.sf.written, on private e-list *fictionmags,* and on various online SF news and information sites. I contacted about a dozen "name" authors (or their agents) to determine if each author was open to my using a particular story in a reprint anthology of this nature. Jeremy and I further discussed the project on Saturday, February 28, 2010, at Potlatch 18, held at the Domain Hotel in Sunnyvale (California). And I made another trip to the city on Thursday, June 10, 2010, to visit the new Night Shade warehouse (they had moved the previous November), at which time Jeremy and I had yet another opportunity to chat about the project. (You can't say that I'm not persistent!)

However, due to scheduling, the down economy, and other such factors, my alien contact anthology was sort of like the ongoing SETI project: just out of range of discovery.[6] Finally, on October 20, 2010, I received an email from Jeremy with the subject line: "Alien Contact: Let's Do It!"

I've been maintaining an online database of alien contact stories[7], which currently has nearly 175 stories listed. And yet, I'm sure this list of stories barely puts a dent in the subject matter. So there is certainly no shortage of quality stories.

I've had an extremely difficult time deciding on the twenty-six stories that I eventually selected for *Alien Contact.* I even had some friends and contacts read a few of the stories just to garner additional opinions. At least a half-dozen of the stories I selected were from authors who each had two (or more) stories that were perfect fits for the book—some of these stories award winners—and it nearly drove me crazy having to make a decision between the two. I also did my best to avoid overlapping plots and/or content—though I found it intriguing that so many stories have aliens as bug/insectlike beings, but the similarity ends there. And,

---

6 Sadly, after I published this introduction on my blog on April 25, the *San Jose Mercury News* online posted an article that evening with the headline: "SETI Institute to shut down alien-seeking radio dishes"—"Lacking the money to pay its operating expenses, Mountain View's SETI Institute has pulled the plug on the renowned Allen Telescope Array, a field of radio dishes that scan the skies for signals from extraterrestrial civilizations": http://www.mercurynews.com/science/ci_17926565?nclick_check=1.

7 A link to the Google Docs-based online database can be found here: http://martyhalpern.blogspot.com/p/alien-contact.html.

quite often, length was simply the deciding factor on whether I included a story or not.

I could discuss each of the stories here, with little tidbits like "art as an expression of the alien" or "the alien as both self and other"—isn't that what an introduction is all about?—but to do each story justice I would need far more words than any publisher ought to allow for a book's introduction. Besides, I would rather the stories—and their respective authors—speak for themselves.

Via email, Twitter, and posts to my Facebook page, readers had been requesting the list of stories selected for the anthology. And, as is their wont, the authors also wanted to know who their fellow contributors were. Most editors, when they've finalized the contents of an anthology, simply post the list of stories; but that list is neither intriguing nor exciting, it's merely, well, a list. Sure, a reader might become interested in a book that includes fiction by, say, Cory Doctorow, Neil Gaiman, Ursula K. Le Guin, and Charles Stross, but it's still merely a list of names and story titles. So, I decided to reveal the contents of *Alien Contact* in a rather different way: I blogged about one story each week, in their order of appearance in the book, beginning the first week of May, and on through the next twenty-five weeks. Thus by the end of October, readers—and authors—had the full contents of the anthology, just in time for the book's publication in November. The blog posts contained comments, when available, from the author on the origin of their story, and when I felt it appropriate—and not too great a spoiler—I also included quoted text from the story. At least I knew at the end of April what I would be blogging about for the next twenty-six weeks.

If you think of this book as a DVD, then these DVD extras can be found on my blog, More Red Ink, on the dedicated *Alien Contact* page: http://martyhalpern.blogspot.com/p/alien-contact.html.

I hope you enjoy reading these stories as much as I enjoyed gathering them all together in this volume.

Marty Halpern
May 2011

THE THOUGHT WAR

PAUL McAULEY

L isten:

Don't try to speak. Don't try to move. Listen to me. Listen to my story.

Everyone remembers their first time. The first time they saw a zombie and knew it for what it was. But my first time was one of the first times ever. It was so early in the invasion that I wasn't sure what was happening. So early we didn't yet call them zombies.

It was in the churchyard of St Pancras Old Church, in the fabulous, long lost city of London. Oh, it's still there, more or less; it's one of the few big cities that didn't get hit in the last, crazy days of global spasm. But it's lost to us now because it belongs to them.

Anyway, St Pancras Old Church was one of the oldest sites of Christian worship in Europe. There'd been a church there, in one form or another, for one and a half thousand years; and although the railway lines to St Pancras station ran hard by its north side it was an isolated and slightly spooky place, full of history and romance. Mary Wollstonecraft Godwin was buried there, and it was at her graveside that her daughter, who later wrote *Frankenstein*, first confessed her love to the poet Shelley, and he to her. In his first career as an architect's assistant, the novelist Thomas Hardy supervised the removal of bodies when the railway was run through part of the churchyard, and set some of the displaced gravestones around an ash tree that was later named after him.

I lived nearby. I was a freelance science journalist then, and when I was working at home and the weather was good I often ate my lunch in the churchyard. That's where I was when I saw my first zombie.

I can see that you don't understand much of this. It's all right. You are young. Things had already changed when you were born and much that was known then is unknowable now. But I'm trying to set a mood. An emotional tone. Because it's how you respond to the mood and emotions of my story that's important. That's why you have to listen carefully. That's why you are gagged and bound, and wired to my machines.

Listen:

It was a hot day in June in that ancient and hallowed ground. I was sitting on a bench in the sun-dappled shade of Hardy's ash tree and eating an egg-and-cress sandwich and thinking about the article I was writing on cosmic rays when I saw him. It looked like a man, anyway. A ragged man in a long black raincoat, ropy hair down around his face as he limped towards me with a slow and stiff gait. Halting and raising his head and looking all around, and then shambling on, the tail of his black coat dragging behind.

I didn't pay much attention to him at first. I thought he was a vagrant. We are all of us vagrants now, but in the long ago most of us had homes and families and only the most unfortunate, slaves to drink or drugs, lost souls brought down by misfortune or madness, lived on the streets. Vagrants were drawn to churchyards by the quietness and sense of ancient sanctuary, and there was a hospital at the west end of the churchyard of Old St Pancras where they went to fill their prescriptions and get treatment for illness or injury. So he wasn't an unusual sight, shambling beneath the trees in a slow and wavering march past Mary Godwin's grave towards Hardy's ash and the little church.

Then a dog began to bark. A woman with several dogs on leads and several more trotting freely called to the little wire-haired terrier that was dancing around the vagrant in a fury of excitement. Two more dogs ran up to him and began to bark too, their coats bristling and ears laid flat. I saw the vagrant stop and shake back the ropes from his face and look all around, and for the first time I saw his face.

It was dead white and broken. Like a vase shattered and badly mended. My first thought was that he'd been in a bad accident, something involving glass or industrial acids. Then I saw that what I had thought were ropes of matted hair were writhing with slow and awful independence like the tentacles of a sea creature; saw that the tattered raincoat wasn't a garment. It was his skin, falling stiff and black around him like the wings of a bat.

The dog woman started screaming. She'd had a clear look at the vagrant too. Her dogs pranced and howled and whined and barked. I was on my feet. So were the handful of other people who'd been spending a lazy lunch hour in the warm and shady churchyard. One of them must have had the presence of mind to call the police, because almost at once, or so it seemed, there was the wail of a siren and a prickle of blue lights beyond the churchyard fence and two policemen in their yellow stab vests came running.

They stopped as soon as they saw the vagrant. One talked into the radio clipped to his vest; the other began to round everyone up and lead us to the edge of the churchyard. And all the while the vagrant stood at the centre of a seething circle of maddened dogs, looking about, clubbed hands held out in a gesture of supplication. A hole yawned redly in his broken white face and shaped hoarse and wordless sounds of distress.

More police came. The road outside the churchyard was blocked off. A helicopter clattered above the tops of the trees. Men in hazmat suits entered the park. One of them carried a rifle. By this time everyone who had been in the park was penned against a police van. The police wouldn't answer our questions and we were speculating in a fairly calm and English way about terrorism. That was the great fear, in the long ago. Ordinary men moving amongst us, armed with explosives and hateful certainty.

We all started when we heard the first shot. The chorus of barks doubled, redoubled. A dog ran pell-mell out of the churchyard gate and a marksman shot it there in the road and the woman who still held the leashes of several dogs cried out. Men in hazmat suits separated us and made us walk one by one through a shower frame they'd assembled on the pavement and made us climb one by one in our wet and stinking clothes into cages in the backs of police vans.

I was in quarantine for a hundred days. When I was released, the world had changed forever. I had watched it change on TV and now I was out in it. Soldiers everywhere on the streets. Security checks and sirens and a constant low-level dread. Lynch mobs. Public hangings and burnings. Ten or twenty menezesings in London alone, each and every day. Quarantined areas cleared and barricaded. Invaders everywhere.

By now, everyone was calling them zombies. We knew that they weren't our own dead come back to walk the Earth, of course, but that's what they most looked like. More and more of them were appearing at random everywhere in the world, and they were growing more and more like us. The first zombies had been only approximations. Barely human in appearance, with a brain and lungs and a heart but little else by way of internal organs, only slabs of muscle that stored enough electrical energy to keep them alive for a day or so. But they were changing. Evolving. Adapting. After only a hundred days, they were almost human. The first had seemed monstrous and pitiful. Now, they looked like dead men walking. Animated showroom dummies. Almost human, but not quite.

After I was released from quarantine, I went back to my trade. Interviewing scientists about the invasion, writing articles. There were dozens of theories, but no real evidence to support any of them. The most popular was that we had been targeted for invasion by aliens from some far star. That the zombies were like the robot probes we had dispatched to other planets and moons in the Solar System, growing ever more sophisticated as they sent back information to their controllers. It made a kind of sense, although it didn't explain why, although they had plainly identified us as the dominant species, their controllers didn't try to contact us. Experiments of varying degrees of cruelty showed that the zombies were intelligent and self-aware, yet they ignored us unless we tried to harm or kill them. Otherwise they simply walked amongst us, and no matter how many were detected and destroyed, there were always more of them.

The most unsettling news came from an old and distinguished physicist, a Nobel laureate, who told me that certain of the fundamental physical constants seemed to be slowly and continuously changing. He had been trying to convey the urgent importance of this to the government but as I discovered when I tried to use my contacts to bring his findings to the attention of ministers and members of parliament and civil servants, the government was too busy dealing with the invasion and the consequences of the invasion.

There was an old and hopeful lie that an alien invasion would cause the nations of Earth to set aside their differences and unite against the common enemy. It didn't happen. Instead, global paranoia and suspicion ratcheted up daily. The zombies were archetypal invaders from within. Hatreds and prejudices that once had been cloaked in diplomatic evasions were now nakedly expressed. Several countries used the invasion as an excuse to attack troublesome minorities or to accuse old enemies of complicity with the zombies. There were genocidal massacres and brush fire wars across the globe. Iran attacked Iraq and Israel with nuclear weapons and what was left of Israel wiped out the capital cities of its neighbours. India attacked Pakistan. China and Russia fought along their long border. The United States invaded Cuba and Venezuela, tried to close its borders with Canada and Mexico, and took sides with China against Russia. And so on, and so on. The zombies didn't have to do anything to destroy us. We were tearing ourselves apart. We grew weaker as we fought each other and the zombies grew stronger by default.

In Britain, everyone under thirty was called up for service in the armed forces. And then everyone under forty was called up too. Three years after my first encounter, I found myself in a troop ship at the tail end of a convoy wallowing through the Bay of Biscay towards the Mediterranean. Huge columns of zombies were straggling out of the Sahara Desert. We were supposed to stop them. Slaughter them. But as we approached the Straits of Gibraltar, someone, it was never clear who, dropped a string of nuclear bombs on zombies massing in Algeria, Tunisia, Libya, and Egypt. On our ships, we saw the flashes of the bombs light the horizon. An hour later we were attacked by the remnants of the Libyan and Egyptian air forces. Half our fleet were sunk; the rest limped home. Britain's government was still intact, more or less, but everyone was in the armed forces now. Defending ourselves from the zombies and from waves of increasingly desperate refugees from the continent. There was a year without summer. Snow in July. Crops failed and despite rationing millions died of starvation and cold. There were biblical plagues of insects and all the old sicknesses came back.

And still the zombies kept appearing.

They looked entirely human now, but it was easy to tell what they were because they weren't starving, or haunted, or mad.

We kept killing them and they kept coming.

They took our cities from us and we fled into the countryside and regrouped and they came after us and we broke into smaller groups and still they came after us.

We tore ourselves apart trying to destroy them. Yet we still didn't understand them. We didn't know where they were coming from, what they were, what they wanted. We grew weaker as they grew stronger.

Do you understand me? I think that you do. Your pulse rate and pupil dilation and skin conductivity all show peaks at the key points of my story. That's good. That means that you might be human.

Listen:

Let me tell you what the distinguished old physicist told me. Let me tell you about the observer effect and Boltzmann brains.

In the nineteenth century, the Austrian physicist Ludwig Boltzmann developed the idea that the universe could have arisen from a random thermal fluctuation. Like a flame popping into existence. An explosion from nowhere. Much later, other physicists suggested that similar random fluctuations could give rise to anything imaginable, including conscious entities in any shape or form: Boltzmann brains. It was one of those contra-intuitive and mostly theoretical ideas that helped cosmologists shape their models of the universe, and how we fit into it. It helped to explain why the universe was hospitable to the inhabitants of an undistinguished planet of an average star in a not very special galaxy in a group of a million such, and that group of galaxies one of millions more. We are typical. Ordinary. And because we are ordinary, our universe is ordinary too, because there is no objective reality beyond that which we observe. Because, according to quantum entanglement, pairs of particles share information about each other's quantum states even when distance and timing means that no signal can pass between them. Because observation is not passive. Because our measurements influence the fundamental laws of the universe. They create reality.

But suppose other observers outnumbered us? What would happen then?

The probability of even one Boltzmann brain appearing in the fourteen billion years of the universe's history is vanishingly small. But perhaps something changed the local quantum field and made it more hospitable to them. Perhaps the density of our own consciousness attracted them, as the mass of a star changes the gravitation field and attracts passing comets. Or perhaps the inhabitants of another universe are interfering with our universe. Perhaps the zombies are their avatars: Boltzmann brains that pop out of the energy field and change our universe to suit their masters simply because they think differently and see things differently.

This was what the old physicist told me, in the long ago. He had evidence, too. Simple experiments that measured slow and continuous changes in the position of the absorption lines of calcium and helium and hydrogen in the sun's spectrum, in standards of mass and distance, and in the speed of light. He believed that the fundamental fabric of the universe was being altered by the presence of the zombies, and that those changes were reaching back into the past and forward into the future, just as a pebble dropped into a pond will send ripples spreading out to either side. Every time he checked the historical records of the positions of those absorption lines, they agreed with his contemporaneous measurements, even though those measurements were continuously changing. We are no longer what we once were, but we are not aware of having changed because our memories have been changed too.

Do you see why this story is important? It is not just a matter of my survival, or even the survival of the human species. It is a matter of the survival of the entire known universe. The zombies have already taken so much from us. The few spies and scouts who have successfully mingled with them and escaped to tell the tale say that they are demolishing and rebuilding our cities. Day and night they ebb and flow through the streets in tidal masses, like army ants or swarming bees, under the flickering auroras of strange energies. They are as unknowable to us as we are to them.

Listen:

This is still our world. That it is still comprehensible to us, that we can still survive in it, suggests that the zombies have not yet won an outright victory. It suggests that the tide can be turned. We have become vagrants scattered across the face of the Earth, and now we must come together and go forward together. But the zombies have become so like us that we can't trust any stranger. We can't trust someone like you, who stumbled out of the wilderness into our sanctuary. That's why you must endure this test. Like mantids or spiders, we must stage fearful courtship rituals before we can accept strangers as our own.

I want you to survive this. I really do. There are not many of us left and you are young. You can have many children. Many little observers.

Listen:

This world can be ours again. It has been many years since the war, and its old beauty is returning. Now that civilisation has been shattered, it has become like Eden again. Tell me: Is a world as wild and clean and beautiful as this not worth saving? Was the sky never so green, or grass never so blue?

HOW TO TALK TO GIRLS AT PARTIES

NEIL GAIMAN

"Come on," said Vic. "It'll be great."

"No, it won't," I said, although I'd lost this fight hours ago, and I knew it.

"It'll be brilliant," said Vic, for the hundredth time. "Girls! Girls! Girls!" He grinned with white teeth.

We both attended an all-boys' school in South London. While it would be a lie to say that we had no experience with girls—Vic seemed to have had many girlfriends, while I had kissed three of my sister's friends—it would, I think, be perfectly true to say that we both chiefly spoke to, interacted with, and only truly understood, other boys. Well, I did, anyway. It's hard to speak for someone else, and I've not seen Vic for thirty years. I'm not sure that I would know what to say to him now if I did.

We were walking the back-streets that used to twine in a grimy maze behind East Croydon station—a friend had told Vic about a party, and Vic was determined to go whether I liked it or not, and I didn't. But my parents were away that week at a conference, and I was Vic's guest at his house, so I was trailing along beside him.

"It'll be the same as it always is," I said. "After an hour you'll be off somewhere snogging the prettiest girl at the party, and I'll be in the kitchen listening to somebody's mum going on about politics or poetry or something."

"You just have to *talk* to them," he said. "I think it's probably that road at the end here." He gestured cheerfully, swinging the bag with the bottle in it.

"Don't you know?"

"Alison gave me directions and I wrote them on a bit of paper, but I left it on the hall table. S'okay. I can find it."

"How?" Hope welled slowly up inside me.

"We walk down the road," he said, as if speaking to an idiot child. "And we look for the party. Easy."

I looked, but saw no party: just narrow houses with rusting cars or bikes in their concreted front gardens; and the dusty glass fronts of newsagents, which smelled of alien spices and sold everything from birthday cards and secondhand comics to the kind of magazines that were so pornographic that they were sold already sealed in plastic bags. I had been there when Vic had slipped one of those magazines beneath his sweater, but the owner caught him on the pavement outside and made him give it back.

We reached the end of the road and turned into a narrow street of terraced houses. Everything looked very still and empty in the summer's evening. "It's all right for you," I said "They fancy you. You don't actually *have* to talk to them." It was true: one urchin grin from Vic and he could have his pick of the room.

"Nah. S'not like that. You've just got to talk."

The times I had kissed my sister's friends I had not spoken to them. They had been around while my sister was off doing something elsewhere, and they had drifted into my orbit, and so I had kissed them. I do not remember any talking. I did not know what to say to girls, and I told him so.

"They're just girls," said Vic. "They don't come from another planet."

As we followed the curve of the road around, my hopes that the party would prove unfindable began to fade: a low pulsing noise, music muffled by walls and doors, could be heard from a house up ahead. It was eight in the evening, not that early if you aren't yet sixteen, and we weren't. Not quite.

I had parents who liked to know where I was, but I don't think Vic's parents cared that much. He was the youngest of five boys. That in itself seemed magical to me: I merely had two sisters, both younger than I was, and I felt both unique and lonely. I had wanted a brother as far back as I could remember. When I turned thirteen, I stopped wishing on falling stars or first stars, but back when I did, a brother was what I had wished for.

We went up the garden path, crazy paving leading us past a hedge and a solitary rosebush to a pebble-dashed facade. We rang the doorbell, and the door was opened by a girl. I could not have told you how old she was, which was one of the things about girls I had begun to hate: when you start out as kids you're just boys and girls, going through time at the same speed, and you're all five, or seven, or eleven together. And then one day there's a lurch and the girls just sort of sprint off into the future ahead of you, they know all about everything, and they have periods and breasts and make-up and God-only-knew-what-else—for I certainly didn't. The diagrams in biology textbooks were no substitute for being, in a very real sense, young adults. And the girls of our age were.

Vic and I weren't young adults, and I was beginning to suspect that even when I started needing to shave every day, instead of once every couple of weeks, I would still be way behind.

The girl said, "Hello?"

Vic said, "We're friends of Alison's." We had met Alison, all freckles and orange hair and a wicked smile, in Hamburg, on a German Exchange. The exchange organizers had sent some girls with us, from a local girls' school, to balance the sexes. The girls, our age, more or less, were raucous and funny, and had more or less adult boyfriends with cars and jobs and motorbikes and—in the case of one girl with crooked teeth and a raccoon coat, who spoke to me about it sadly at the end of a party in Hamburg, in, of course, the kitchen—a wife and kids.

"She isn't here," said the girl at the door. "No Alison."

"Not to worry," said Vic, with an easy grin. "I'm Vic. This is Enn." A beat, and then the girl smiled back at him. Vic had a bottle of white wine in a plastic bag, removed from his parents' kitchen cabinet. "Where should I put this, then?"

She stood out of the way, letting us enter. "There's a kitchen in the back," she said "Put it on the table there, with the other bottles." She had golden, wavy hair, and she was very beautiful. The hall was dim in the twilight, but I could see that she was beautiful.

"What's your name, then?" said Vic.

She told him it was Stella, and he grinned his crooked white grin and told her that that had to be the prettiest name he had ever heard. Smooth bastard. And what was worse was that he said it like he meant it.

Vic headed back to drop off the wine in the kitchen, and I looked into the front room, where the music was coming from. There were people dancing in there. Stella walked in, and she started to dance, swaying to the music all alone, and I watched her.

This was during the early days of punk. On our own record-players we would play the Adverts and the Jam, the Stranglers and the Clash and the Sex Pistols. At other people's parties you'd hear ELO or 10cc or even Roxy Music. Maybe some Bowie, if you were lucky. During the German Exchange, the only LP that we had all been able to agree on was Neil Young's *Harvest,* and his song "Heart of Gold" had threaded through the trip like a refrain: *I crossed the ocean for a heart of gold…*

The music that was playing in that front room wasn't anything I recognized. It sounded a bit like a German electronic pop group called Kraftwerk, and a bit like an LP I'd been given for my last birthday, of strange sounds made by the BBC Radiophonic Workshop. The music had a beat, though, and the half-dozen girls in that room were moving gently to it, although I was only looking at Stella. She shone.

Vic pushed past me, into the room. He was holding a can of lager. "There's booze back in the kitchen," he told me. He wandered over to Stella and he began to talk to her. I couldn't hear what they were saying over the music, but I knew that there was no room for me in that conversation.

I didn't like beer, not back then. I went off to see if there was something I wanted to drink. On the kitchen table stood a large bottle of Coca-Cola, and I poured myself a plastic tumblerful, and I didn't dare say anything to the pair of girls who were talking in the underlit kitchen. They were animated, and utterly lovely. Each of them had very black skin and glossy hair and movie-star clothes, and their accents were foreign, and each of them was out of my league.

I wandered, Coke in hand.

The house was deeper than it looked, larger and more complex than the two-up two-down model I had imagined. The rooms were underlit—I doubt there was a bulb of more than forty watts in the building—and each room I went into was inhabited: in my memory, inhabited only by girls. I did not go upstairs.

A girl was the only occupant of the conservatory. Her hair was so fair it was white, and long, and straight, and she sat at the glass-topped table, her hands clasped together, staring at the garden outside, and the gathering dusk. She seemed wistful.

"Do you mind if I sit here?" I asked, gesturing with my cup. She shook her head, and then followed it up with a shrug, to indicate that it was all the same to her. I sat down.

Vic walked past the conservatory door. He was talking to Stella, but he looked in at me, sitting at the table, wrapped in shyness and awkwardness, and he opened and closed his hand in a parody of a speaking mouth. *Talk.* Right.

"Are you from round here?" I asked the girl.

She shook her head. She wore a low-cut silvery top, and I tried not to stare at the swell of her breasts.

I said, "What's your name? I'm Enn."

"Wain's Wain," she said, or something that sounded like it. "I'm a second."

"That's uh. That's a different name."

She fixed me with huge liquid eyes. "It indicates that my progenitor was also Wain, and that I am obliged to report back to her. I may not breed."

"Ah. Well. Bit early for that anyway, isn't it?"

She unclasped her hands, raised them above the table, spread her fingers. "You see?" The little finger on her left hand was crooked, and it bifurcated at the top, splitting into two smaller fingertips. A minor deformity. "When I was finished a decision was needed. Would I be retained, or eliminated? I was fortunate that the decision was with me. Now, I travel, while my more perfect sisters remain at home in stasis. They were firsts. I am a second.

"Soon I must return to Wain, and tell her all I have seen. All my impressions of this place of yours."

"I don't actually live in Croydon," I said. "I don't come from here." I wondered if she was American. I had no idea what she was talking about.

"As you say," she agreed, "neither of us comes from here." She folded her six-fingered left hand beneath her right, as if tucking it out of sight. "I had expected it to be bigger, and cleaner, and more colorful. But still, it is a jewel."

She yawned, covered her mouth with her right hand, only for a moment, before it was back on the table again. "I grow weary of the journeying, and I wish sometimes that it would end. On a street in Rio, at Carnival, I saw them on a bridge, golden and tall and insect-eyed and winged, and elated I almost ran to greet them, before I saw that they were only people in costumes. I said to Hola Colt, 'Why do they try so hard to look like us?' and Hola Colt replied, 'Because they hate themselves, all shades of pink and brown, and so small.' It is what I experience, even me, and I am not grown. It is like a world of children, or of elves." Then she smiled, and said, "It was a good thing they could not any of them see Hola Colt."

"Um," I said, "do you want to dance?"

She shook her head immediately. "It is not permitted," she said. "I can do nothing that might cause damage to property. I am Wain's."

"Would you like something to drink, then?"

"Water," she said.

I went back to the kitchen and poured myself another Coke, and filled a cup with water from the tap. From the kitchen back to the hall, and from there into the conservatory, but now it was quite empty.

I wondered if the girl had gone to the toilet, and if she might change her mind about dancing later. I walked back to the front room and stared in. The place was filling up. There were more girls dancing, and several lads I didn't know, who looked a few years older than me and Vic. The lads and the girls all kept their distance, but Vic was holding Stella's hand as they danced, and when the song ended he put an arm around her, casually, almost proprietorially, to make sure that nobody else cut in.

I wondered if the girl I had been talking to in the conservatory was now upstairs, as she did not appear to be on the ground floor.

I walked into the living room, which was across the hall from the room where the people were dancing, and I sat down on the sofa. There was a girl sitting there already. She had dark hair, cut short and spiky; and a nervous manner.

Talk, I thought. "Um, this mug of water's going spare," I told her, "if you want it?"

She nodded, and reached out her hand and took the mug, extremely carefully, as if she were unused to taking things, as if she could trust neither her vision nor her hands.

"I love being a tourist," she said, and smiled, hesitantly. She had a gap between her two front teeth, and she sipped the tap water as if she were an adult sipping a fine wine. "The last tour, we went to sun, and we swam in sunfire pools with the whales. We heard their histories and we shivered in the chill of the outer places, then we swam deepward where the heat churned and comforted us.

"I wanted to go back. This time, I wanted it. There was so much I had not seen. Instead we came to world. Do you like it?"

"Like what?"

She gestured vaguely to the room—the sofa, the armchairs, the curtains, the unused gas fire.

"It's all right, I suppose."

"I told them I did not wish to visit world," she said. "My parent-teacher was unimpressed. 'You will have much to learn,' it told me. I said, 'I could learn more in sun, again. Or in the deeps. Jessa spun webs between galaxies. I want to do that.'

"But there was no reasoning with it, and I came to world. Parent-teacher engulfed me, and I was here, embodied in a decaying lump of meat hanging on a frame of calcium. As I incarnated I felt things deep inside me, fluttering and pumping and squishing. It was my first experience with pushing air through the mouth, vibrating the vocal chords on the way, and I used it to tell parent-teacher that I wished that I would die, which it acknowledged was the inevitable exit strategy from world."

There were black worry beads wrapped around her wrist, and she fiddled with them as she spoke. "But knowledge is there, in the meat," she said, "and I am resolved to learn from it."

We were sitting close at the centre of the sofa now. I decided I should put an arm around her, but casually. I would extend my arm along the back of the sofa and eventually sort of creep it down, almost imperceptibly, until it was touching her. She said, "The thing with the liquid in the eyes, when the world blurs. Nobody told me, and I still do not understand. I have touched the folds of the Whisper and pulsed and flown with the tachyon swans, and I still do not understand."

She wasn't the prettiest girl there, but she seemed nice enough, and she was a girl, anyway. I let my arm slide down a little, tentatively, so that it made contact with her back, and she did not tell me to take it away.

Vic called to me then, from the doorway. He was standing with his arm around Stella, protectively, waving at me. I tried to let him know, by shaking my head, that I was on to something, but he called my name, and, reluctantly, I got up from the sofa, and walked over to the door. "What?"

"Er. Look. The party," said Vic, apologetically. "It's not the one I thought it was. I've been talking to Stella and I figured it out. Well, she sort of explained it to me. We're at a different party."

"Christ. Are we in trouble? Do we have to go?"

Stella shook her head. He leaned down and kissed her, gently, on the lips. "You're just happy to have me here, aren't you, darlin'?"

"You know I am," she told him.

He looked from her back to me, and he smiled his white smile: roguish, loveable, a little bit Artful Dodger, a little bit wide-boy Prince Charming. "Don't worry. They're all tourists here anyway. It's a foreign exchange thing, innit? Like when we all went to Germany."

"It is?"

"Enn. You got to *talk* to them. And that means you got to listen to them too. You understand?"

"I *did*. I already talked to a couple of them."

"You getting anywhere?"

"I was till you called me over."

"Sorry about that. Look, I just wanted to fill you in. Right?"

And he patted my arm and he walked away with Stella. Then, together, the two of them went up the stairs.

Understand me, all the girls at that party, in the twilight, were lovely; they all had perfect faces, but, more important than that, they had whatever strangeness of proportion, of oddness or humanity it is that makes a beauty something more than a shop-window dummy. Stella was the most lovely of any of them, but she, of course, was Vic's, and they were going upstairs together, and that was just how things would always be.

There were several people now sitting on the sofa, talking to the gap-toothed girl. Someone told a joke, and they all laughed. I would have had to push my way in there to sit next to her again, and it didn't look like she was expecting me back, or cared that I had gone, so I wandered out into the hall. I glanced in at the dancers, and found myself wondering where the music was coming from. I couldn't see a record player, or speakers.

From the hall I walked back to the kitchen.

Kitchens are good at parties. You never need an excuse to be there, and, on the good side, at this party I couldn't see any signs of someone's mum. I inspected the various bottles and cans on the kitchen table, then I poured a half an inch of Pernod into the bottom of my plastic cup, which I filled to the top with Coke. I dropped in a couple of ice cubes, and took a sip, relishing the sweet-shop tang of the drink.

"What's that you're drinking?" A girl's voice.

"It's Pernod," I told her. "It tastes like aniseed balls, only it's alcoholic." I didn't say that I'd only tried it because I'd heard someone in the crowd ask for a Pernod on a live Velvet Underground LP.

"Can I have one?" I poured another Pernod, topped it off with Coke, passed it to her. Her hair was a coppery auburn, and it tumbled around her head in ringlets. It's not a hair style you see much now, but you saw it a lot back then.

"What's your name?" I asked.

"Triolet," she said.

"Pretty name," I told her, although I wasn't sure that it was. She was pretty, though.

"It's a verse form," she said, proudly. "Like me."

"You're a poem?"

She smiled, and looked down and away, perhaps bashfully. Her profile was almost flat—a perfect Grecian nose that came down from her forehead in a straight line. We did *Antigone* in the school theatre the previous year. I was the messenger who brings Creon the news of Antigone's death. We wore half-masks that made us look like that. I thought of that play, looking at her face, in the kitchen, and I thought of Barry Smith's drawings of women in the *Conan* comics: five years later I would have thought of the Pre-Raphaelites, of Jane Morris and Lizzie Siddall. But I was only fifteen, then.

"You're a poem?" I repeated.

She chewed her lower lip. "If you want. I am a poem, or I am a pattern, or a race of people whose world was swallowed by the sea."

"Isn't it hard to be three things at the same time?"

"What's your name?"

"Enn."

"So you are Enn," she said. "And you are a male. And you are a biped. Is it hard to be three things at the same time?"

"But they aren't different things. I mean, they aren't contradictory." It was a word I had read many times but never said aloud before that night, and I put the stresses in the wrong places. *Contradictory.*

She wore a thin dress, made of a white, silky fabric. Her eyes were a pale green, a color that would now make me think of tinted contact lenses; but this was thirty years ago: things were different then. I remember wondering about Vic and Stella, upstairs. By now, I was sure that they were in one of the bedrooms, and I envied Vic so much it almost hurt.

Still, I was talking to this girl, even if we were talking nonsense, even if her name wasn't really Triolet (my generation had not been given hippy names: all the Rainbows and the Sunshines and the Moons, they were only six, seven, eight years old back then). She said, "We knew that it would soon be over, and so we put it all into a poem, to tell the universe who we were, and why we were here, and what we said and did and thought and dreamed and yearned for. We wrapped our dreams in words and patterned the words so that they would live forever, un-forgettable. Then we sent the poem as a pattern of flux, to wait in the heart of a star, beaming out its message in pulses and bursts and fuzzes across the electromagnetic spectrum, until the time when, on worlds a thousand sun-systems distant, the pattern would be decoded and read, and it would become a poem once again."

"And then what happened?"

She looked at me with her green eyes, and it was as if she stared out at me from her own Antigone half-mask; but as if her pale green eyes were just a different, deeper, part of the mask. "You cannot hear a poem without it changing you," she told me. "They heard it, and it colonized them. It inherited them and it inhabited them, its rhythms becoming part of the way that they thought; its images permanently transmuting their metaphors; its verses, its outlook, its aspirations becoming their lives. Within a generation their children would be born already knowing the poem, and, sooner rather than later, as these things go, there were no more children born. There was no need for them, not any longer. There was only a poem, which took flesh and walked and spread itself across the vastness of the known."

I edged closer to her, so I could feel my leg pressing against hers.

She seemed to welcome it: she put her hand on my arm, affectionately, and I felt a smile spreading across my face.

"There are places that we are welcomed," said Triolet, "and places where we are regarded as a noxious weed, or as a disease, something immediately to be quarantined and eliminated. But where does contagion end and art begin?"

"I don't know," I said, still smiling. I could hear the unfamiliar music as it pulsed and scattered and boomed in the front room.

She leaned into me then and—I suppose it was a kiss…I suppose. She pressed her lips to my lips, anyway, and then, satisfied, she pulled back, as if she had now marked me as her own.

"Would you like to hear it?" she asked, and I nodded, unsure what she was offering me, but certain that I needed anything she was willing to give me.

She began to whisper something in my ear. It's the strangest thing about poetry—you can tell it's poetry, even if you don't speak the language. You can hear Homer's Greek without understanding a word, and you still know it's poetry. I've heard Polish poetry; and Inuit poetry, and I knew what it was without knowing. Her whisper was like that. I didn't know the language, but her words washed through me, perfect, and in my mind's eye I saw towers of glass and diamond; and people with eyes of the palest green; and, unstoppable, beneath every syllable, I could feel the relentless advance of the ocean.

Perhaps I kissed her properly. I don't remember. I know I wanted to.

And then Vic was shaking me violently. "Come on!" he was shouting. "Quickly. Come on!"

In my head I began to come back from a thousand miles away.

"Idiot. Come on. Just get a move on," he said, and he swore at me. There was fury in his voice.

For the first time that evening I recognized one of the songs being played in the front room. A sad saxophone wail followed by a cascade of liquid chords, a man's voice singing cut-up lyrics about the sons of the silent age. I wanted to stay and hear the song.

She said, "I am not finished. There is yet more of me."

"Sorry, love," said Vic, but he wasn't smiling any longer. "There'll be another time," and he grabbed me by the elbow and he twisted and pulled, forcing me from the room. I did not resist. I knew from experience that Vic could beat the stuffing out me if he got it into his head to do so. He wouldn't do it unless he was upset or angry, but he was angry now.

Out into the front hall. As Vic pulled open the door, I looked back one last time, over my shoulder, hoping to see Triolet in the doorway to the kitchen, but she was not there. I saw Stella, though, at the top of the stairs. She was staring down at Vic, and I saw her face.

This all happened thirty years ago. I have forgotten much, and I will forget more, and in the end I will forget everything; yet, if I have any certainty of life beyond death, it is all wrapped up not in psalms or hymns, but in this one thing alone: I cannot believe that I will ever forget that moment, or forget the expression on Stella's face as she watched Vic hurrying away from her. Even in death I shall remember that.

Her clothes were in disarray, and there was make-up smudged across her face, and her eyes—

You wouldn't want to make a universe angry. I bet an angry universe would look at you with eyes like that.

We ran then, me and Vic, away from the party and the tourists and the twilight, ran as if a lightning storm was on our heels, a mad helter-skelter dash down the confusion of streets, threading through the maze, and we did not look back, and we did not stop until we could not breathe; and then we stopped and panted, unable to run any longer. We were in pain. I held on to a wall, and Vic threw up, hard and long, into the gutter.

He wiped his mouth.

"She wasn't a—" He stopped.

He shook his head.

Then he said, "You know... I think there's a thing. When you've gone as far as you dare. And if you go any further, you wouldn't be you anymore? You'd be the person who'd done that? The places you just can't go.... I think that happened to me tonight."

I thought I knew what he was saying. "Screw her, you mean?" I said.

He rammed a knuckle hard against my temple, and twisted it violently. I wondered if I was going to have to fight him—and lose—but after a moment he lowered his hand and moved away from me, making a low, gulping noise.

I looked at him curiously, and I realized that he was crying: his face was scarlet; snot and tears ran down his cheeks. Vic was sobbing in the street, as unselfconsciously and heartbreakingly as a little boy.

He walked away from me then, shoulders heaving, and he hurried down the road so he was in front of me and I could no longer see his face. I wondered what had occurred in that upstairs room to make him behave like that, to scare him so, and I could not even begin to guess.

The streetlights came on, one by one; Vic went on ahead, while I trudged down the street behind him in the dusk, my feet treading out the measure of a poem that, try as I might, I could not properly remember and would never be able to repeat.

FACE VALUE

KAREN JOY FOWLER

I t was almost like being alone. Taki, who had been alone one way or another most of his life, recognized this and thought he could deal with it. What choice did he have? It was only that he had allowed himself to hope for something different. A second star, small and dim, joined the sun in the sky, making its appearance over the rope bridge which spanned the empty river. Taki crossed the bridge in a hurry to get inside before the hottest part of the day began.

Something flashed briefly in the dust at his feet and he stooped to pick it up. It was one of Hesper's poems, half finished, left out all night. Taki had stopped reading Hesper's poetry. It reflected nothing, not a whisper of her life here with him, but was filled with longing for things and people behind her. Taki pocketed the poem on his way to the house, stood outside the door, and removed what dust he could with the stiff brush which hung at the entrance. He keyed his admittance; the door made a slight sucking sound as it resealed behind him.

Hesper had set out an iced glass of ade for him. Taki drank it at a gulp, superimposing his own dusty fingerprints over hers sketched lightly in

29

the condensation on the glass. The drink was heavily sugared and only made him thirstier.

A cloth curtain separated one room from another, a blue sheet, Hesper's innovation since the dwelling was designed as a single, multifunctional space. Through the curtain Taki heard a voice and knew Hesper was listening again to her mother's letter—earth weather, the romances of her younger cousins. The letter had arrived weeks ago, but Taki was careful not to remind Hesper how old its news really was. If she chose to imagine the lives of her family moving along the same timeline as her own, then this must be a fantasy she needed. She knew the truth. In the time it had taken her to travel here with Taki, her mother had grown old and died. Her cousins had settled into marriages happy or unhappy or had faced life alone. The letters which continued to arrive with some regularity were an illusion. A lifetime later Hesper would answer them.

Taki ducked through the curtain to join her. "Hot," he told her as if this were news. She lay on their mat stomach down, legs bent at the knees, feet crossed in the air. Her hair, the color of dried grasses, hung over her face. Taki stared for a moment at the back of her head. "Here," he said. He pulled her poem from his pocket and laid it by her hand. "I found this out front."

Hesper switched off the letter and rolled onto her back away from the poem. She was careful not to look at Taki. Her cheeks were stained with irregular red patches so that Taki knew she had been crying again. The observation caused him a familiar mixture of sympathy and impatience. His feelings for Hesper always came in these uncomfortable combinations; it tired him.

"'Out front,'" Hesper repeated, and her voice held a practiced tone of uninterested nastiness. "And how did you determine that one part of this featureless landscape was the 'front'?"

"Because of the door. We have only the one door so it's the front door."

"No," said Hesper. "If we had two doors then one might arguably be the front door and the other the back door, but with only one it's just the door." Her gaze went straight upward. "You use words so carelessly. Words from another world. They mean nothing here." Her eyelids fluttered briefly, the lashes darkened with tears. "It's not just an annoyance to me, you know," she said. "It can't help but damage your work."

"My work is the study of the mene," Taki answered. "Not the creation of a new language," and Hesper's eyes closed.

"I really don't see the difference," she told him. She lay a moment longer without moving, then opened her eyes and looked at Taki directly. "I don't want to have this conversation. I don't know why I started it. Let's rewind, run it again. I'll be the wife this time. You come in and say, 'Honey, I'm home!' and I'll ask you how your morning was."

Taki began to suggest that this was a scene from another world and would mean nothing here. He had not yet framed the sentence when he heard the door seal release and saw Hesper's face go hard and white. She reached for her poem and slid it under the scarf at her waist. Before she could get to her feet the first of the mene had joined them in the bedroom. Taki ducked through the curtain to fasten the door before the temperature inside the house rose. The outer room was filled with dust and the hands which reached out to him as he went past left dusty streaks on his clothes and his skin. He counted eight of the mene, fluttering about him like large moths, moths the size of human children, but with furry vestigial wings, hourglass abdomens, sticklike limbs. They danced about him in the open spaces, looked through the cupboards, pulled the tapes from his desk. When they had their backs to him he could see the symmetrical arrangement of dark spots which marked their wings in a pattern resembling a human face. A very sad face, very distinct. Masculine, Taki had always thought, but Hesper disagreed.

The party which had made initial contact under the leadership of Hans Mene so many years ago had wisely found the faces too whimsical for mention in their report. Instead they had included pictures and allowed them to speak for themselves. Perhaps the original explorers had been asking the same question Hesper posed the first time Taki showed her the pictures. Was the face really there? Or was this only evidence of the ability of humans to see their own faces in everything? Hesper had a poem entitled "The Kitchen God," which recounted the true story of a woman about a century ago who had found the image of Christ in the burn-marks on a tortilla. "Do *they* see it, too?" she had asked Taki, but there was as yet no way to ask this of the mene, no way to know if they had reacted with shock and recognition to the faces of the first humans they had seen, though studies of the mene eye suggested a finer depth perception which might significantly distort the flat image.

Taki thought that Hesper's own face had changed since the day, only six months ago calculated as Travel-time, when she had said she would come here with him and he thought it was because she loved him. They had sorted through all the information which had been collected to date on the mene and her face had been all sympathy then. "What would it be like," she asked him, "to be able to fly and then to lose this ability? To outgrow it? What would a loss like that do to the racial consciousness of a species?"

"It happened so long ago, I doubt it's even noticed as a loss," Taki had answered. "Legends, myths not really believed perhaps. Probably not even that. In the racial memory not even a whisper."

Hesper had ignored him. "What a shame they don't write poetry," she had said. She was finding them less romantic now as she joined Taki in the outer room, her face stoic. The mene surrounded her, ran their string-fingered hands all over her body, inside her clothing. One mene attempted to insert a finger into her mouth, but Hesper tightened her lips together resolutely, dust on her chin. Her eyes were fastened on Taki. Accusingly? Beseechingly? Taki was no good at reading people's eyes. He looked away.

Eventually the mene grew bored. They left in groups, a few lingering behind to poke among the boxes in the bedroom, then following the others until Hesper and Taki were left alone. Hesper went to wash herself as thoroughly as their limited water supply allowed; Taki swept up the loose dust. Before he finished, Hesper returned, showing him her empty jewelry box without a word. The jewelry had all belonged to her mother.

"I'll get them when it cools," Taki told her.

"Thank you."

It was always Hesper's things that the mene took. The more they disgusted her, pawing over her, rummaging through her things, no way to key the door against clever mene fingers even if Taki had agreed to lock them out, which he had not, the more fascinating they seemed to find her. They touched her twice as often as they touched Taki and much more insistently. They took her jewelry, her poems, her letters, all the things she treasured most, and Taki believed, although it was far too early in his studies really to speculate with any assurance, that the mene read something off the objects. The initial explorers had concluded that mene communication was entirely telepathic, and if this was accurate, then Taki's speculation was not such a leap. Certainly the mene didn't value the objects for themselves. Taki always found them discarded in the dust on this side of the rope bridge.

The fact that everything would be easily recovered did nothing to soften Hesper's sense of invasion. She mixed herself a drink, stirring it with the metal straw which poked through the dust-proof lid. "You shouldn't allow it," she said at last, and Taki knew from the time that had elapsed that she had tried not to begin this familiar conversation. He appreciated her effort as much as he was annoyed by her failure.

"It's part of my job," he reminded her. "We have to be accessible to them. I study them. They study us. There's no way to differentiate the two activities and certainly no way to establish communication except simultaneously."

"You're letting them study us, but you're giving them a false picture. You're allowing them to believe that humans intrude on each other in this way. Does it occur to you that they may be involved in similar charades? If so, what can either of us learn?"

Taki took a deep breath. "The need for privacy may not be as intrinsically human as you imagine. I could point to many societies which afforded very little of this. As for any deliberate misrepresentations on their part—well, isn't that the whole rationale for not sending a study team? Wouldn't I be farther along if I were working with environmentalists, physiologists, linguists? But the risk of contamination increases exponentially with each additional human. We would be too much of a presence. Of course, I will be very careful. I am far from the stage in my study where I can begin to draw conclusions. When I visit them..."

"Reinforcing the notion that such visits are ordinary human behavior..." Hesper was looking at Taki with great coolness.

"When I visit them I am much more circumspect," Taki finished. "I conduct my study as unobtrusively as possible."

"And what do you imagine you are studying?" Hesper asked. She closed her lips tightly over the straw and drank. Taki regarded her steadily and with exasperation.

"Is this a trick question?" he asked. "I imagine I am studying the mene. What do you imagine I am studying?"

"What humans always study," said Hesper. "Humans."

• • •

You never saw one of the mene alone. Not ever. One never wandered off to watch the sun set or took its food to a solitary hole to eat without sharing. They did everything in groups and although Taki had been observing them for weeks now and was able to identify individuals and had compiled charts of the groupings he had seen, trying to isolate families or friendships or work-castes, still the results were inconclusive.

His attempts at communication were similarly discouraging. He had tried verbalizations, but had not expected a response to them; he had no idea how they processed audio information although they could hear. He had tried clapping and gestures, simple hand signals for the names of common objects. He had no sense that these efforts were noticed. They were so unfocused when he dealt with them, fluttering here, fluttering there. Taki's ESP quotient had never been measurable, yet he tried that route, too. He tried to send a simple command. He would trap a mene hand and hold it against his own cheek, trying to form in his mind the picture which corresponded to the action. When he released the hand, sticky mene fingers might linger for a moment or they might slip away immediately, tangle in his hair instead, or tap his teeth. Mene teeth were tiny and pointed like wires. Taki saw them only when the mene ate. At other times they were hidden inside the folds of skin which almost hid their eyes as well. Taki speculated that the skin flaps protected their mouths and eyes from the dust. Taki found mene faces less expressive than their backs. Head-on they appeared petaled and blind as flowers. When he wanted to differentiate one mene from another, Taki looked at their wings.

Hesper had warned him there would be no art and he had asked her how she could be so sure. "Because their communication system is perfect," she said. "Out of one brain and into the next with no loss of meaning, no need for abstraction. Art arises from the inability to communicate. Art is the imperfect symbol. Isn't it?" But Taki, watching the mene carry water up from their underground deposits, asked himself where the line between tools and art objects should be drawn. For no functional reason that he could see, the water containers curved in the centers like the shapes of the mene's own abdomens.

Taki followed the mene below ground, down some shallow, rough-cut stairs into the darkness. The mene themselves were slightly luminescent

when there was no other light; at times and seasons some were spec-
tacularly so and Taki's best guess was that this was sexual. Even with
the dimmer members, Taki could see well enough. He moved through
a long tunnel with a low ceiling which made him stoop. He could hear
water at the other end of it, not the water itself, but a special quality to
the silence which told him water was near. The lake was clearly artificial, collected during the rainy season which no human had seen yet.
The tunnel narrowed sharply. Taki could have gone forward, but felt
suddenly claustrophobic and backed out instead. What did the mene
think, he wondered, of the fact that he came here without Hesper. Did
they notice this at all? Did it teach them anything about humans that
they were capable of understanding?

"Their lives together are perfect," Hesper said. "Except for those useless wings. If they are ever able to talk with us at all it will be because
of those wings."

Of course Hesper was a poet. The world was all language as far as she
was concerned.

When Taki first met Hesper, at a party given by a colleague of his, he
had asked her what she did. "I name things," she had said. "I try to find
the right names for things." In retrospect Taki thought it was bullshit. He
couldn't remember why he had been so impressed with it at the time, a
deliberate miscommunication, when a simple answer, "I write poetry,"
would have been so clear and easy to understand. He felt the same way
about her poetry itself, needlessly obscure, slightly evocative, but it left
the reader feeling that he had fallen short somehow, that it had been a
test and he had flunked it. It was unkind poetry and Taki had worked
so hard to read it then.

"Am I right?" he would ask her anxiously when he finished. "Is that
what you're saying?" but she would answer that the poem spoke for itself.

"Once it's on the page, I've lost control over it. Then the reader deter-
mines what it says or how it works." Hesper's eyes were gray, the irises
so large and intense within their dark rings, that they made Taki dizzy
"So you're always right. By definition. Even if it's not remotely close to
what I intended."

What Taki really wanted was to find himself in Hesper's poems. He
would read them anxiously for some symbol which could be construed
as him, some clue as to his impact on her life. But he was never there.

• • •

It was against policy to send anyone into the field alone. There were pros and cons, of course, but ultimately the isolation of a single professional was seen as too cruel. For shorter projects there were advantages in sending a threesome, but during a longer study the group dynamics in a trio often became difficult. Two were considered ideal and Taki knew that Rawji and Heyen had applied for this post, a husband and wife team in which both members were trained for this type of study. He had never stopped being surprised that the post had been offered to him instead. He could not have even been considered if Hesper had not convinced the members of the committee of her willingness to accompany him, but she must have done much more. She must have impressed someone very much for them to decide that one trained xenologist and one poet might be more valuable than two trained xenologists. The committee had made some noises about "contamination" occurring between the two trained professionals, but Taki found this argument specious. "What did you say to them?" he asked her after her interview and she shrugged.

"You know," she said. "Words."

Taki had hidden things from the committee during his own interview. Things about Hesper. Her moods, her deep attachment to her mother, her unreliable attachment to him. He must have known it would never work out, but he walked about in those days with the stunned expression of a man who has been given everything. Could he be blamed for accepting it? Could he be blamed for believing in Hesper's unexpected willingness to accompany him? It made a sort of equation for Taki. *If* Hesper was willing to give up everything and come with Taki, *then* Hesper loved Taki. An ordinary marriage commitment was reviewable every five years; this was something much greater. No other explanation made any sense.

The equation still held a sort of inevitability for Taki. *Then* Hesper loved Taki, *if* Hesper were willing to come with him. So somehow, sometime, Taki had done something which lost him Hesper's love. If he could figure out what, perhaps he could make her love him again. "Do you love me?" he had asked Hesper, only once; he had too much pride for these thinly disguised pleadings. "Love is such a difficult word," she had answered, but her voice had been filled with a rare softness and had not hurt Taki as much as it might.

The daystar was appearing again when Taki returned home. Hesper had made a meal which suggested she was coping well today. It included a sort of pudding made of a local fruit they found themselves able to tolerate. Hesper called the pudding "boxty." It was apparently a private joke. Taki was grateful for the food and the joke, even if he didn't understand it. He tried to keep the conversation lighthearted, talking to Hesper about the mene water jars. Taki's position was that when the form of a practical object was less utilitarian than it might be, then it was art. Hesper laughed. She ran through a list of human artifacts and made him classify them.

"A paper clip," she said.

"The shape hasn't changed in centuries," he told her. "Not art."

"A safety pin."

Taki hesitated. How essential was the coil at the bottom of the pin? Very. "Not art," he decided.

"A hair brush."

"Boar bristle?"

"Wood handle."

"Art. Definitely."

She smiled at him. "You're confusing ornamentation with art. But why not? It's as good a definition as any," she told him. "Eat your boxty."

They spend the whole afternoon alone, uninterrupted. Taki transcribed the morning's notes into his files, reviewed his tapes. Hesper recorded a letter whose recipient would never hear it and sang softly to herself.

That night he reached for her, his hand along the curve at her waist. She stiffened slightly, but responded by putting her hand on his face. He kissed her and her mouth did not move. His movements became less gentle. It might have been passion; it might have been anger. She told him to stop, but he didn't. Couldn't. Wouldn't. "Stop," she said again and he heard she was crying. "They're here. Please stop. They're watching us."

"Studying us," Taki said. "Let them," but he rolled away and released her. They were alone in the room. He would have seen the mene easily in the dark. "Hesper," he said. "There's no one here."

She lay rigid on her side of their bed. He saw the stitching of her backbone disappearing into her neck and had a sudden feeling that he could see everything about her, how she was made, how she was held together. It made him no less angry.

"I'm sorry," Hesper told him, but he didn't believe her. Even so, he was asleep before she was. He made his own breakfast the next morning without leaving anything out for her. He was gone before she had gotten out of bed.

The mene were gathering food, dried husks thick enough to protect the liquid fruit during the two-star dry season. They punctured the husks with their needle-thin teeth. Several crowded about him, greeting him with their fingers, checking his pockets, removing his recorder and passing it about until one of them dropped it in the dust. When they returned to work, Taki retrieved it, wiped it as clean as he could. He sat down to watch them, logged everything he observed. He noted in particular how often they touched each other and wondered what each touch meant. Affection? Communication? Some sort of chain of command?

Later he went underground again, choosing another tunnel, looking for one which wouldn't narrow so as to exclude him, but finding himself beside the same lake with the same narrow access ahead. He went deeper this time until it gradually became too close for his shoulders. Before him he could see a luminescence; he smelled the dusty odor of the mene and could just make out a sound, too, a sort of movement, a grass-rubbing-together sound. He stooped and strained his eyes to see something in the faint light. It was like looking into the wrong end of a pair of binoculars. The tunnel narrowed and narrowed. Beyond it must be the mene homes and he could never get into them. He contrasted this with the easy access they had to his home. At the end of his vision he thought he could just see something move, but he wasn't sure. A light touch on the back of his neck and another behind his knee startled him. He twisted around to see a group of the mene crowded into the tunnel behind him. It gave him a feeling of being trapped and he had to force himself to be very gentle as he pushed his way back and let the mene go through. The dark pattern of their wings stood in high relief against the luminescent bodies. The human faces grew smaller and smaller until they disappeared.

• • •

"Leave me alone," Hesper told him. It took Taki completely by surprise. He had done nothing but enter the bedroom; he had not even spoken yet. "Just leave me alone."

Taki saw no signs that Hesper had ever gotten up. She lay against the pillow and her cheek was still creased from the wrinkles in the sheets. She had not been crying. There was something worse in her face, something which alarmed Taki.

"Hesper?" he asked. "Hesper? Did you eat anything? Let me get you something to eat."

It took Hesper a moment to answer. When she did, she looked ordinary again. "Thank you," she said. "I am hungry." She joined him in the outer room, wrapped in their blanket, her hair tangled around her face. She got a drink for herself, dropping the empty glass once, stooping to retrieve it. Taki had the strange impression that the glass fell slowly. When they had first arrived, the gravitational pull had been light, just perceptibly lighter than Earth's. Without quite noticing, this had registered on him in a sort of lightheartedness. But Hesper had complained of feelings of dislocation, disconnection. Taki put together a cold breakfast, which Hesper ate slowly, watching her own hands as if they fascinated her. Taki looked away. "Fork," she said. He looked back. She was smiling at him.

"What?"

"Fork."

He understood. "Not art."

"Four tines?"

He didn't answer.

"Roses carved on the handle."

"Well then, art. Because of the handle. Not because of the tines." He was greatly reassured.

The mene came while he was telling her about the tunnel. They put their dusty fingers in her food, pulled it apart. Hesper set her fork down and pushed the plate away. When they reached for her she pushed them away, too. They came back. Hesper shoved harder.

"Hesper," said Taki.

"I just want to be left alone. They never leave me alone." Hesper stood up, towering above the mene. The blanket fell to the floor. "We flew here," Hesper said to the mene. "Did you see the ship? Didn't you see the pod? Doesn't that interest you? Flying?" She laughed and flapped her arms until they froze, horizontal at her sides. The mene reached for her again and she brought her arms in to protect her breasts, pushing the mene away repeatedly, harder and harder, until they tired of approaching her and went into the bedroom, reappearing with her poems in their hands. The door sealed behind them.

"I'll get them back for you," Taki promised, but Hesper told him not to bother.

"I haven't written in weeks," she said. "In case you hadn't noticed. I haven't finished a poem since I came here. I've lost that. Along with everything else." She brushed at her hair rather frantically with one hand. "It doesn't matter," she added. "My poems? Not art."

"Are you the best person to judge that?" Taki asked.

"Don't patronize me." Hesper returned to the table, looked again at the plate which held her unfinished breakfast, dusty from handling. "My critical faculties are still intact. It's just the poetry that's gone." She took the dish to clean it, scraped the food away. "I was never any good," she said. "Why do you think I came here? I had no poetry of my own so I thought I'd write the mene's. I came to a world without words. I hoped it would be clarifying. I knew there was a risk." Her hands moved very fast. "I want you to know I don't blame you."

"Come and sit down a moment, Hesper," Taki said, but she shook her head. She looked down at her body and moved her hands over it.

"They feel sorry for us. Did you know that? They feel sorry about our bodies."

"How do *you* know that?" Taki asked.

"Logic. We have these completely functional bodies. No useless wings. Not art." Hesper picked up the blanket and headed for the bedroom. At the cloth curtain she paused a moment. "They love our loneliness, though. They've taken all mine. They never leave me alone now." She thrust her right arm suddenly out into the air. It made the curtain ripple. "Go away," she said, ducking behind the sheet.

Taki followed her. He was very frightened. "No one is here but us, Hesper," he told her. He tried to put his arms around her but she pushed him back and began to dress.

"Don't touch me all the time," she said. He sank onto the bed and watched her. She sat on the floor to fasten her boots.

"Are you going out, Hesper?" he asked and she laughed.

"Hesper is out," she said. "Hesper is out of place, out of time, out of luck, and out of her mind. Hesper has vanished completely. Hesper was broken into and taken."

Taki fastened his hands tightly together. "Please don't do this to me, Hesper," he pleaded. "It's really so unfair. When did I ask so much of you? I took what you offered me; I never took anything else. Please don't do this."

Hesper had found the brush and was pulling it roughly through her hair. He rose and went to her, grabbing her by the arms, trying to turn her to face him. "Please, Hesper!"

She shook loose from him without really appearing to notice his hands, continued to work through the worst of her tangles. When she did turn around, her face was familiar, but somehow not Hesper's face. It was a face which startled him.

"Hesper is gone," it said. "We have her. You've lost her. We are ready to talk to you. Even though you will never, never, never understand." She reached out to touch him, laying her open palm against his cheek and leaving it there.

THE ROAD NOT TAKEN

Harry Turtledove

Captain Togram was using the chamberpot when the *Indomitable* broke out of hyperdrive. As happened all too often, nausea surged through the Roxolan officer. He raised the pot and was abruptly sick into it.

When the spasm was done, he set the thundermug down and wiped his streaming eyes with the soft, gray-brown fur of his forearm. "The gods curse it!" he burst out. "Why don't the shipmasters warn us when they do that?" Several of his troopers echoed him more pungently.

At that moment, a runner appeared in the doorway. "We're back in normal space," the youth squeaked, before dashing on to the next chamber. Jeers and oaths followed him: "No shit!" "Thanks for the news!" "Tell the steerers—they might not have got the word!"

Togram sighed and scratched his muzzle in annoyance at his own irritability. As an officer, he was supposed to set an example for his soldiers. He was junior enough to take such responsibilities seriously, but had had enough service to realize he should never expect too much from anyone more than a couple of notches above him. High ranks went to those with ancient blood or fresh money.

Sighing again, he stowed the chamberpot in its niche. The metal cover he slid over it did little to relieve the stench. After sixteen days in space, the *Indomitable* reeked of ordure, stale food, and staler bodies. It was no better in any other ship of the Roxolan fleet, or any other. Travel between the stars was simply like that. Stinks and darkness were part of the price the soldiers paid to make the kingdom grow.

Togram picked up a lantern and shook it to rouse the glowmites inside. They flashed silver in alarm. Some races, the captain knew, lit their ships with torches or candles, but glowmites used less air, even if they could only shine intermittently.

Ever the careful soldier, Togram checked his weapons while the light lasted. He always kept all four of his pistols loaded and ready to use; when landing operations began, one pair would go on his belt, the other in his boottops. He was more worried about his sword. The perpetually moist air aboard ship was not good for the blade. Sure enough, he found a spot of rust to scour away.

As he polished the rapier, he wondered what the new system would be like. He prayed for it to have a habitable planet. The air in the *Indomitable* might be too foul to breathe by the time the ship could get back to the nearest Roxolan-held planet. That was one of the risks starfarers took. It was not a major one—small yellow suns usually shepherded a life-bearing world or two—but it was there.

He wished he hadn't let himself think about it; like an aching fang, the worry, once there, would not go away. He got up from his pile of bedding to see how the steerers were doing.

As usual with them, both Ransisc and his apprentice Olgren were complaining about the poor quality of the glass through which they trained their spyglasses. "You ought to stop whining," Togram said, squinting in from the doorway. "At least you have light to see by." After seeing so long by glowmite lantern, he had to wait for his eyes to adjust to the harsh raw sunlight flooding the observation chamber before he could go in.

Olgren's ears went back in annoyance. Ransisc was older and calmer. He set his hand on his apprentice's arm. "If you rise to all of Togram's jibes, you'll have time for nothing else—he's been a troublemaker since he came out of the egg. Isn't that right, Togram?"

"Whatever you say." Togram liked the white-muzzled senior steerer. Unlike most of his breed, Ransisc did not act as though he believed his important job made him something special in the gods' scheme of things.

Olgren stiffened suddenly; the tip of his stumpy tail twitched. "This one's a world!" he exclaimed.

"Let's see," Ransisc said. Olgren moved away from his spyglass. The two steerers had been examining bright stars one by one looking for those that would show discs and prove themselves actually to be planets.

"It's a world," Ransisc said at length, "but not one for us—those yellow, banded planets always have poisonous air, and too much of it." Seeing Olgren's dejection, he added, "It's not a total loss—if we look along a line from that planet to its sun, we should find others fairly soon."

"Try that one," Togram said, pointing toward a ruddy star that looked brighter than most of the others he could see.

Olgren muttered something haughty about knowing his business better than any amateur, but Ransisc said sharply, "The captain has seen more worlds from space than you, sirrah. Suppose you do as he asks." Ears drooping dejectedly, Olgren obeyed.

Then his pique vanished. "A planet with green patches!" he shouted.

Ransisc had been aiming his spyglass at a different part of the sky, but that brought him hurrying over. He shoved his apprentice aside, fiddled with the spyglass' focus, peered long at the magnified image. Olgren was hopping from one foot to the other, his muddy-brown fur puffed out with impatience to hear the verdict.

"Maybe," said the senior steerer, and Olgren's face lit, but it fell again as Ransisc continued, "I don't see anything that looks like open water. If we find nothing better, I say we try it, but let's search a while longer."

"You've just made a luof very happy," Togram said. Ransisc chuckled. The Roxolani brought the little creatures along to test new planets' air. If a luof could breathe it in the airlock of a flyer, it would also be safe for the animal's masters.

The steerers growled in irritation as several stars in a row stubbornly stayed mere points of light. Then Ransisc stiffened at his spyglass. "Here it is," he said softly. "This is what we want. Come here, Olgren."

"Oh, my, yes," the apprentice said a moment later.

"Go report it to Warmaster Slevon, and ask him if his devices have picked up any hyperdrive vibrations except for the fleet's." As Olgren hurried away, Ransisc beckoned Togram over. "See for yourself."

The captain of foot bent over the eyepiece. Against the black of space, the world in the spyglass field looked achingly like Roxolan: deep ocean blue, covered with swirls of white cloud. A good-sized moon hung nearby. Both were in approximately half-phase, being nearer their star than was the *Indomitable*.

"Did you spy any land?" Togram asked.

"Look near the top of the image, below the ice cap," Ransisc said. "Those browns and greens aren't colors water usually takes. If we want any world in this system, you're looking at it now."

They took turns examining the distant planet and trying to sketch its features until Olgren came back. "Well?" Togram said, though he saw the apprentice's ears were high and cheerful.

"Not a hyperdrive emanation but ours in the whole system!" Olgren grinned. Ransisc and Togram both pounded him on the back, as if he were the cause of the good news and not just its bearer.

The captain's smile was even wider than Olgren's. This was going to be an easy one, which, as a professional soldier, he thoroughly approved of. If no one hereabouts could build a hyperdrive, either the system had no intelligent life at all or its inhabitants were still primitives, ignorant of gunpowder, fliers, and other aspects of warfare as it was practiced among the stars.

He rubbed his hands. He could hardly wait for landfall.

•••

Buck Herzog was bored. After four months in space, with five and a half more staring him in the face, it was hardly surprising. Earth was a bright star behind the *Ares III*, with Luna a dimmer companion; Mars glowed ahead.

"It's your exercise period, Buck," Art Snyder called. Of the five-person crew, he was probably the most officious.

"All right, Pancho." Herzog sighed. He pushed himself over to the bicycle and began pumping away, at first languidly, then harder. The work helped keep calcium in his bones in spite of free fall. Besides, it was something to do.

Melissa Ott was listening to the news from home. "Fernando Valenzuela died last night," she said.

"Who?" Snyder was not a baseball fan.

Herzog was, and a Californian to boot. "I saw him at an old-timers' game once, and I remember my dad and my grandfather always talking about him," he said. "How old was he, Mel?"

"Seventy-nine," she answered.

"He always was too heavy," Herzog said sadly.

"Jesus Christ!"

Herzog blinked. No one on the *Ares III* had sounded that excited since liftoff from the American space station. Melissa was staring at the radar screen. "Freddie!" she yelled.

Frederica Lindstrom, the ship's electronics expert, had just gotten out of the cramped shower space. She dove for the control board, still trailing a stream of water droplets. She did not bother with a towel; modesty aboard the *Ares III* had long since vanished.

Melissa's shout even made Claude Jonnard stick his head out of the little biology lab where he spent most of his time. "What's wrong?" he called from the hatchway.

"Radar's gone to hell," Melissa told him.

"What do you mean, gone to hell?" Jonnard demanded indignantly. He was one of those annoying people who thought quantitatively all the time, and thought everyone else did, too.

"There are about a hundred, maybe a hundred fifty, objects on the screen that have no right to be there," answered Frederica Lindstrom, who had a milder case of the same disease. "Range appears to be a couple of million kilometers."

"They weren't there a minute ago, either," Melissa said. "I hollered when they showed up."

As Frederica fiddled with the radar and the computer, Herzog stayed on the exercise bike, feeling singularly useless: What good is a geologist millions of kilometers away from rocks? He wouldn't even get his name in the history books—no one remembers the crew of the third expedition to anywhere.

Frederica finished her checks. "I can't find anything wrong," she said, sounding angry at herself and the equipment both.

"Time to get on the horn to Earth, Freddie," Art Snyder said. "If I'm going to land this beast, I can't have the radar telling me lies."

Melissa was already talking into the microphone. "Houston, this is *Ares III*. We have a problem—"

Even at light-speed, there were a good many minutes of waiting. They crawled past, one by one. Everyone jumped when the speaker crackled to life. "*Ares III*, this is Houston Control. Ladies and gentlemen, I don't quite know how to tell you this, but we see them too."

The communicator kept talking, but no one was listening to her anymore. Herzog felt his scalp tingle as his hair, in primitive reflex, tried to stand on end. Awe filled him. He had never thought he would live to see humanity contact another race. "Call them, Mel," he said urgently.

She hesitated. "I don't know, Buck. Maybe we should let Houston handle this."

"Screw Houston," he said, surprised at his own vehemence. "By the time the bureaucrats down there figure out what to do, we'll be coming down on Mars. We're the people on the spot. Are you going to throw away the most important moment in the history of the species?"

Melissa looked from one of her crewmates to the next. Whatever she saw in their faces must have satisfied her, for she shifted the aim to the antenna and began to speak: "This is the spacecraft *Ares III*, calling the unknown ships. Welcome from the people of Earth." She turned off the transmitter for a moment. "How many languages do we have?"

The call went out in Russian, Mandarin, Japanese, French, German, Spanish, even Latin. "Who knows the last time, they may have visited?" Frederica said when Snyder gave her an odd look.

If the wait for a reply from Earth had been long, this one was infinitely worse. The delay stretched far, far past the fifteen-second speed-of-light round trip. "Even if they don't speak any of our languages, shouldn't they say something?" Melissa demanded of the air. It did not answer, nor did the aliens.

Then, one at a time, the strange ships began darting away sunward, toward Earth. "My God, the acceleration!" Snyder said. "Those are no rockets!" He looked suddenly sheepish; "I don't suppose starships would have rockets, would they?"

The *Ares III* lay alone again in its part of space, pursuing its Hohmann orbit inexorably toward Mars. Buck Herzog wanted to cry.

•••

As was their practice, the ships of the Roxolan fleet gathered above the pole of the new planet's hemisphere with the most land. Because everyone would be coming to the same spot, the doctrine made visual rendezvous easy. Soon only four ships were unaccounted for. A scoutship hurried around to the other pole, found them, and brought them back.

"Always some waterlovers every trip," Togram chuckled to the steerers as he brought them the news. He took every opportunity he could to go to their dome, not just for the sunlight but also because, unlike many soldiers, he was interested in planets for their own sake. With any head for figures, he might have tried to become a steerer himself.

He had a decent hand with quill and paper, so Ransisc and Olgren were willing to let him spell them at the spyglass and add to the sketchmaps they were making of the world below.

"Funny sort of planet," he remarked. "I've never seen one with so many forest fires or volcanoes or whatever they are on the dark side."

"I still think they're cities," Olgren said, with a defiant glance at Ransisc.

"They're too big and too bright," the senior steerer said patiently; the argument, plainly, had been going on for some time.

"This is your first trip off-planet, isn't it, Olgren?" Togram asked.

"Well, what if it is?"

"Only that you don't have enough perspective. Egelloc on Roxolan has almost a million people, and from space it's next to invisible at night. It's nowhere near as bright as those lights, either. Remember, this is a primitive planet. I admit it looks like there's intelligent life down there, but how could a race that hasn't even stumbled across the hyperdrive build cities ten times as great as Egelloc?"

"I don't know," Olgren said sulkily. "But from what little I can see by moonlight, those lights look to be in good spots for cities—on coasts, or along rivers, or whatever."

Ransisc sighed. "What are we going to do with him, Togram? He's so sure he knows everything, he won't listen to reason. Were you like that when you were young?"

"Till my clanfathers beat it out of me, anyway. No need getting all excited, though. Soon enough the flyers will go down with their luofi, and then we'll know." He swallowed a snort of laughter, then sobered abruptly, hoping he hadn't been as gullible as Olgren when he was young.

•••

"I have one of the alien vessels on radar," the SR-81 pilot reported. "It's down to 80,000 meters and still descending." He was at his own plane's operational ceiling, barely half as high as the ship entering atmosphere.

"For God's sake, hold your fire," ground control ordered. The command had been drummed into him before he took off, but the brass were not about to let him forget. He did not really blame them. One trigger-happy idiot could ruin humanity forever.

"I'm beginning to get a visual image," he said, glancing at the head-up display projected in front of him. A moment later he added, "It's one damn funny-looking ship, I can tell you that already. Where are the wings?"

"We're picking up the image now too," the ground control officer said. "They must use the same principle for their in-atmosphere machines as they do for their spacecraft: some sort of antigravity that gives them both lift and drive capability."

The alien ship kept ignoring the SR-81, just as all the aliens had ignored every terrestrial signal beamed at them. The craft continued its slow descent, while the SR-81 pilot circled below, hoping he would not have to go down to the aerial tanker to refuel.

"One question answered," he called to the ground. "It's a warplane." No craft whose purpose was peaceful would have had those glaring eyes and that snarling, fang-filled mouth painted on its belly. Some USAF ground-attack aircraft carried similar markings.

At last the alien reached the level at which the SR-81 was loitering. The pilot called the ground again. "Permission to pass in front of the aircraft?" he asked. "Maybe everybody's asleep in there and I can wake 'em up."

After a long silence, ground control gave grudging ascent. "No hostile gestures," the controller warned.

"What do you think I'm going to do, flip him the finger?" the pilot muttered, but his radio was off. Acceleration pushed him back in his seat as he guided the SR-81 into a long, slow turn that would carry it about half a kilometer in front of the vessel from the spacefleet.

His airplane's camera gave him a brief glimpse of the alien pilot, who was sitting behind a small, dirty windscreen.

The being from the stars saw him, too. Of that there was no doubt.

The alien jinked like a startled fawn, performing maneuvers that would have smeared the SR-81 pilot against the walls of his pressure cabin—if his aircraft could have matched them in the first place.

"I'm giving pursuit!" he shouted. Ground control screamed at him, but he was the man on the spot. The surge from his afterburner made the pressure he had felt before a love pat by comparison.

Better streamlining made his plane faster than the craft from the starships, but that did not do him much good. Every time its pilot caught sight of him, the alien ship danced away with effortless ease. The SR-81 pilot felt like a man trying to kill a butterfly with a hatchet.

To add to his frustration, his fuel warning light came on. In any case, his aircraft was designed for the thin atmosphere at the edge of space, not the increasingly denser air through which the alien flew. He swore, but he had to pull away.

As his SR-81 gulped kerosene from the tanker, he could not help wondering what would have happened if he'd turned a missile loose. There were a couple of times he'd had a perfect shot. That was one thought he kept firmly to himself. What his superiors would do if they knew about it was too gruesome to contemplate.

•••

The troopers crowded round Togram as he came back from the officers' conclave. "What's the word, Captain?" "Did the luof live?" "What's it like down there?"

"The luof lived, boys!" Togram said with a broad smile.

His company raised a cheer that echoed deafeningly in the barracks room. "We're going down!" they whooped. Ears stood high in excitement. Some soldiers waved plumed hats in the fetid air. Others, of a bent more like their captain's, went over to their pallets and began seeing to their weapons.

"How tough are they going to be, sir?" a gray-furred veteran named Ilingua asked as Togram went by. "I hear the flier pilot saw some funny things."

Togram's smile got wider. "By the heavens and hells, Ilingua, haven't you done this often enough to know better than pay heed to rumors you hear before planetfall?"

"I hope so, sir," Ilingua said, "but these are so strange I thought there might be something to them." When Togram did not answer, the trooper shook his head at his own foolishness and shook up a lantern so he could examine his dagger's edge.

As inconspicuously as he could, the captain let out a sigh. He did not know what to believe himself, and he had listened to the pilot's report. How could the locals have flying machines when they did not know contragravity? Togram had heard of a race that used hot air balloons before it discovered the better way of doing things, but no balloon could have reached the altitude the locals' flier had achieved, and no balloon could have changed direction, as the pilot had violently insisted this craft had done.

Assume he was wrong, as he had to be. But how was one to take his account of towns as big as the ones whose possibility Ransisc had ridiculed, of a world so populous there was precious little open space? And lantern signals from other ships showed their scout pilots were reporting the same wild improbabilities.

Well, in the long run it would not matter if this race was as numerous as reffo at a picnic. There would simply be that many more subjects here for Roxolan.

•••

"This is a terrible waste," Billy Cox said to anyone who would listen as he slung his duffel bag over his shoulder and tramped out to the waiting truck. "We should be meeting the star people with open arms, not with a show of force."

"You tell 'em, Professor," Sergeant Santas Amoros chuckled from behind him. "Me, I'd sooner stay on my butt in a nice, air-conditioned barracks than face L.A. summer smog and sun any old day. Damn shame you're just a Spec-1. If you was president, you could give the orders any way you wanted, instead o' takin' 'em."

Cox didn't think that was very fair either. He'd been just a few units short of his M.A. in poli sci when the big buildup after the second Syrian crisis sucked him into the army.

He had to fold his lanky length like a jackknife to get under the olive-drab canopy of the truck and down into the passenger compartment.

The seats were too hard and too close together. Jamming people into the vehicle counted for more than their comfort while they were there. Typical military thinking, Cox thought disparagingly.

The truck filled. The big diesel rumbled to life. A black soldier dug out a deck of cards and bet anyone that he could turn twenty-five cards into five pat poker hands. A couple of greenhorns took him up on it. Cox had found out the expensive way that it was a sucker bet. The black man was grinning as he offered the deck to one of his marks to shuffle.

Riffff! The ripple of the pasteboards was authoritative enough to make everybody in the truck turn their heads. "Where'd you learn to handle cards like that, man?" demanded the black soldier, whose name was Jim but whom everyone called Junior.

"Dealing blackjack in Vegas." *Riffff!*

"Hey, Junior," Cox called, "all of a sudden I want ten bucks of your action."

"Up yours too, pal," Junior said, glumly watching the cards move as if they had lives of their own.

The truck rolled northward, part of a convoy of trucks, MICVs, and light tanks that stretched for miles. An entire regiment was heading into Los Angeles, to be billeted by companies in different parts of the sprawling city. Cox approved of that; it made it less likely that he would personally come face-to-face with any of the aliens.

"Sandy," he said to Amoros, who was squeezed in next to him, "even if I'm wrong and the aliens aren't friendly, what the hell good will hand weapons do? It'd be like taking on an elephant with a safety pin."

"Professor, like I told you already, they don't pay me to think, or you neither. Just as well, too. I'm gonna do what the lieutenant tells me, and you're gonna do what I tell you, and everything is gonna be fine, right?"

"Sure," Cox said, because Sandy, while he wasn't a bad guy, was a sergeant. All the same, the Neo-Armalite between Cox's boots seemed very futile, and his helmet and body armor as thin and gauzy as a stripper's negligee.

•••

The sky outside the steerers' dome began to go from black to deep blue as the *Indomitable* entered atmosphere. "There," Olgren said, pointing.

"That's where we'll land."

"Can't see much from this height," Togram remarked.

"Let him use your spyglass, Olgren," Ransisc said. "He'll be going back to his company soon."

Togram grunted; that was more than a comment—it was also a hint. Even so, he was happy to peer through the eyepiece. The ground seemed to leap toward him. There was a moment of disorientation as he adjusted to the inverted image, which put the ocean on the wrong side of the field of view. But he was not interested in sightseeing. He wanted to learn what his soldiers and the rest of the troops aboard the *Indomitable* would have to do to carve out a beachhead and hold it against the locals.

"There's a spot that looks promising," he said. "The greenery there in the midst of the buildings in the eastern—no, the western—part of the city. That should give us a clear landing zone, a good campground, and a base for landing reinforcements."

"Let's see what you're talking about," Ransisc said, elbowing him aside. "Hmm, yes, I see the stretch you mean. That might not be bad. Olgren, come look at this. Can you find it again in the warmaster's spyglass? All right then, go point it out to him. Suggest it as our set down point."

The apprentice hurried away. Ransisc bent over the eyepiece again. "Hmm," he repeated. "They build tall down there, don't they?"

"I thought so," Togram said. "And there's a lot of traffic on those roads. They've spent a fortune cobblestoning them all, too; I didn't see any dust kicked up."

"This should be a rich conquest," Ransisc said.

Something swift, metallic, and predator-lean flashed past the observation window. "By the gods, they do have fliers, don't they?" Togram said. In spite of the pilots' claims, deep down he hadn't believed it until he saw it for himself.

He noticed Ransisc's ears twitching impatiently, and realized he really had spent too much time in the observation room. He picked up his glowmite lantern and went back to his troopers.

A couple of them gave him a resentful look for being away so long, but he cheered them up by passing on as much as he could about their landing site. Common soldiers loved nothing better than inside information. They second-guessed their superiors without it, but the game was even more fun when they had some idea of what they were talking about.

A runner appeared in the doorway. "Captain Togram, your company will planet from airlock three."

"Three," Togram acknowledged, and the runner trotted off to pass orders to other ground troop leaders. The captain put his plumed hat on his head (the plume was scarlet, so his company could recognize him in combat), checked his pistols one last time, and ordered his troopers to follow him.

The reeking darkness was as oppressive in front of the inner airlock door as anywhere else aboard the *Indomitable,* but somehow easier to bear. Soon the doors would swing open and he would feel fresh breezes riffling his fur, taste sweet clean air, enjoy sunlight for more than a few precious units at a stretch. Soon he would measure himself against these new beings in combat.

He felt the slightest of jolts as the *Indomitable*'s fliers launched themselves from the mother ship. There would be no luofi aboard them this time, but musketeers to terrorize the natives with fire from above, and jars of gunpowder to be touched off and dropped. The Roxolani always strove to make as savage a first impression as they could. Terror doubled their effective numbers.

Another jolt came, different from the one before. They were down.

•••

A shadow spread across the UCLA campus. Craning his neck, Junior said, "Will you look at the size of the mother!" He had been saying that for the last five minutes, as the starship slowly descended.

Each time, Billy Cox could only nod, his mouth dry, his hands clutching the plastic grip and cool metal barrel of his rifle. The Neo-Armalite seemed totally impotent against the huge bulk floating so arrogantly downward. The alien flying machines around it were as minnows beside a whale, while they in turn dwarfed the USAF planes circling at a greater distance. The roar of their jets assailed the ears of the nervous troops and civilians on the ground. The aliens' engines were eerily silent.

The starship landed in the open quad between New Royce, New Haines, New Kinsey, and New Powell halls. It towered higher than any of the two-story redbrick buildings, each a reconstruction of one overthrown in the earthquake of 2034. Cox heard saplings splinter under the weight of the alien craft. He wondered what it would have done to the big trees that had fallen five years ago along with the famous old halls.

"All right, they've landed. Let's move on up," Lieutenant Shotton ordered. He could not quite keep the wobble out of his voice, but he trotted south toward the starship. His platoon followed him past Dickson Art Center, past New Bunche Hall. Not so long ago, Billy Cox had walked this campus barefoot. Now his boots thudded on concrete.

The platoon deployed in front of Dodd Hall, looking west toward the spacecraft. A little breeze toyed with the leaves of the young, hopeful trees planted to replace the stalwarts lost to the quake.

"Take as much cover as you can," Lieutenant Shotton ordered quietly. The platoon scrambled into flowerbeds, snuggled down behind thin treetrunks. Out on Hilgard Avenue, diesels roared as armored fighting vehicles took positions with good lines of fire.

It was all such a waste, Cox thought bitterly. The thing to do was to make friends with the aliens, not to assume automatically they were dangerous.

Something, at least, was being done along those lines. A delegation came out of Murphy Hall and slowly walked behind a white flag from the administration building toward the starship. At the head of the delegation was the mayor of Los Angeles: the president and governor were busy elsewhere. Billy Cox would have given anything to be part of the delegation instead of sprawled here on his belly in the grass. If only the aliens had waited until he was fifty or so, had given him a chance to get established.

Sergeant Amoros nudged him with an elbow. "Look there, man. Something's happening—"

Amoros was right. Several hatchways which had been shut were swinging open, allowing Earth's air to mingle with the ship's.

The westerly breeze picked up. Cox's nose twitched. He could not name all the exotic odors wafting his way, but he recognized sewage and garbage when he smelled them. "God, what a stink!" he said.

• • •

"By the gods, what a stink!" Togram exclaimed. When the outer airlock doors went down, he had expected real fresh air to replace the stale, overused gases inside the *Indomitable*. This stuff smelled like smoky peat fires, or lamps whose wicks hadn't quite been extinguished. And it stung! He felt the nictitating membranes flick across his eyes to protect them.

"Deploy!" he ordered, leading his company forward. This was the tricky part. If the locals had nerve enough, they could hit the Roxolani just as the latter were coming out of their ship, and cause all sorts of trouble. Most races without hyperdrive, though, were too overawed by the arrival of travelers from the stars to try anything like that. And if they didn't do it fast, it would be too late.

They weren't doing it here. Togram saw a few locals, but they were keeping respectful distance. He wasn't sure how many there were. Their mottled skins—or was that clothing?—made them hard to notice and count. But they were plainly warriors, both by the way they acted and by the weapons they bore.

His own company went into its familiar two-line formation, the first crouching, the second standing and aiming their muskets over the heads of the troops in front.

"Ah, there we go." Togram said happily. The bunch approaching behind the white banner had to be the local nobles. The mottling, the captain saw, was clothing, for these beings wore entirely different garments, somber except for strange, narrow neckcloths. They were taller and skinnier than Roxolani, with muzzleless faces.

"Ilingua!" Togram called. The veteran trooper led the right flank squad of the company.

"Sir!"

"Your troops, quarter-right face. At the command, pick off the leaders there. That will demoralize the rest," Togram said, quoting standard doctrine.

"Slowmatches ready!" Togram said. The Roxolani lowered the smoldering cords to the touchholes of their muskets. "Take your aim!" The guns moved, very slightly. "Fire!"

• • •

"Teddy bears!" Sandy Amoros exclaimed. The same thought had leaped into Cox's mind. The beings emerging from the spaceship were round, brown, and furry, with long noses and big ears. Teddy bears, however, did not normally carry weapons. They also, Cox thought, did not commonly live in a place that smelled like sewage. Of course it might have been perfume to them. But if it was, they and Earthpeople were going to have trouble getting along.

He watched the Teddy bears as they took their positions. Somehow their positioning did not suggest that they were forming an honor guard for the mayor and his party. Yet it did look familiar to Cox, although he could not quite figure out why.

Then he had it. If he had been anywhere but at UCLA, he would not have made the connection. But he remembered a course he had taken on the rise of the European nation-states in the sixteenth century, and on the importance of the professional, disciplined armies the kings had created. Those early armies had performed evolutions like this one.

It was a funny coincidence. He was about to mention it to his sergeant when the world blew up.

Flames spurted from the aliens' guns. Great gouts of smoke puffed into the sky. Something that sounded like an angry wasp buzzed past Cox's ear. He heard shouts and shrieks from either side. Most of the mayor's delegation was down, some motionless, others thrashing.

There was a crash from the starship, and another one an instant later as a roundshot smashed into the brickwork of Dodd Hall. A chip stung Cox in the back of the neck. The breeze brought him the smell of fireworks, one he had not smelled for years.

•••

"Reload!" Togram yelled. "Another volley, then at 'em with the bayonet!" His troopers worked frantically, measuring powder charges and ramming round bullets home.

"So that's how they wanna play!" Amoros shouted. "Nail their hides to the wall!" The tip of his little finger had been shot away. He did not seem to know it.

Cox's Neo-Armalite was already barking, spitting a stream of hot brass cartridges, slamming against his shoulder. He rammed in clip after clip, playing the rifle like a hose. If one bullet didn't bite, the next would.

Others from the platoon were also firing. Cox heard bursts of automatic weapons fire from different parts of the campus, too, and the deeper blasts of rocket-propelled grenades and field artillery. Smoke not of the aliens' making began to envelop their ship and the soldiers around it.

One or two shots came back at the platoon, and then a few more, but so few that Cox, in stunned disbelief, shouted to his sergeant, "This isn't fair!"

"Fuck 'em!" Amoros shouted back. "They wanna throw their weight around, they take their chances. Only good thing they did was knock over the mayor. Always did hate that old crackpot."

The harsh tac-tac-tac did not sound like any gunfire Togram had heard. The shots came too close together, making a horrible sheet of noise. And if the locals were shooting back at his troopers, where were the thick, choking clouds of gunpowder smoke over their position?

He did not know the answer to that. What he did know was that his company was going down like grain before a scythe. Here a soldier was hit by three bullets at once and fell awkwardly, as if his body could not tell in which direction to twist. There another had the top of his head gruesomely removed.

The volley the captain had screamed for was stillborn. Perhaps a squad's worth of soldiers moved toward the locals, the sun glinting bravely off their long, polished bayonets. None of them got more than a half-sixteen of paces before falling.

Ilingua looked at Togram, horror in his eyes, his ears flat against his head. The captain knew his were the same. "What are they doing to us?" Ilingua howled.

Togram could only shake his head helplessly. He dove behind a corpse, fired one of his pistols at the enemy. There was still a chance, he thought— how would these demonic aliens stand up under their first air attack?

A flier swooped toward the locals. Musketeers blasted away from firing ports, drew back to reload.

"Take that, you whoresons!" Togram shouted. He did not, however, raise his fist in the air. That, he had already learned, was dangerous.

"Incoming aircraft!" Sergeant Amoros roared. His squad, those not already prone, flung themselves on their faces. Cox heard shouts of pain through the combat din as men were wounded.

The Cottonmouth crew launched their shoulder-fired AA missile at the alien flying machine. The pilot must have had reflexes like a cat's. He sidestepped his machine in midair; no plane built on Earth could have matched that performance. The Cottonmouth shot harmlessly past.

The flier dropped what looked like a load of crockery. The ground jumped as the bombs exploded. Cursing, deafened, Billy Cox stopped worrying whether the fight was fair.

But the flier pilot had not seen the F-29 fighter on his tail. The USAF plane released two missiles from point-blank range, less than a mile. The infrared seeker found no target and blew itself up, but the missile that homed on radar streaked straight toward the flier. The explosion made Cox bury his face in the ground and clap his hands over his ears.

So this is war, he thought: I can't see, I can barely hear, and my side is winning. What must it be like for the losers?

•••

Hope died in Togram's hearts when the first flier fell victim to the locals' aircraft. The rest of the *Indomitable*'s machines did not last much longer. They could evade, but had even less ability to hit back than the Roxolan ground forces. And they were hideously vulnerable when attacked in their pilots' blind spots, from below or behind.

One of the starship's cannon managed to fire again, and quickly drew a response from the traveling fortresses Togram got glimpses of as they took their positions in the streets outside this parklike area.

When the first shell struck, the luckless captain thought for an instant that it was another gun going off aboard the *Indomitable*. The sound of the explosion was nothing like the crash a solid shot made when it smacked into a target. A fragment of hot metal buried itself in the ground by Togram's hand. That made him think a cannon had blown up, but more explosions on the ship's superstructure and fountains of dirt flying up from misses showed it was just more from the locals' fiendish arsenal.

Something large and hard struck the captain in the back of the neck. The world spiraled down into blackness.

•••

"Cease fire!" The order reached the field artillery first, then the infantry units at the very front line. Billy Cox pushed up his cuff to look at his watch, stared in disbelief. The whole firefight had lasted less than twenty minutes.

He looked around. Lieutenant Shotton was getting up from behind an ornamental palm. "Let's see what we have," he said. His rifle still at the ready, he began to walk slowly toward the starship. It was hardly more than a smoking ruin. For that matter, neither were the buildings around it. The damage to their predecessors had been worse in the big quake, but not much.

Alien corpses littered the lawn. The blood splashing the bright green grass was crimson as any man's. Cox bent to pick up a pistol. The weapon was beautifully made, with scenes of combat carved into the grayish wood of the stock. But he recognized it as a single-shot piece, a small arm obsolete for at least two centuries. He shook his head in wonderment.

Sergeant Amoros lifted a conical object from where it had fallen beside a dead alien. "What the hell is this?" he demanded.

Again Cox had the feeling of being caught up in something he did not understand. "It's a powderhorn," he said.

"Like in the movies? Pioneers and all that good shit?"

"The very same."

"Damn," Amoros said feelingly. Cox nodded in agreement.

Along with the rest of the platoon, they moved closer to the wrecked ship. Most of the aliens had died still in the two neat rows from which they had opened fire on the soldiers.

Here, behind another corpse, lay the body of the scarlet-plumed officer who had given the order to begin that horrifyingly uneven encounter. Then, startling Cox, the alien moaned and stirred, just as might a human starting to come to. "Grab him; he's a live one!" Cox exclaimed.

Several men jumped on the reviving alien, who was too groggy to fight back. Soldiers began peering into the holes torn in the starship, and even going inside. There they were still wary; the ship was so incredibly much bigger than any human spacecraft that there were surely survivors despite the shellacking it had taken.

As always happens, the men did not get to enjoy such pleasures long. The fighting had been over for only minutes when the first team of experts came thuttering in by helicopter, saw common soldiers in their private preserve, and made horrified noises. The experts also promptly relieved the platoon of its prisoner.

Sergeant Amoros watched resentfully as they took the alien away. "You must've known it would happen, Sandy," Cox consoled him. "We do the dirty work and the brass take over once things get cleaned up again."

"Yeah, but wouldn't it be wonderful if just once it was the other way round?" Amoros laughed without humor. "You don't need to tell me: fat friggin' chance."

•••

When Togram woke up on his back, he knew something was wrong. Roxolani always slept prone. For a moment he wondered how he had got to where he was...too much water-of-life the night before? His pounding head made that a good possibility.

Then memory came flooding back. Those damnable locals with their sorcerous weapons! Had his people rallied and beaten back the enemy after all? He vowed to light votive lamps to Edieva, mistress of battles, for the rest of his life if that were true.

The room he was in began to register. Nothing was familiar, from the bed he lay on to the light in the ceiling that glowed bright as sunshine and neither smoked nor flickered. No, he did not think the Roxolani had won their fight.

Fear settled like ice in his vitals. He knew how his own race treated prisoners, had heard spacers' stories of even worse things among other folk. He shuddered to think of the refined tortures a race as ferocious as his captors could invent.

He got shakily to his feet. By the end of the bed he found his hat, some smoked meat obviously taken from the *Indomitable,* and a translucent jug made of something that was neither leather nor glass nor baked clay nor metal. Whatever it was, it was too soft and flexible to make a weapon.

The jar had water in it: not water from the *Indomitable.* That was already beginning to taste stale. This was cool and fresh and so pure as to have no taste whatever, water so fine he had only found its like in a couple of mountain springs.

The door opened on noiseless hinges. In came two of the locals. One was small and wore a white coat—a female, if those chest projections were breasts. The other was dressed in the same clothes the local warriors had worn, though those offered no camouflage here. That one carried what was plainly a rifle and, the gods curse him, looked extremely alert.

To Togram's surprise, the female took charge. The other local was merely a bodyguard. Some spoiled princess, curious about these outsiders, the captain thought. Well, he was happier about treating with her than meeting the local executioner.

She sat down, waved for him also to take a seat. He tried a chair, found it uncomfortable—too low in the back, not built for his wide rump and short legs. He sat on the floor instead.

She set a small box on the table by the chair. Togram pointed at it. "What's that?" he asked.

He thought she had not understood—no blame to her for that; she had none of his language. She was playing with the box, pushing a button here, a button there. Then his ears went back and his hackles rose, for the box said, "What's that?" in Roxolani. After a moment he realized it was speaking in his own voice. He swore and made a sign against witchcraft.

She said something, fooled with the box again. This time it echoed her. She pointed at it. "Recorder," she said. She paused expectantly.

What was she waiting for, the Roxolanic name for that thing? "I've never seen one of those in my life, and I hope I never do again," he said. She scratched her head. When she made the gadget again repeat what he had said, only the thought of the soldier with the gun kept him from flinging it against the wall.

Despite that contretemps, they did eventually make progress on the language. Togram had picked up snatches of a good many tongues in the course of his adventurous life; that was one reason he had made captain in spite of low birth and paltry connections. And the female—Togram heard her name as Hildachesta—had a gift for them, as well as the box that never forgot.

"Why did your people attack us?" she asked one day, when she had come far enough in Roxolanic to be able to frame the question.

He knew he was being interrogated, no matter how polite she sounded. He had played that game with prisoners himself. His ears twitched in a shrug. He had always believed in giving straight answers; that was one reason he was only a captain. He said, "To take what you grow and make and use it for ourselves. Why would anyone want to conquer anyone else?"

"Why indeed?" she murmured, and was silent a little while; his forthright reply seemed to have closed off a line of questioning. She tried again: "How are your people able to walk—I mean, travel—faster than light, when the rest of your arts are so simple?"

His fur bristled with indignation.

"They are not! We make gunpowder, we cast iron and smelt steel, we have spyglasses to help our steerers guide us from star to star. We are no savages huddling in caves or shooting at each other with bows and arrows."

His speech, of course, was not that neat or simple. He had to backtrack, to use elaborate circumlocutions, to play act to make Hildachesta understand. She scratched her head in the gesture of puzzlement he had come to recognize. She said, "We have known all these things you mention for hundreds of years, but we did not think anyone could walk—damn, I keep saying that instead of 'travel'—faster than light. How did your people learn to do that?"

"We discovered it for ourselves," he said proudly. "We did not have to learn it from some other starfaring race, as many folk do."

"But how did you discover it?" she persisted.

"How do I know? I'm a soldier; what do I care for such things? Who knows who invented gunpowder or found out about using bellows in a smithy to get the fire hot enough to melt iron? These things happen, that's all."

She broke off the questions early that day.

"It's humiliating," Hilda Chester said. "If these fool aliens had waited a few more years before they came, we likely would have blown ourselves to kingdom come without ever knowing there was more real estate around. Christ, from what the Roxolani say, races that scarcely know how to work iron fly starships and never think twice about it."

"Except when the starships don't get home," Charlie Ebbets answered. His tie was in his pocket and his collar open against Pasadena's fierce summer heat, although the Caltech Athenaeum was efficiently air-conditioned. Along with so many other engineers and scientists, he depended on linguists like Hilda Chester for a link to the aliens.

"I don't quite understand it myself," she said. "Apart from the hyperdrive and contragravity, the Roxolani are backward, almost primitive. And the other species out there must be the same, or someone would have overrun them long since."

Ebbets said, "Once you see it, the drive is amazingly simple. The research crews say anybody could have stumbled over the principle at almost any time in our history. The best guess is that most races did come across it, and once they did, why, all their creative energy would naturally go into refining and improving."

"But we missed it," Hilda said slowly, "and so our technology developed in a different way."

"That's right. That's why the Roxolani don't know anything about controlling electricity, to say nothing of atomics. And the thing is, as well as we can tell so far, the hyperdrive and contragravity don't have the ancillary applications the electromagnetic spectrum does. All they do is move things from here to there in a hurry."

"That should be enough at the moment," Hilda said. Ebbets nodded. There were almost nine billion people jammed onto the Earth, half of them hungry. Now, suddenly, there were places for them to go and a means to get them there.

"I think," Ebbets said musingly, "we're going to be an awful surprise to the people out there."

It took Hilda a second to see what he was driving at. "If that's a joke, it's not funny. It's been a hundred years since the last war of conquest."

"Sure—they've gotten too expensive and too dangerous. But what kind of fight could the Roxolani or anyone else at their level of technology put up against us? The Aztecs and Incas were plenty brave. How much good did it do them against the Spaniards?"

"I hope we've gotten smarter in the last five hundred years." Hilda said. All the same, she left her sandwich half-eaten. She found she was not hungry anymore.

•••

"Ransisc!" Togram exclaimed as the senior steerer limped into his cubicle. Ransisc was thinner than he had been a few moons before, aboard the misnamed *Indomitable*. His fur had grown out white around several scars Togram did not remember.

His air of amused detachment had not changed, though. "Tougher than bullets, are you, or didn't the humans think you were worth killing?"

"The latter, I suspect. With their firepower, why should they worry about one soldier more or less?" Togram said bitterly. "I didn't know you were still alive, either."

"Through no fault of my own, I assure you," Ransisc said. "Olgren, next to me—" His voice broke off. It was not possible to be detached about everything.

"What are you doing here?" the captain asked. "Not that I'm not glad to see you, but you're the first Roxolan face I've set eyes on since—" It was his turn to hesitate.

"Since we landed." Togram nodded in relief at the steerer's circumlocution. Ransisc went on, "I've seen several others before you. I suspect we're being allowed to get together so the humans can listen to us talking with each other."

"How could they do that?" Togram asked, then answered his own question: "Oh, the recorders, of course." He perforce used the English word. "Well, we'll fix that."

He dropped into Oyag, the most widely spoken language on a planet the Roxolani had conquered fifty years before. "What's going to happen to us, Ransisc?"

"Back on Roxolan, they'll have realized something's gone wrong by now," the steerer answered in the same tongue.

That did nothing to cheer Togram. "There are so many ways to lose ships," he said gloomily. "And even if the High Warmaster does send another fleet after us, it won't have any more luck than we did. These gods-accursed humans have too many war-machines." He paused and took a long, moody pull at a bottle of vodka. The flavored liquors the locals brewed made him sick, but vodka he liked. "How is it they have all these machines and we don't, or any race we know of? They must be wizards, selling their souls to the demons for knowledge."

Ransisc's nose twitched in disagreement. "I asked one of their savants the same question. He gave me back a poem by a human named Hail or Snow or something of that sort. It was about someone who stood at a fork in the road and ended up taking the less-used track. That's what the humans did. Most races find the hyperdrive and go traveling. The humans never did, and so their search for knowledge went in a different direction."

"Didn't it!" Togram shuddered at the recollection of that brief, terrible combat. "Guns that spit dozens of bullets without reloading, cannon mounted on armored platforms that move by themselves, rockets that follow their targets by themselves. And there are the things we didn't see, the ones the humans only talk about—the bombs that can blow up a whole city, each one by itself."

"I don't know if I believe that," Ransisc said.

"I do. They sound afraid when they speak of them."

"Well, maybe. But it's not just the weapons they have. It's the machines that let them see and talk to one another from far away; the machines that do their reckoning for them; their recorders and everything that has to do with them. From what they say of their medicine, I'm almost tempted to believe you and think they are wizards—they actually know what causes their diseases, and how to cure or even prevent them. And their farming: this planet is far more crowded than any I've seen or heard of, but it grows enough for all these humans."

Togram sadly waggled his ears. "It seems so unfair. All that they got, just by not stumbling onto the hyperdrive."

"They have it now," Ransisc reminded him. "Thanks to us."

The Roxolani looked at each other, appalled. They spoke together: "What have we done?"

THE ALIENS WHO KNEW, I MEAN, *EVERYTHING*

GEORGE ALEC EFFINGER

I was sitting at my desk, reading a report on the brown pelican situation, when the secretary of state burst in. "Mr. President," he said, his eyes wide, "the aliens are here!" Just like that. "The aliens are here!" As if I had any idea of what to do about them.

"I see," I said. I learned early in my first term that "I see" was one of the safest and most useful comments I could possibly make in any situation. When I said, "I see," it indicated that I had digested the news and was waiting intelligently and calmly for further data. That knocked the ball back into my advisors' court. I looked at the secretary of state expectantly. I was all prepared with my next utterance, in the event that he had nothing further to add. My next utterance would be "Well?" That would indicate that I was on top of the problem, but that I couldn't be expected to make an executive decision without sufficient information, and that he should have known better than to burst into the Oval Office unless he had that information. That's why we had protocol; that's why

69

we had proper channels; that's why I had advisors. The voters out there didn't want me to make decisions without sufficient information. If the secretary didn't have anything more to tell me, he shouldn't have burst in, in the first place. I looked at him awhile longer. "Well?" I asked at last.

"That's about all we have at the moment," he said uncomfortably. I looked at him sternly for a few seconds, scoring a couple of points while he stood there all flustered. I turned back to the pelican report, dismissing him. I certainly wasn't going to get all flustered. I could think of only one president in recent memory who was ever flustered in office, and we all know what happened to him. As the secretary of state closed the door to my office behind him, I smiled. The aliens were probably going to be a bitch of a problem eventually, but it wasn't my problem yet. I had a little time.

But I found that I couldn't really keep my mind on the pelican question. Even the president of the United States has *some* imagination, and if the secretary of state was correct, I was going to have to confront these aliens pretty damn soon. I'd read stories about aliens when I was a kid, I'd seen all sorts of aliens in movies and television, but these were the first aliens who'd actually stopped by for a chat. Well, I wasn't going to be the first American president to make a fool of himself in front of visitors from another world. I was going to be briefed. I telephoned the secretary of defense. "We must have some contingency plans drawn up for this," I told him. "We have plans for every other possible situation." This was true; the Defense Department has scenarios for such bizarre events as the rise of an imperialist fascist regime in Liechtenstein or the spontaneous depletion of all the world's selenium.

"Just a second, Mr. President," said the secretary. I could hear him muttering to someone else. I held the phone and stared out the window. There were crowds of people running around hysterically out there. Probably because of the aliens. "Mr. President?" came the voice of the secretary of defense. "I have one of the aliens here, and he suggests that we use the same plan that President Eisenhower used."

I closed my eyes and sighed. I hated it when they said stuff like that. I wanted information, and they told me these things knowing that I would have to ask four or five more questions just to understand the answer to the first one. "You have an alien with you?" I said, in a pleasant enough voice.

"Yes, sir. They prefer not to be called 'aliens.' He tells me he's a nup. That's their word for 'man,' in the sense of 'human being.' The plural is 'nuhp.'"

"Thank you, Luis. Tell me, why do you have an al—Why do you have a nup and I don't?"

Luis muttered the question to his nup. "He says it's because they wanted to go through proper channels. They learned all about that from President Eisenhower."

"Very good, Luis." This was going to take all day, I could see that; and I had a photo session with Mick Jagger's granddaughter. "My second question, Luis, is what the hell does he mean by 'the same plan that President Eisenhower used'?"

Another muffled consultation. "He says that this isn't the first time that the nuhp have landed on Earth. A scout ship with two nuhp aboard landed at Edwards Air Force Base in 1954. The two nuhp met with President Eisenhower. It was apparently a very cordial occasion, and President Eisenhower impressed the nuhp as a warm and sincere old gentleman. They've been planning to return to Earth ever since but they've been very busy, what with one thing and another. President Eisenhower requested that the nuhp not reveal themselves to the people of Earth in general, until our government decided how to control the inevitable hysteria. My guess is that the government never got around to that, and when the nuhp departed, the matter was studied and then shelved. As the years passed, few people were even aware that the first meeting ever occurred. The nuhp have returned now in great numbers, expecting that we'd have prepared the populace by now. It's not their fault that we haven't. They just sort of took it for granted that they'd be welcome."

"Uh huh," I said. That was my usual utterance when I didn't know what the hell else to say. "Assure them that they are, indeed, welcome. I don't suppose the study they did during the Eisenhower administration was ever completed. I don't suppose there really is a plan to break the news to the public."

"Unfortunately, Mr. President, that seems to be the case."

"Uh huh." That's Republicans for you, I thought. "Ask your nup something for me, Luis. Ask him if he knows what they told Eisenhower. They must be full of outer space wisdom. Maybe they have some ideas about how we should deal with this."

There was yet another pause. "Mr. President, he says all they discussed with Mr. Eisenhower was his golf game. They helped to correct his putting stroke. But they are definitely full of wisdom. They know all sorts of things. My nup—that is, his name is Hurv—anyway, he says that they'd be happy to give you some advice."

"Tell him that I'm grateful, Luis. Can they have someone meet with me in, say, half an hour?"

"There are three nuhp on their way to the Oval Office at this moment. One of them is the leader of their expedition, and one of the others is the commander of their mother ship."

"Mother ship?" I asked.

"You haven't seen it? It's tethered on the Mall. They're real sorry about what they did to the Washington Monument. They say they can take care of it tomorrow."

I just shuddered and hung up the phone. I called my secretary. "There are going to be three—"

"They're here now, Mr. President."

I sighed. "Send them in." And that's how I met the nuhp. Just as President Eisenhower had.

They were handsome people. Likable, too. They smiled and shook hands and suggested that photographs be taken of the historic moment, so we called in the media; and then I had to sort of wing the most important diplomatic meeting of my entire political career. I welcomed the nuhp to Earth. "Welcome to Earth," I said, "and welcome to the United States."

"Thank you," said the nup I would come to know as Pleen. "We're glad to be here."

"How long do you plan to be with us?" I hated myself when I said that, in front of the Associated Press and the UPI and all the network news people. I sounded like a desk clerk at a Holiday Inn.

"We don't know, exactly," said Pleen. "We don't have to be back to work until a week from Monday."

"Uh huh," I said. Then I just posed for pictures and kept my mouth shut. I wasn't going to say or do another goddamn thing until my advisors showed up and started advising.

•••

Well, of course, the people panicked. Pleen told me to expect that, but I had figured it out for myself. We've seen too many movies about visitors from space. Sometimes they come with a message of peace and universal brotherhood and just the inside information mankind has been needing for thousands of years. More often, though, the aliens come to enslave and murder us because the visual effects are better, and so when the nuhp arrived everyone was all prepared to hate them. People didn't trust their good looks. People were suspicious of their nice manners and their quietly tasteful clothing. When the nuhp offered to solve all our problems for us, we all said, sure, solve our problems—*but at what cost?*

That first week, Pleen and I spent a lot of time together, just getting to know one another and trying to understand what the other one wanted. I invited him and Commander Toag and the other nuhp bigwigs to a reception at the White House. We had a church choir from Alabama singing gospel music and a high school band from Michigan playing a medley of favorite collegiate fight songs and talented clones of the original stars nostalgically re-creating the Steve and Eydie Experience and an improvisational comedy troupe from Los Angeles or someplace and the New York Philharmonic under the baton of a twelve-year-old girl genius. They played Beethoven's Ninth Symphony in an attempt to impress the nuhp with how marvelous Earth culture was.

Pleen enjoyed it all very much. "Men are as varied in their expressions of joy as we nuhp," he said, applauding vigorously. "We are all very fond of human music. We think Beethoven composed some of the most beautiful melodies we've ever heard, anywhere in our galactic travels."

I smiled. "I'm sure we are all pleased to hear that," I said.

"Although the Ninth Symphony is certainly not the best of his work."

I faltered in my clapping. "Excuse me?" I said.

Pleen gave me a gracious smile. "It is well known among us that Beethoven's finest composition is his Piano Concerto Number Five in E Flat Major."

I let out my breath. "Of course, that's a matter of opinion. Perhaps the standards of the nuhp—"

"Oh, no," Pleen hastened to assure me, "taste does not enter into it at all. The Concerto Number Five is Beethoven's best, according to very rigorous and definite critical principles. And even that lovely piece is by no means the best music ever produced by mankind."

I felt just a trifle annoyed. What could this nup, who came from some weirdo planet God alone knows how far away, from some society with not the slightest connection to our heritage and culture, what could this nup know of what Beethoven's Ninth Symphony aroused in our human souls? "Tell me, then, Pleen," I said in my ominously soft voice, "what is the best human musical composition?"

"The score from the motion picture *Ben Hur*, by Miklos Rozsa," he said simply. What could I do but nod my head in silence. It wasn't worth starting an interplanetary incident over.

So from fear our reaction to the nuhp changed to distrust. We kept waiting for them to reveal their real selves; we waited for the pleasant masks to slip off and show us the true nightmarish faces we all suspected lurked beneath. The nuhp did not go home a week from Monday, after all. They liked Earth, and they liked us. They decided to stay a little longer. We told them about ourselves and our centuries of trouble; and they mentioned, in an off-hand nuhp way, that they could take care of a few little things, make some small adjustments, and life would be a whole lot better for everybody on Earth. They didn't want anything in return. They wanted to give us these things in gratitude for our hospitality, for letting them park their mother ship on the Mall and for all the free refills of coffee they were getting all around the world. We hesitated, but our vanity and our greed won out. "Go ahead," we said, "make our deserts bloom. Go ahead, end war and poverty and disease. Show us twenty exciting new things to do with leftovers. Call us when you're done."

The fear changed to distrust, but soon the distrust changed to hope. The nuhp made the deserts bloom, all right. They asked for four months. We were perfectly willing to let them have all the time they needed. They put a tall fence all around the Namib and wouldn't let anyone in to watch what they were doing. Four months later, they had a big cocktail party and invited the whole world to see what they'd accomplished. I sent the secretary of state as my personal representative. He brought back some wonderful slides: The vast desert had been turned into a botanical miracle. There were miles and miles of flowering plants now, instead of the monotonous dead sand and gravel sea. Of course, the immense garden contained nothing but hollyhocks, many millions of hollyhocks. I mentioned to Pleen that the people of Earth had been hoping for a little more in the way of variety, and something just a trifle more practical, too.

"What do you mean, 'practical'?" he asked.

"You know," I said. "Food."

"Don't worry about food," said Pleen. "We're going to take care of hunger pretty soon."

"Good, good. But hollyhocks?"

"What's wrong with hollyhocks?"

"Nothing," I admitted.

"Hollyhocks are the single prettiest flower grown on Earth."

"Some people like orchids," I said. "Some people like roses."

"No," said Pleen firmly. "Hollyhocks are it. I wouldn't kid you."

So we thanked the nuhp for a Namibia full of hollyhocks and stopped them before they did the same thing to the Sahara, the Mojave, and the Gobi.

• • •

On the whole, everyone began to like the nuhp, although they took just a little getting used to. They had very definite opinions about everything, and they wouldn't admit that what they had were *opinions*. To hear a nup talk, he had a direct line to some categorical imperative that spelled everything out in terms that were unflinchingly black and white. Hollyhocks were the best flower. Alexander Dumas was the greatest novelist. Powder blue was the prettiest color. Melancholy was the most ennobling emotion. *Grand Hotel* was the finest movie. The best car ever built was the 1956 Chevy Bel Air, but it had to be aqua and white. And there just wasn't room for discussion: the nuhp made these pronouncements with the force of divine revelation.

I asked Pleen once about the American presidency. I asked him who the nuhp thought was the best president in our history. I felt sort of like the Wicked Queen in *Snow White*. Mirror, mirror, on the wall. I didn't really expect Pleen would tell me that I was the best president, but my heart pounded while I waited for his answer; you never know, right? To tell the truth, I expected him to say Washington, Lincoln, Roosevelt, or Akiwara. His answer surprised me: James K. Polk.

"Polk?" I asked. I wasn't even sure I could recognize Polk's portrait.

"He's not the most familiar," said Pleen, "but he was an honest if unexciting president. He fought the Mexican War and added a great amount of territory to the United States. He saw every bit of his platform become law. He was a good, hard-working man who deserves a better reputation."

"What about Thomas Jefferson?" I asked.

Pleen just shrugged. "He was okay, too, but he was no James Polk."

My wife, the First Lady, became very good friends with the wife of Commander Toag, whose name was Doim. They often went shopping together, and Doim would make suggestions to the First Lady about fashion and hair care. Doim told my wife which rooms in the White House needed redecoration, and which charities were worthy of official support. It was Doim who negotiated the First Lady's recording contract, and it was Doim who introduced her to the Philadelphia cheese steak, one of the nuhp's favorite treats (although they asserted that the best cuisine on Earth was Tex-Mex).

One day, Doim and my wife were having lunch. They sat at a small table in a chic Washington restaurant, with a couple dozen Secret Service people and nuhp security agents disguised elsewhere among the patrons.

"I've noticed that there seems to be more nuhp here in Washington every week," said the First Lady.

"Yes," said Doim, "new mother ships arrive daily. We think Earth is one of the most pleasant planets we've ever visited."

"We're glad to have you, of course," said my wife, "and it seems that our people have gotten over their initial fears."

"The hollyhocks did the trick," said Doim.

"I guess so. How many nuhp are there on Earth now?"

"About five or six million, I'd say."

The First Lady was startled. "I didn't think it would be that many."

Doim laughed. "We're not just here in America, you know. We're all over. We really like Earth. Although, of course, Earth isn't absolutely the best planet. Our own home, Nupworld, is still Number One; but Earth would certainly be on any Top Ten list."

"Uh huh." (My wife has learned many important oratorical tricks from me.)

"The hollyhocks were nice," said the First Lady. "But when are you going to tackle the really vital questions?"

"Don't worry about that," said Doim, turning her attention to her cottage cheese salad.

"When are you going to take care of world hunger?"

"Pretty soon. Don't worry."

"Urban blight."

"Pretty soon."

"Man's inhumanity to man?"

Doim gave my wife an impatient look. "We haven't even been here for six months yet. What do you want, miracles? We've already done more than your husband accomplished in his entire first term."

"Hollyhocks," muttered the First Lady.

"I heard that," said Doim. "The rest of the universe absolutely *adores* hollyhocks. We can't help it if humans have no taste."

They finished their lunch in silence, and my wife came back to the White House fuming.

That same week, one of my advisors showed me a letter that had been sent by a young man in New Mexico. Several nuhp had moved into a condo next door to him and had begun advising him about the best investment possibilities (urban respiratory spas), the best fabrics and colors to wear to show off his coloring, the best holo system on the market (the Esmeraldas F-64 with hexphased Libertad screens and a Ruy Challenger argon solipsizer), the best place to watch sunsets (the revolving restaurant on top of the Weyerhaeuser Building in Yellowstone City), the best wines to go with everything (too numerous to mention—send SASE for list), and which of the two women he was dating to marry (Candi Marie Esterhazy). "Mr. President," said the bewildered young man, "I realize that we must be gracious hosts to our benefactors from space, but I am having some difficulty keeping my temper. The nuhp are certainly knowledgeable and willing to share the benefits of their wisdom, but they don't even wait to be asked. If they were people, regular human beings who lived next door, I would have punched their lights out by now. Please advise. And hurry: they are taking me downtown next Friday to pick out an engagement ring and new living room furniture. I don't even *want* new living room furniture!"

Luis, my secretary of defense, talked to Hurv about the ultimate goals of the nuhp. "We don't have any goals," he said. "We're just taking it easy."

"Then why did you come to Earth?" asked Luis.

"Why do you go bowling?"

"I don't go bowling."

"You should," said Hurv. "Bowling is the most enjoyable thing a person can do."

"What about sex?"

"Bowling *is* sex. Bowling is a symbolic form of intercourse, except you don't have to bother about the feelings of some other person. Bowling is sex without guilt. Bowling is what people have wanted down through all the millennia: sex without the slightest responsibility. It's the very distillation of the essence of sex. Bowling is sex without fear and shame."

"Bowling is sex without pleasure," said Luis.

There was a brief silence. "You mean," said Hurv, "that when you put that ball right into the pocket and see those pins explode off the alley, you don't have an orgasm?"

"Nope," said Luis.

"*That's* your problem, then. I can't help you there, you'll have to see some kind of therapist. It's obvious this subject embarrasses you. Let's talk about something else."

"Fine with me," said Luis moodily. "When are we going to receive the real benefits of your technological superiority? When are you going to unlock the final secrets of the atom? When are you going to free mankind from drudgery?"

"What do you mean, 'technological superiority'?" asked Hurv.

"There must be scientific wonders beyond our imagining aboard your mother ships."

"Not so's you'd notice. We're not even so advanced as you people here on Earth. We've learned all sorts of wonderful things since we've been here."

"What?" Luis couldn't imagine what Hurv was trying to say.

"We don't have anything like your astonishing bubble memories or silicon chips. We never invented anything comparable to the transistor, even. You know why the mother ships are so big?"

"My God."

"That's right," said Hurv, "vacuum tubes. All our spacecraft operate on vacuum tubes. They take up a hell of a lot of space. And they burn out. Do you know how long it takes to find the goddamn tube when it burns out? Remember how people used to take bags of vacuum tubes from their television sets down to the drugstore to use the tube tester? Think of doing that with something the size of our mother ships. And we can't just zip off into space when we feel like it. We have to let a mother ship warm up first. You have to turn the key and let the thing warm up for a couple of minutes, *then* you can zip off into space. It's a goddamn pain in the neck."

"I don't understand," said Luis, stunned. "If your technology is so primitive, how did you come here? If we're so far ahead of you, we should have discovered your planet, not the other way around."

Hurv gave a gentle laugh. "Don't pat yourself on the back, Luis. Just because your electronics are better than ours, you aren't necessarily superior in any way. Look, imagine that you humans are a man in Los Angeles with a brand-new Trujillo and we are a nup in New York with a beat-up old Ford. The two fellows start driving toward St. Louis. Now, the guy in the Trujillo is doing a hundred and twenty on the interstates, and the guy in the Ford is putting along at fifty-five; but the human in the Trujillo stops in Vegas and puts all of his gas money down the hole of a blackjack table, and the determined little nup cruises along for days until at last he reaches his goal. It's all a matter of superior intellect and the will to succeed. Your people talk a lot about going to the stars, but you just keep putting your money into other projects, like war and popular music and international athletic events and resurrecting the fashions of previous decades. If you wanted to go into space, you would have."

"But we *do* want to go."

"Then we'll help you. We'll give you the secrets. And you can explain your electronics to our engineers, and together we'll build wonderful new mother ships that will open the universe to both humans and nuhp."

Luis let out his breath. "Sounds good to me," he said.

Everyone agreed that this looked better than hollyhocks. We all hoped that we could keep from kicking their collective asses long enough to collect on that promise.

• • •

When I was in college, my roommate in my sophomore year was a tall, skinny guy named Barry Rintz. Barry had wild, wavy black hair and a sharp face that looked like a handsome normal face that had been sat on and folded in the middle. He squinted a lot, not because he had any defect in his eyesight, but because he wanted to give the impression that he was constantly evaluating the world. This was true. Barry could tell you the actual and market values of any object you happened to come across.

We had a double date one football weekend with two girls from another college in the same city. Before the game, we met the girls and took them to the university's art museum, which was pretty large and owned an impressive collection. My date, a pretty Elementary Ed major named Brigid, and I wandered from gallery to gallery, remarking that our tastes in art were very similar. We both liked the Impressionists, and we both liked Surrealism. There were a couple of little Renoirs that we admired for almost half an hour, and then we made a lot of silly sophomore jokes about what was happening in the Magritte and Dali and de Chirico paintings.

Barry and his date, Dixie, ran across us by accident as all four of us passed through the sculpture gallery. "There's a terrific Seurat down there," Brigid told her girlfriend.

"Seurat," Barry said. There was a lot of amused disbelief in his voice.

"I like Seurat," said Dixie.

"Well, of course," said Barry, "there's nothing really *wrong* with Seurat."

"What do you mean by that?" asked Brigid.

"Do you know F. E. Church?" he asked.

"Who?" I said.

"Come here." He practically dragged us to a gallery of American paintings. F. E. Church was a remarkable American landscape painter (1826–1900) who achieved an astonishing and lovely luminance in his works. "Look at that light!" cried Barry. "Look at that space! Look at that air!"

Brigid glanced at Dixie. "Look at that air?" she whispered.

It was a fine painting and we all said so, but Barry was insistent. F. E. Church was the greatest artist in American history, and one of the best the world has ever known. "I'd put him right up there with Van Dyck and Canaletto."

"Canaletto?" said Dixie. "The one who did all those pictures of Venice?"

"Those skies!" murmured Barry ecstatically. He wore the expression of a satisfied voluptuary.

"Some people like paintings of puppies or naked women," I offered. "Barry likes light and air."

We left the museum and had lunch. Barry told us which things on the menu were worth ordering, and which things were an abomination. He made us all drink an obscure imported beer from Ecuador. To Barry, the world was divided up into masterpieces and abominations. It made life so much simpler for him, except that he never understood why his friends could never tell one from the other.

At the football game, Barry compared our school's quarterback to Y. A. Tittle. He compared the other team's punter to Ngoc Van Vinh. He compared the halftime show to the Ohio State band's Script Ohio formation. Before the end of the third quarter it was very obvious to me that Barry was going to have absolutely no luck at all with Dixie. Before the clock ran out in the fourth quarter, Brigid and I had made whispered plans to dump the other two as soon as possible and sneak away by ourselves. Dixie would probably find an excuse to ride the bus back to her dorm before suppertime. Barry, as usual, would spend the evening in our room, reading *The Making of the President 1996*.

On other occasions, and with little or no provocation, Barry would lecture me about subjects as diverse as American literature (the best poet was Edwin Arlington Robinson, the best novelist James T. Farrell), animals (the only correct pet was the golden retriever), clothing (in anything other than a navy blue jacket and gray slacks, a man was just asking for trouble), and even hobbies (Barry collected military decorations of czarist Imperial Russia; he wouldn't talk to me for days after I told him my father collected barbed wire).

Barry was a wealth of information. He was the campus arbiter of good taste. Everyone knew Barry was the man to ask.

But no one ever did. We all hated his guts. I moved out of our dorm room before the end of the fall semester. Shunned, lonely, and bitter, Barry Rintz wound up as a guidance counselor in a high school in Ames, Iowa. The job was absolutely perfect for him; few people are so lucky in finding a career.

If I didn't know better, I might have believed that Barry was the original advance spy for the nuhp.

• • •

When the nuhp had been on Earth for a full year, they gave us the gift of interstellar travel. It was surprisingly inexpensive. The nuhp explained their propulsion system, which was cheap and safe and adaptable to all sorts of other earthbound applications. The revelations opened up an entirely new area of scientific speculation. Then the nuhp taught us their navigational methods, and about the "shortcuts" they had discovered in space. People called them spacewarps, although technically speaking the shortcuts had nothing to do with Einsteinian theory or curved space or anything like that. Not many humans understood what the nuhp were talking about, but that didn't make very much difference. The nuhp didn't understand the shortcuts either; they just used them. The matter was presented to us like a Thanksgiving turkey on a platter. We bypassed the whole business of cautious scientific experimentation and leaped right into commercial exploitation. Mitsubishi of La Paz and Martin Marietta used nuhp schematics to begin construction of three luxury passenger ships, each capable of transporting a thousand tourists anywhere in our galaxy. Although man had yet to set foot on the moons of Jupiter, certain selected travel agencies began booking passage for a grand tour of the dozen nearest inhabited worlds.

Yes, it seemed that space was teeming with life, humanoid life on planets circling half the G-type stars in the heavens. "We've been trying to communicate with extraterrestrial intelligence for decades," complained one Soviet scientist. "Why haven't they responded?"

A friendly nup merely shrugged. "Everybody's trying to communicate out there," he said. "Your messages are like Publishers Clearinghouse mail to them." At first that was a blow to our racial pride, but we got over it. As soon as we joined the interstellar community, they'd begin to take us more seriously. And the nuhp made that possible.

We were grateful to the nuhp, but that didn't make them any easier to live with. They were still insufferable. As my second term as president came to an end, Pleen began to advise me about my future career. "Don't write a book," he told me (after I had already written the first two hundred pages of *A President Remembers*). "If you want to be an elder statesman, fine; but keep a low profile and wait for the people to come to you."

"What am I supposed to do with my time then?" I asked.

"Choose a new career," Pleen said. "You're not all that old. Lots of people do it. Have you considered starting a mail-order business? You can operate it from your home. Or go back to school and take courses in some subject that's always interested you. Or become active in church or civic projects. Find a new hobby, raising hollyhocks or collecting military decorations."

"Pleen," I begged, "just leave me alone."

He seemed hurt. "Sure, if that's what you want." I regretted my harsh words.

All over the country, all over the world, everyone was having the same trouble with the nuhp. It seemed that so many of them had come to Earth, every human had his own personal nup to make endless personal suggestions. There hadn't been so much tension in the world since the 1992 Miss Universe contest, when the most votes went to No Award.

That's why it didn't surprise me very much when the first of our own mother ships returned from its twenty-eight-day voyage among the stars with only two hundred seventy-six of its one thousand passengers still aboard. The other seven hundred twenty-four had remained behind on one lush, exciting, exotic, friendly world or another. These planets had one thing in common: They were all populated by charming, warm, intelligent, humanlike people who had left their own home worlds after being discovered by the nuhp. Many races lived together in peace and harmony on these planets, in spacious cities newly built to house the fed-up expatriates. Perhaps these alien races had experienced the same internal jealousies and hatreds we human beings had known for so long, but no more. Coming together from many planets throughout our galaxy, these various peoples dwelt contentedly beside each other, united by a single common aversion: their dislike for the nuhp.

Within a year of the launching of our first interstellar ship, the population of Earth had declined by one half of one percent. Within two years, the population had fallen by almost fourteen million. The nuhp were too sincere and too eager and too sympathetic to fight with. That didn't make them any less tedious. Rather than make a scene, most people just up and left. There were plenty of really lovely worlds to visit, and it didn't cost very much, and the opportunities in space were unlimited. Many people who were frustrated and disappointed on Earth were able to build new and fulfilling lives for themselves on planets that we didn't even know existed until the nuhp arrived.

The nuhp knew this would happen. It had already happened dozens, hundreds of times in the past, wherever their mother ships touched down. They had made promises to us and they had kept them, although we couldn't have guessed just how things would turn out.

Our cities were no longer decaying warrens imprisoning the impoverished masses. The few people who remained behind could pick and choose among the best housing. Landlords were forced to reduce rents and keep properties in perfect repair just to attract tenants.

Hunger was ended when the ratio of consumers to food producers dropped drastically. Within ten years, the population of Earth was cut in half, and was still falling.

For the same reason, poverty began to disappear. There were plenty of jobs for everyone. When it became apparent that the nuhp weren't going to compete for those jobs, there were more opportunities than people to take advantage of them.

Discrimination and prejudice vanished almost overnight. Everyone cooperated to keep things running smoothly despite the large-scale emigration. The good life was available to everyone, and so resentments melted away. Then, too, whatever enmity people still felt could be focused solely on the nuhp; the nuhp didn't mind, either. They were oblivious to it all.

I am now mayor and postmaster of the small human community of New Dallas, here on Thir, the fourth planet of a star known in our old catalog as Struve 2398. The various alien races we encountered here call the star by another name, which translates into "God's Pineal." All the aliens here are extremely helpful and charitable, and there are few nuhp.

All through the galaxy, the nuhp are considered the messengers of peace. Their mission is to travel from planet to planet, bringing reconciliation, prosperity, and true civilization. There isn't an intelligent race in the galaxy that doesn't love the nuhp. We all recognize what they've done and what they've given us.

But if the nuhp started moving in down the block, we'd be packed and on our way somewhere else by morning.

I AM THE DOORWAY

STEPHEN KING

Richard and I sat on my porch, looking out over the dunes to the Gulf. The smoke from his cigar drifted mellowly in the air, keeping the mosquitoes at a safe distance. The water was a cool aqua, the sky a deeper, truer blue. It was a pleasant combination.

"You are the doorway," Richard repeated thoughtfully. "You are sure you killed the boy—you didn't just dream it?"

"I didn't dream it. And I didn't kill him, either—I told you that. They did. I am the doorway."

Richard sighed. "You buried him?"

"Yes."

"You remember where?"

"Yes." I reached into my breast pocket and got a cigarette. My hands were awkward with their covering of bandages. They itched abominably. "If you want to see it, you'll have to get the dune buggy. You can't roll this"—I indicated my wheelchair—"through the sand." Richard's dune buggy was a 1959 VW with pillow-sized tires. He collected driftwood in it. Ever since he retired from the real estate business in Maryland he had

85

been living on Key Caroline and building driftwood sculptures which he sold to the winter tourists at shameless prices.

He puffed his cigar and looked out at the Gulf. "Not yet. Will you tell me once more?"

I sighed and tried to light my cigarette. He took the matches away from me and did it himself. I puffed twice, dragging deep. The itch in my fingers was maddening.

"All right," I said. "Last night at seven I was out here, looking at the Gulf and smoking, just like now, and—"

"Go further back," he invited.

"Further?"

"Tell me about the flight."

I shook my head. "Richard, we've been through it and through it. There's nothing—"

The seamed and fissured face was as enigmatic as one of his own driftwood sculptures. "You may remember," he said. "Now you may remember."

"Do you think so?"

"Possibly. And when you're through, we can look for the grave."

"The grave," I said. It had a hollow, horrible ring, darker than anything, darker even than all that terrible ocean Cory and I had sailed through five years ago. Dark, dark, dark.

Beneath the bandages, my new eyes stared blindly into the darkness the bandages forced on them. They itched.

• • •

Cory and I were boosted into orbit by the Saturn 16, the one all the commentators called the Empire State Building booster. It was a big beast, all right. It made the old Saturn 1-B look like a Redstone, and it took off from a bunker two hundred feet deep—it had to, to keep from taking half of Cape Kennedy with it.

We swung around the Earth, verifying all our systems, and then did our inject. Headed out for Venus. We left a Senate fighting over an appropriations bill for further deep-space exploration, and a bunch of NASA people praying that we would find something, anything.

"It don't matter what," Don Lovinger, Project Zeus's private whiz kid, was very fond of saying when he'd had a few. "You got all the gadgets, plus five souped-up TV cameras and a nifty little telescope with a zillion lenses and filters. Find some gold or platinum. Better yet, find some nice, dumb little blue men for us to study and exploit and feel superior to. Anything. Even the ghost of Howdy Doody would be a start."

Cory and I were anxious enough to oblige, if we could. Nothing had worked for the deep-space program. From Borman, Anders, and Lovell, who orbited the moon in '68 and found an empty, forbidding world that looked like dirty beach sand, to Markhan and Jacks, who touched down on Mars eleven years later to find an arid wasteland of frozen sand and a few struggling lichens, the deep-space program had been an expensive bust. And there had been casualties—Pedersen and Lederer, eternally circling the sun when all at once nothing worked on the second-to-last Apollo flight. John Davis, whose little orbiting observatory was holed by a meteoroid in a one-in-a-thousand fluke. No, the space program was hardly swinging along. The way things looked, the Venus orbit might be our last chance to say we told you so.

It was sixteen days out—we ate a lot of concentrates, played a lot of gin, and swapped a cold back and forth—and from the tech side it was a milk run. We lost an air-moisture converter on the third day out, went to backup, and that was all, except for nits and nats, until re-entry. We watched Venus grow from a star to a quarter to a milky crystal ball, swapped jokes with Huntsville Control, listened to tapes of Wagner and the Beatles, tended to automated experiments which had to do with everything from measurements of the solar wind to deep-space navigation. We did two midcourse corrections, both of them infinitesimal, and nine days into the flight Cory went outside and banged on the retractable DESA until it decided to operate. There was nothing else out of the ordinary until…

"DESA," Richard said. "What's that?"

"An experiment that didn't pan out. NASA-ese for Deep Space Antenna—we were broadcasting pi in high-frequency pulses for anyone who cared to listen." I rubbed my fingers against my pants, but it was no good; if anything, it made it worse. "Same idea as that radio telescope in West Virginia—you know, the one that listens to the stars. Only instead of listening, we were transmitting, primarily to the deeper space planets—Jupiter, Saturn, Uranus. If there's any intelligent life out there, it was taking a nap."

"Only Cory went out?"

"Yes. And if he brought in any interstellar plague, the telemetry didn't show it."

"Still—"

"It doesn't matter," I said crossly. "Only the here and now matters. They killed the boy last night, Richard. It wasn't a nice thing to watch—or feel. His head...it exploded. As if someone had scooped out his brains and put a hand grenade in his skull."

"Finish the story," he said.

I laughed hollowly. "What's to tell?"

...

We went into an eccentric orbit around the planet. It was radical and deteriorating, three twenty by seventy-six miles. That was on the first swing. The second swing our apogee was even higher, the perigee lower. We had a max of four orbits. We made all four. We got a good look at the planet. Also over six hundred stills and God knows how many feet of film.

The cloud cover is equal parts methane, ammonia, dust, and flying shit. The whole planet looks like the Grand Canyon in a wind tunnel. Cory estimated windspeed at about 600 mph near the surface. Our probe beeped all the way down and then went out with a squawk. We saw no vegetation and no sign of life. Spectroscope indicated only traces of the valuable minerals. And that was Venus. Nothing but nothing—except it scared me. It was like circling a haunted house in the middle of deep space. I know how unscientific that sounds, but I was scared gutless until we got out of there. I think if our rockets hadn't gone off, I would have cut my throat on the way down. It's not like the moon. The moon is desolate but somehow antiseptic. That world we saw was utterly unlike anything that anyone has ever seen. Maybe it's a good thing that cloud cover is there. It was like a skull that's been picked clean—that's the closest I can get.

On the way back we heard the Senate had voted to halve space-exploration funds. Cory said something like "looks like we're back in the weather-satellite business, Artie." But I was almost glad. Maybe we don't belong out there.

Twelve days later Cory was dead and I was crippled for life. We bought all our trouble on the way down. The chute was fouled. How's that for life's little ironies? We'd been in space for over a month, gone further than any humans had ever gone, and it all ended the way it did because some guy was in a hurry for his coffee break and let a few lines get fouled.

We came down hard. A guy that was in one of the copters said it looked like a gigantic baby falling out of the sky, with the placenta trailing after it. I lost consciousness when we hit.

I came to when they were taking me across the deck of the *Portland*. They hadn't even had a chance to roll up the red carpet we were supposed to've walked on. I was bleeding. Bleeding and being hustled up to the infirmary over a red carpet that didn't look anywhere near as red as I did...

•••

"...I was in Bethesda for two years. They gave me the Medal of Honor and a lot of money and this wheelchair. I came down here the next year. I like to watch the rockets take off."

"I know," Richard said. He paused. "Show me your hands."

"No." It came out very quickly and sharply. "I can't let them see. I've told you that."

"It's been five years," Richard said. "Why now, Arthur? Can you tell me that?"

"I don't know. I don't know! Maybe whatever it is has a long gestation period. Or who's to say I even got it out there? Whatever it was might have entered me in Fort Lauderdale. Or right here on this porch, for all I know."

Richard sighed and looked out over the water, now reddish with the late-evening sun. "I'm trying. Arthur, I don't want to think that you are losing your mind."

"If I have to, I'll show you my hands," I said. It cost me an effort to say it. "But only if I have to."

Richard stood up and found his cane. He looked old and frail. "I'll get the dune buggy. We'll look for the boy."

"Thank you, Richard."

He walked out toward the rutted dirt track that led to his cabin—I could just see the roof of it over the Big Dune, the one that runs almost the whole length of Key Caroline. Over the water toward the Cape, the sky had gone an ugly plum color, and the sound of thunder came faintly to my ears.

•••

I didn't know the boy's name but I saw him every now and again, walking along the beach at sunset, with his sieve under his arm. He was tanned almost black by the sun, and all he was ever clad in was a frayed pair of denim cutoffs. On the far side of Key Caroline there is a public beach, and an enterprising young man can make perhaps as much as five dollars on a good day, patiently sieving the sand for buried quarters or dimes. Every now and then I would wave to him and he would wave back, both of us noncommittal, strangers yet brothers, year-round dwellers set against a sea of money-spending, Cadillac-driving, loud-mouthed tourists. I imagine he lived in the small village clustered around the post office about a half mile further down.

When he passed by that evening I had already been on the porch for an hour, immobile, watching. I had taken off the bandages earlier. The itching had been intolerable, and it was always better when they could look through their eyes.

It was a feeling like no other in the world—as if I were a portal just slightly ajar through which they were peeking at a world which they hated and feared. But the worst part was that I could see, too, in a way. Imagine your mind transported into a body of a housefly, a housefly looking into your own face with a thousand eyes. Then perhaps you can begin to see why I kept my hands bandaged even when there was no one around to see them.

It began in Miami. I had business there with a man named Cresswell, an investigator from the Navy Department. He checks up on me once a year—for a while I was as close as anyone ever gets to the classified stuff our space program has. I don't know just what it is he looks for; a shifty gleam in the eye, maybe, or maybe a scarlet letter on my forehead. God knows why. My pension is large enough to be almost embarrassing.

Cresswell and I were sitting on the terrace of his hotel room, sipping drinks and discussing the future of the U.S. space program. It was about three-fifteen. My fingers began to itch. It wasn't a bit gradual. It was switched on like electric current. I mentioned it to Cresswell.

"So you picked up some poison ivy on that scrofulous little island," he said, grinning.

"The only foliage on Key Caroline is a little palmetto scrub," I said. "Maybe it's the seven-year itch." I looked down at my hands. Perfectly ordinary hands. But itchy.

Later in the afternoon I signed the same old paper ("I do solemnly swear that I have neither received nor disclosed and divulged information which would…") and drove myself back to the Key. I've got an old Ford, equipped with hand-operated brake and accelerator. I love it—it makes me feel self-sufficient.

It's a long drive back, down Route 1, and by the time I got off the big road and onto the Key Caroline exit ramp, I was nearly out of my mind. My hands itched maddeningly. If you have ever suffered through the healing of a deep cut or a surgical incision, you may have some idea of the kind of itch I mean. Live things seemed to be crawling and boring in my flesh.

The sun was almost down and I looked at my hands carefully in the glow of the dash lights. The tips of them were red now, red in tiny, perfect circlets, just above the pad where the fingerprint is, where you get calluses if you play guitar. There were also red circles of infection on the space between the first and second joint of each thumb and finger, and on the skin between the second joint and the knuckle. I pressed my right fingers to my lips and withdrew them quickly, with a sudden loathing. A feeling of dumb horror had risen in my throat, woolen and choking. The flesh where the red spots had appeared was hot, feverish, and the flesh was soft and gelid, like the flesh of an apple gone rotten.

I drove the rest of the way trying to persuade myself that I had indeed caught poison ivy somehow. But in the back of my mind there was another ugly thought. I had an aunt, back in my childhood, who lived the last ten years of her life closed off from the world in an upstairs room. My mother took her meals up, and her name was a forbidden topic. I found out later that she had Hansen's disease—leprosy.

When I got home I called Dr. Flanders on the mainland. I got his answering service instead. Dr. Flanders was on a fishing cruise, but if it was urgent, Dr. Ballenger—

"When will Dr. Flanders be back?"

"Tomorrow afternoon at the latest. Would that—"

"Sure."

I hung up slowly, then dialed Richard. I let it ring a dozen times before hanging up. After that I sat indecisive for a while. The itching had deepened. It seemed to emanate from the flesh itself.

I rolled my wheelchair over to the bookcase and pulled down the battered medical encyclopedia that I'd had for years. The book was maddeningly vague. It could have been anything, or nothing.

I leaned back and closed my eyes. I could hear the old ship's clock ticking on the shelf across the room. There was the high, thin drone of a jet on its way to Miami. There was the soft whisper of my own breath.

I was still looking at the book.

The realization crept on me, then sank home with a frightening rush. My eyes were closed, but I was still looking at the book. What I was seeing was smeary and monstrous, the distorted, fourth-dimensional counterpart of a book, yet unmistakable for all that.

And I was not the only one watching.

I snapped my eyes open, feeling the constriction of my heart. The sensation subsided a little, but not entirely. I was looking at the book, seeing the print and diagrams with my own eyes, perfectly normal everyday experience, and I was also seeing it from a different, lower angle and seeing it with other eyes. Seeing not a book but an alien thing, something of monstrous shape and ominous intent.

I raised my hands slowly to my face, catching an eerie vision of my living room turned into a horror house.

I screamed.

There were eyes peering up at me through splits in the flesh of my fingers. And even as I watched the flesh was dilating, retreating, as they pushed their mindless way up to the surface.

But that was not what made me scream. I had looked into my own face and seen a monster.

•••

The dune buggy nosed over the hill and Richard brought it to a halt next to the porch. The motor gunned and roared choppily. I rolled my wheelchair down the inclined plane to the right of the regular steps and Richard helped me in.

"All right, Arthur," he said. "It's your party. Where to?"

I pointed down toward the water, where the Big Dune finally begins to peter out. Richard nodded. The rear wheels spun sand and we were off. I usually found time to rib Richard about his driving, but I didn't bother tonight. There was too much else to think about—and to feel: they didn't want the dark, and I could feel them straining to see through the bandages, willing me to take them off.

The dune buggy bounced and roared through the sand toward the water, seeming almost to take flight from the tops of the small dunes. To the left the sun was going down in bloody glory. Straight ahead and across the water, the thunderclouds were beating their way toward us. Lightning forked at the water.

"Off to your right," I said. "By that lean-to."

Richard brought the dune buggy to a sand-spraying halt beside the rotted remains of the lean-to, reached into the back, and brought out a spade. I winced when I saw it. "Where?" Richard asked expressionlessly.

"Right there." I pointed to the place.

He got out and walked slowly through the sand to the spot, hesitated for a second, then plunged the shovel into the sand. It seemed that he dug for a very long time. The sand he was throwing back over his shoulder looked damp and moist. The thunderheads were darker, higher, and the water looked angry and implacable under their shadow and the reflected glow of the sunset.

I knew long before he stopped digging that he was not going to find the boy. They had moved him. I hadn't bandaged my hands last night, so they could see—and act. If they had been able to use me to kill the boy, they could use me to move him, even while I slept.

"There's no boy, Arthur." He threw the dirty shovel into the dune buggy and sat tiredly on the seat. The coming storm cast marching, crescent-shaped shadows along the sand. The rising breeze rattled sand against the buggy's rusted body. My fingers itched.

"They used me to move him," I said dully. "They're getting the upper hand, Richard. They're forcing their doorway open, a little at a time. A hundred times a day I find myself standing in front of some perfectly familiar object—a spatula, a picture, even a can of beans—with no idea how I got there, holding my hands out, showing it to them, seeing it as they do, as an obscenity, something twisted and grotesque—"

"Arthur," he said. "Arthur, don't. Don't." In the failing light his face was wan with compassion. "*Standing* in front of something, you said. *Moving* the boy's body, you said. *But you can't walk, Arthur.* You're dead from the waist down."

I touched the dashboard of the dune buggy. "This is dead, too. But when you enter it, you can make it go. You could make it kill. It couldn't stop you even if it wanted to." I could hear my voice rising hysterically. "I am the doorway, can't you understand that? They killed the boy, Richard! They moved the body!"

"I think you'd better see a medical man," he said quietly. "Let's go back. Let's—"

"Check! Check on the boy, then! Find out—"

"You said you didn't know his name."

"He must have been from the village. It's a small village. Ask—"

"I talked to Maud Harrington on the phone when I got the dune buggy. If anyone in the state has a longer nose, I've not come across her. I asked if she'd heard of anyone's boy not coming home last night. She said she hadn't."

"But he's a local! He has to be!"

He reached for the ignition switch, but I stopped him. He turned to look at me and I began to unwrap my hands.

From the Gulf, thunder muttered and growled.

•••

I didn't go to the doctor and I didn't call Richard back. I spent three weeks with my hands bandaged every time I went out. Three weeks just blindly hoping it would go away. It wasn't a rational act; I can admit that. If I had been a whole man who didn't need a wheelchair for legs or who had spent a normal life in a normal occupation, I might have gone to Doc Flanders or to Richard. I still might have, if it hadn't been for the memory of my aunt, shunned, virtually a prisoner, being eaten alive by her own failing flesh. So I kept a desperate silence and prayed that I would wake up some morning and find it had been an evil dream.

And little by little, I felt them. Them. An anonymous intelligence. I never really wondered what they looked like or where they had come from. It was moot. I was their doorway, and their window on the world. I got enough feedback from them to feel their revulsion and horror, to know that our world was very different from theirs. Enough feedback to feel their blind hate. But still they watched. Their flesh was embedded in my own. I began to realize that they were using me, actually manipulating me.

When the boy passed, raising one hand in his usual noncommittal salute, I had just about decided to get in touch with Cresswell at his Navy Department number. Richard had been right about one thing—I was certain that whatever had gotten hold of me had done it in deep space or in that weird orbit around Venus. The Navy would study me, but they would not freakify me. I wouldn't have to wake up anymore into the creaking darkness and stifle a scream as I felt them watching, watching, watching.

My hands went out toward the boy and I realized that I had not bandaged them. I could see the eyes in the dying light, watching silently. They were huge, dilated, golden-irised. I had poked one of them against the tip of a pencil once, and had felt excruciating agony slam up my arm. The eye seemed to glare at me with a chained hatred that was worse than physical pain. I did not poke again.

And now they were watching the boy. I felt my mind sideslip. A moment later my control was gone. The door was open. I lurched across the sand toward him, legs scissoring nervelessly, so much driven deadwood. My own eyes seemed to close and I saw only with those alien eyes—saw a monstrous alabaster seascape overtopped with a sky like a great purple way, saw a leaning, eroded shack that might have been the carcass of some unknown, flesh-devouring creature, saw an abominated creature that moved and respired and carried a device of wood and wire under its arm, a device constructed of geometrically impossible right angles.

I wonder what he thought, that wretched, unnamed boy with his sieve under his arm and his pockets bulging with an odd conglomerate of sandy tourist coins, what he thought when he saw me lurching at him like a blind conductor stretching out his hands over a lunatic orchestra, what he thought as the last of the light fell across my hands, red and split and shining with their burden of eyes, what he thought when the hands made that sudden, flailing gesture in the air, just before his head burst.

I know what I thought.

I thought I had peeked over the rim of the universe and into the fires of hell itself.

•••

The wind pulled at the bandages and made them into tiny, whipping streamers as I unwrapped them. The clouds had blotted the red remnants of the sunset, and the dunes were dark and shadow-cast. The clouds raced and boiled above us.

"You must promise me one thing, Richard," I said over the rising wind. "You must run if it seems I might try...to hurt you. Do you understand that?"

"Yes." His open-throated shirt whipped and rippled with the wind. His face was set, his own eyes little more than sockets in early dark.

The last of the bandages fell away.

I looked at Richard and they looked at Richard. I saw a face I had known for five years and come to love. They saw a distorted, living monolith.

"You see them," I said hoarsely. "Now you see them."

He took an involuntary step backward. His face became stained with a sudden unbelieving terror. Lightning slashed out of the sky. Thunder walked in the clouds and the water had gone black as the river Styx.

"Arthur—"

How hideous he was! How could I have lived near him, spoken with him? He was not a creature, but mute pestilence. He was—

"Run! Run, Richard!"

And he did run. He ran in huge, bounding leaps. He became a scaffold against the looming sky. My hands flew up, flew over my head in a screaming, orlesque gesture, the fingers reaching to the only familiar thing in this nightmare world—reaching to the clouds.

And the clouds answered.

There was a huge, blue-white streak of lightning that seemed like the end of the world. It struck Richard, it enveloped him. The last thing I remember is the electric stench of ozone and burnt flesh.

When I awoke I was sitting calmly on my porch, looking out toward the

Big Dune. The storm had passed and the air was pleasantly cool. There was a tiny sliver of moon. The sand was virginal—no sign of Richard or of the dune buggy.

I looked down at my hands. The eyes were open but glazed. They had exhausted themselves. They dozed.

I knew well enough what had to be done. Before the door could be wedged open any further, it had to be locked. Forever. Already I could notice the first signs of structural change in the hands themselves. The fingers were beginning to shorten…and to change.

There was a small hearth in the living room, and in season I had been in the habit of lighting a fire against the damp Florida cold. I lit one now, moving with haste. I had no idea when they might wake up to what I was doing.

When it was burning well I went out back to the kerosene drum and soaked both hands. They came awake immediately, screaming with agony. I almost didn't make it back to the living room, and to the fire.

But I did make it.

•••

That was all seven years ago.

I'm still here, still watching the rockets take off. There have been more of them lately. This is a space-minded administration. There has even been talk of another series of manned Venus probes.

I found out the boy's name, not that it matters. He was from the village, just as I thought. But his mother had expected him to stay with a friend on the mainland that night, and the alarm was not raised until the following Monday. Richard—well, everyone thought Richard was an odd duck, anyway. They suspect he may have gone back to Maryland or taken up with some woman.

As for me, I'm tolerated, although I have quite a reputation for eccentricity myself. After all, how many ex-astronauts regularly write their elected Washington officials with the idea that space-exploration money could be better spent elsewhere?

I get along just fine with these hooks. There was terrible pain for the first year or so, but the human body can adjust to almost anything. I shave with them and even tie my own shoelaces. And as you can see, my typing is nice and even. I don't expect to have any trouble putting the shotgun into my mouth or pulling the trigger. It started again three weeks ago, you see.

There is a perfect circle of twelve golden eyes on my chest.

RECYCLING STRATEGIES FOR THE INNER CITY

PAT MURPHY

I see the metal claw lying in the gutter among the broken bottles and litter, and I recognize it immediately: a piece of an alien spaceship. Before I pick it up, I glance in both directions to make sure no one is watching. The only person nearby is a hooker waiting for a john, and she is watching the cars drive past. A young couple is walking by, but they are looking away, determined to ignore both the hooker and me. They, like so many other people, don't really want to see what's around them.

I scoop up the alien artifact. The claw has three digits, joined together at a thick stalk. The end of the stalk is rough, as if it had broken off a larger piece. Though the day is foggy, the metal is warm to the touch. When I touch the claw, I feel its digits flex in response to my touch, but when I examine it more closely, it lies still.

I add the claw to the treasures in my pink plastic shopping bag, and I hurry to the hotel where I live. Harold is at the front desk when I come in. He's wearing the same dingy white shirt, burgundy tie, and frayed blue suit jacket he always wears. I think he believes that the suit jacket gives him an air of respectability. Harold calls himself the hotel manager, but he's really just the desk clerk. He's a middle-aged man with delusions of grandeur.

He looks up when I walk in. "Your social worker was looking for you today," he grumbled. "She said you had missed your last two appointments." Harold doesn't look at me when he speaks. He looks past me, at a point somewhere over my head.

"I must have forgotten," I tell him. A month ago, I was assigned to a new social worker, a bright young woman just out of graduate school. I suspect that she is an agent of the CIA. The one time that I mentioned the aliens to her, I caught a look in her eyes, a flicker of joyous discovery. She hid her elation, but not before I noticed.

"She left this." He holds out a slip of industrial green paper. It is an official notification that I have an appointment with the city Department of Social Services tomorrow.

I take the paper, drop it in my shopping bag, and head for my room. On my way through the lobby, I pass Mr. Johnson, Mrs. Danneman, and Mrs. Goldman. They sit in the grimy armchairs in the lobby, watching people walk by the hotel's front windows. I nod to them and smile, but they do not respond. They stare past me, like zombies who are trying to remember what life was like. I may be old, but I hope I will never be that close to dead. I punch the button for the elevator.

On the top floor of the hotel, the hallway stinks of other people's food: tomato soup heated on illegal hot plates, greasy burgers from the take-out place on the corner, Chinese food in soggy cardboard containers. Down the center of the hall, there's a long strip of bright red carpet that covers the path where the gray wall-to-wall carpet has worn through. The runner is wearing too: a trail of footprints and dirt marks the center and the edges are starting to fray.

I carry my shopping bag down the hall to my room—a cozy cubicle furnished with a single bed, a battered chest of drawers, and a chair upholstered in turquoise blue vinyl. The room is small, but I've made it my own. Along the walls, I've stacked cardboard boxes filled with the things that I've collected. The paper bags that hold my other treasures fill most of the floor space. A narrow path leads from the door to the chair.

I make my way to the chair and set my shopping bag on the worn gray carpet. This is the best part of the day. Now I sort the treasures I have found, putting each one where it belongs: the buttons go into the bag of buttons, the bottle caps into the box of bottle caps, the broken umbrella into the stack of broken umbrellas. The green slip from the Department of Social Services goes in the trash.

There is no proper place for the metal claw. I set it on the arm of the chair. I will put it with the other spaceship parts, when I find more.

•••

The government does not want people to know about the alien space-ships. They deny all reports of UFOs and flying saucers. The government is good at hiding the things people would rather not see: the old men and women in the lobby, the hookers on the corners, the aliens who visit our world.

But I know about the aliens. Late at night, I sit on the narrow metal balcony of the fire escape outside my window and I watch the sky. The city lights wash out the stars, but there are other lights in the sky: planes landing at the San Francisco airport, police helicopters on patrol, and, of course, the alien spaceships, small sparks that dance just above the buildings of downtown. Sometimes, I can barely see them. I have to squint my eyes and concentrate, staring into the darkness until at last they become clear.

It was drizzling, night before last, when I tried to communicate with the aliens. I had been watching one particular alien spaceship through the rain-streaked window. Its faint wavering light reminded me of fire-flies that I had seen as a child. The light blinked on and off, on and off: a dash, a series of dots. I knew it had to be a message, but I could not translate the signal.

The light came lower, hovering just above the buildings a few blocks away. I left the window and stood by my door, flicking the light switch so that the bare bulb in the ceiling went on and off, on and off, repeating the pattern I had seen. I didn't know how the aliens responded; from my post by the light switch I could not see out the window. As I was repeat-ing the pattern for the third time, I heard the wailing of a siren and the muffled thunder of a police helicopter. I abandoned the light switch and hurried to the window.

The helicopter was circling nearby. The roving beams of its spotlights reflected from the raindrops, forming bright shafts of light that seemed to connect the copter to the ground. The spotlights moved in a frantic, erratic pattern, rippling over the cars, the alleys, the walls of buildings.

Sirens in the street, bright lights flashing blue and red and blue and red, the rattle of gunfire, a distant explosion—I backed away from the window, suddenly frightened. I turned off my light and crawled into bed, pulling the covers up under my chin. I hadn't meant to lure the space-ship in too close. I hadn't meant to cause trouble. For a long time, I lay awake, listening to the sirens.

The next day, Harold said that there had been a drug bust down the street. "Thank God they're doing something to clean up the neighbor-hood," he said to Mrs. Goldman, who wasn't listening.

Harold believes what he reads in the newspapers. He doesn't know about the aliens. He doesn't see the world as it really is.

•••

With the alien claw on the arm of my chair, I lie in my bed, trying to sleep. My room is not a quiet place. The bathroom faucet drips, a delicate tap, tap, tapping in the darkness. The wheezing of buses and the rattling of Muni trains drift up to my window from the street below. My next-door-neighbor's TV rumbles through the walls—he's a little deaf, and he keeps the sound turned up loud.

On this particular night I notice a new noise: a furtive scrabbling that stops each time I move. I sit up in the bed and look around, thinking it might be a rat. I've seen rats on the stairs, nasty gray shadows that flee at the sound of footsteps.

The metal claw is no longer on the arm of the chair. I wait, remaining very still. Finally, by the pale moonlight that filters through my window, I see the claw crouching among the bags and boxes. As I watch, it begins to move again, pulling itself along with its three digits and dragging its broken stalk across the carpet. I shift my weight, the bed creaks, and the claw stops, freezing in position.

It seems so frightened and helpless, crouching on the floor in the dark-ness. "It's all right," I say to it softly. "Don't worry. I won't hurt you. I'm your friend." I remain very still.

Eventually, the claw moves again. I hear a soft rustling as it pushes between the paper bags. I hear it rattling among the broken umbrellas. I fall asleep to the gentle clicking as its digits flex and straighten, flex and straighten again.

• • •

In the morning, I see the claw sunning itself in the pale morning light that comes in the window. When I was a girl on my grandfather's farm, the morning light was yellow—like the corn that grew in the fields, like the sunflowers on the edge of the garden. But the city light is gray. I remember reading somewhere that different stars cast light of different colors. I wonder what color light the claw is used to.

During the night, the claw has improved itself. It has six legs now—the original three and three more that look like they were constructed from the ribs of a broken umbrella. When I sit up in bed, the claw scurries away, seeking refuge among the boxes and bags. I watch it go.

It's comforting to have something alive here in my room. I had a kitten once, a scrawny black alley cat that I found hiding under a dumpster in an alley. But Harold found out about it and told me cats weren't allowed. When I was out, he got into my room and took the kitten away. I don't think he could catch the claw and take it away. I'll bet that the claw would hide so well that he wouldn't even see it.

I get up and wash my face. In a cracked cup, I make myself a cup of instant coffee, using hot water from the bathroom tap. I eat a sweet roll from a bag of day-old donuts that I bought from the shop on the corner. As I eat my breakfast and get dressed, I talk softly to the claw that I know is hidden somewhere among my things. "No one will find you here," I tell the claw. "I'll make sure of that. You'll be okay with me."

The claw does not respond, but I know it's there, hidden and silent. I finish dressing, take my shopping bag, and go out to see what I can find.

• • •

The day is cold and a bitter wind has swept the gutters almost clean. Though I search for hours, I can't find any other spaceship parts. I find other things: a few aluminum cans, a rhinestone brooch with a broken pin, a stray button from someone's coat. Near a construction site, I find a one-foot length of cable made up of many strands of copper wire. But nothing else from the spaceship. Finally, late in the afternoon, I return to my room.

The claw has been busy while I was out. In the narrow space between the bed and the bags of things, it has built a metal framework from the narrow ribs of broken umbrellas. In my absence, it seems to have gained confidence. As I make my way to the chair, it continues working.

The framework forms a cylinder that is maybe six feet long and two feet across. As I watch, the claw neatly snips another rib from a broken umbrella. Carrying the strip of metal in its two front feet, it makes its way to the end of the cylinder, then begins to weave the strip in with the others, pushing it over and under the crisscrossing strips of the framework. It's a clever little machine, busy about its own business. I wonder if it even notices that I'm home.

I set the shopping bag on the floor at my feet and begin to sort through my acquisitions. Boldly, the claw comes over to investigate these additions to my collection. It examines the cable closely, gently separating the individual copper strands. I watch for a moment and then put my hand down by the floor, wiggling my fingers as if coaxing a cat to come nearer. The claw abandons the cable and turns toward my hand, approaching cautiously. It touches me delicately with two of its digits, hesitates, then clambers onto my outstretched hand.

My hands are still cold from being outside. The claw radiates a comforting warmth, like the glow of a wood fire. Moving slowly, I bring it to my lap. It folds its legs beneath it, snuggling down. I stroke it gently and the claw responds by vibrating pleasantly, like a cat purring.

"Were you lonely before I found you?" I ask the claw. "Were you lost and all alone?"

The claw just keeps on purring. I can feel its heat through the fabric of my dress. The warmth soothes my aching legs. It feels so right to hold the claw and just sit.

"You must have been frightened," I say. "It's much better when someone's with you."

I stroke the claw, knowing that I should get up and heat up some soup on the hotplate. But I'm not hungry now, though I haven't eaten since the sweet roll I had for breakfast. Through my window, I watch the sky grow darker. I relax, reluctant to move, and I consider the framework that the claw has constructed.

It could be something dangerous, I suppose, but I rather doubt that. The claw seems like a friendly creature. I study the structure and think about what it might be. Back in school, I remember experimenting with a worm called the planaria. If you cut off a piece of a planaria, the piece will grow into a whole planaria again. All you need is a piece, and the piece re-creates the rest.

Suppose that the alien spaceship was like a planaria. Each part of it contained all the information about the whole thing. Break off one piece, and that piece would go about reconstructing the rest. I consider the framework that the claw has built.

"I'll tell you what I think," I say to the claw. "I think you are rebuilding the spaceship that blew up."

The claw shows no interest in my theories. After a time, it scrambles off my lap and gets back to work, busily weaving the copper wire in and out through the framework it has built. Every now and then, it selects a metal button from the box of buttons, threads the wire through the holes in the button, and then continues its weaving. I can see no pattern to its selection or placement of buttons. That night, I lie awake, listening to the rustlings of the claw as it searches among my things and assembles them into an alien pattern.

I wake to the rattle of aluminum. The claw is hard at work. Flattened aluminum cans fill the gaps in the framework, held in place by a lacework of copper wire. Pearl buttons and rhinestone brooches, scavenged from my bags and boxes, sparkle among the cans. The claw scrambles over the surface, tirelessly weaving copper wire over the can that it is adding. It looks so natural there: like a spider on its web.

I don't want to leave. I'm afraid that if I leave, the claw will be gone when I come back. I sit on the edge of the bed to watch it work. As I watch, it hesitates for a moment, and then leaves its work to rest on the floor at my feet. When I reach out to touch it, it clambers onto my hand and lets me put it in my lap. For a time, it sits in my lap and purrs, then it returns to work.

I feel sad, watching the claw build the craft that will take it away. Eventually, I go out on my usual rounds, unwilling to watch any longer.

•••

It is a cold, bleak day, and I find nothing of interest. A few aluminum cans, a few bottle caps. Maybe the claw can use them to complete its work. I carry them back to the hotel.

My social worker is waiting for me in the lobby, perched uncomfortably on the dingy sofa. She sits between Mrs. Goldman and Mr. Johnson. She is talking brightly about something, but they are ignoring her, lost in their own hazy thoughts. She catches me before I can slip past.

"I'm so glad to see you," she said. "I was quite worried when you missed your appointment. I asked the manager to check your room." She glanced at Harold, but he was busy with his papers, refusing to look up. "You know, we really must clean up all that trash beside your bed."

I stare at her. "What are you talking about?"

"All those cans and things. It's really a health hazard. I've already arranged to have someone come in tomorrow and—"

"You can't do that," I protested. "Those are my things."

"Now just relax," she said, her voice dripping with understanding. "It really isn't safe. Imagine if there were a fire. You'd never be able to get out of your room with all that clutter. It's really best—"

"If there were a fire, we'd all roast like marshmallows," I say, but she isn't listening.

"—best if we clean it all up for you. I wouldn't be doing my job if I didn't—"

I back away from her and flee to my room. Fortunately, she doesn't follow. Even if she isn't an agent of the government, she is dangerous. She wants to teach me to overlook things, to look past things, to ignore the world. She thinks there is only one way of looking at the world—her way. I don't agree.

• • •

I rush into my room and close the door. The spaceship fills the space between the bed and the boxes. A hinged lid, like the lid of a pirate chest, stands open, poised to close. I put my hand on the tail section. I can feel a faint trembling, as if something were humming inside. The claw crouches beside the lid, waiting.

"You'd better get out of here," I tell the claw. "They're closing in on us. They'll lock us both up."

I open the window so that the spaceship can take off. When I stand back, nothing happens. The claw just sits by the lid, remaining motionless.

"Look, you'd really better leave," I say. It doesn't move. I sit in the chair and watch it, frustrated by its inaction. From the TV next door, I hear the *Star Trek* theme song.

The claw climbs to the armrest of the chair. With two of its legs, it takes hold of my finger. Gently, it tugs on my hand, trying to move me in the direction of the cylinder.

"What do you want?" I ask, but it only tugs again, more strongly this time.

I pick up the claw in my other hand and go to the spaceship. The hollow place inside it is just my height and just wide enough for my shoulders. The claw had arranged some old sweaters inside: it looks soft and rather inviting.

Maybe I wasn't quite right the other night when I was thinking about planaria. I should have thought a little longer. Consider, for instance, the difference between a horse and a car. A horse has a mind of his own. You develop a relationship with a horse. If you like the horse and the horse likes you, you get along; if not, you don't. A horse can miss you. If you leave a horse behind, the horse can come looking for you. A car is just a hunk of metal—no loyalty. If you sell your car, you may miss it, but it won't miss you.

Suppose, just suppose, that someone somewhere built a spaceship that was more like a horse than a car. A spaceship that could rebuild itself from pieces. That someone went away and left the spaceship behind—died maybe, because otherwise why would anyone leave behind such a wonderful spaceship? And the spaceship waited for a while, and then came looking for its creator, its master. Maybe it couldn't find its original master—but it found someone else. Someone who wanted to travel. The claw is purring in my hand.

I take off my shoes and step gingerly into the opening. Carefully, I slide my legs into the cylinder. At my feet, I can feel the warmth of the hidden engines. The claw curls up beside me, snuggling into the crook of my neck.

"Ready?" I ask. Reaching up, I close the lid. And we go.

THE 43 ANTAREAN DYNASTIES

MIKE RESNICK

To thank the Maker Of All Things for the birth of his first male off-spring, the Emperor Maloth IV ordered his architects to build a temple that would forever dwarf all other buildings on the planet. It was to be made entirely of crystal, and the spire-covered roof, which looked like a million glistening spear-points aimed at the sun, would be supported by 217 columns, to honor his 217 forebears. When struck, each column would sound a musical note that could be heard for kilometers, calling the faithful to prayer.

The structure would be known as the Temple of the Honored Sun, for his heir had been born exactly at midday, when the sun was highest in the sky. The temple took 27 Standard years to complete, and although races from all across the galaxy would come to Antares III to marvel at it, Maloth further decreed that no aliens or non-believers would ever be allowed to enter it and desecrate its sacred corridors with their presence...

•••

A man, a woman, and a child emerge from the Temple of the Honored Sun. The woman holds a camera to her eye, capturing the same image from a dozen unimaginative angles. The child, his lip sparsely covered with hair that is supposed to imply maturity, never sees beyond the game he is playing on his pocket computer. The man looks around to make sure no one is watching him, grinds out a smokeless cigar beneath his heel, and then increases his pace until he joins them.

They approach me, and I will myself to become one with my surroundings, to insinuate myself into the marble walls and stone walkways before they can speak to me.

I am invisible. You cannot see me. You will pass me by.

"Hey, fella—we're looking for a guide," says the man. "You interested?"

I stifle a sigh and bow deeply. "I am honored," I say, glad that they do not understand the subtleties of Antarean inflection.

"Wow!" exclaims the woman, aiming her camera at me. "I never saw anything like that! It's almost as if you folded your torso in half! Can you do it again?"

I am reminded of an ancient legend, possibly apocryphal though I choose to believe it. An ambassador who was equally fascinated by the way the Antarean body is jointed, once asked Komarith I, the founder of the 38th Dynasty, to bow a second time. Komarith merely stared at him without moving until the embarrassed ambassador slunk away. He went on to rule for twenty-nine years and was never known to bow again.

It has been a long time since Komarith, almost seven millennia now, and Antares and the universe have changed. I bow for the woman while she snaps her holographs.

"What's your name?" asks the man.

"You could not pronounce it," I reply. "When I conduct members of your race, I choose the name Hermes."

"Herman, eh?"

"Hermes," I correct him.

"Right. Herman."

The boy finally looks up. "He said Hermes, Dad."

The man shrugs. "Whatever." He looks at his timepiece. "Well, let's get started."

"Yeah," chimes in the child. "They're piping in the game from Roosevelt III this afternoon. I've got to get back for it."

"You can watch sports anytime," says the woman. "This may be your only chance to see Antares."

"I should be so lucky," he mutters, returning his attention to his computer.

I recite my introductory speech almost by rote. "Allow me to welcome you to Antares III, and to its capital city of Kalimetra, known throughout the galaxy as the City of a Million Spires."

"I didn't see any million spires when we took the shuttle in from the spaceport," says the child, who I could have sworn was not listening. "A thousand or two, maybe."

"There was a time when there were a million," I explain. "Today only 16,304 remain. Each is made of quartz or crystal. In late afternoon, when the sun sinks low in the sky, they act as a prism for its rays, creating a flood of exotic colors that stretches across the thoroughfares of the city. Races have come from halfway across the galaxy to experience the effect."

"Sixteen thousand," murmurs the woman. "I wonder what happened to the rest?"

• • •

No one knew why Antareans found the spires so aesthetically pleasing. They towered above the cities, casting their shadows and their shifting colors across the landscape. Tall, delicate, exquisite, they reflected a unique grandness of vision and sensitivity of spirit. The rulers of Antares III spent almost 38,000 years constructing their million spires.

During the Second Invasion, it took the Canphorite armada less than two weeks to destroy all but 16,304 of them...

• • •

The woman is still admiring the spires that she can see in the distance. Finally she asks who built them, as if they are too beautiful to have been created by Antareans.

"The artisans and craftsmen of my race built everything you will see today," I answer.

"All by yourselves?"

"Is it so difficult for you to believe?" I ask gently.

"No," she says defensively. "Of course not. It's just that there's so much..."

"Kalimetra was not created in a day or a year, or even a millennium," I point out. "It is the cumulative achievement of 43 Antarean Dynasties."

"So we're in the 43rd Dynasty now?" she asks.

•••

It was Zelorean IX who officially declared Kalimetra to be the Eternal City. Neither war nor insurrection had ever threatened its stability, and even the towering temples of his forefathers gave every promise of lasting for all eternity. It was a Golden Age, and he could see no reason why it should not go on forever...

•••

"The last absolute ruler of the 43rd Dynasty has been dust for almost three thousand years," I explain. "Since then we have been governed by a series of conquerors, each alien race superseding the last."

"Thank goodness they didn't destroy your buildings," says the woman, turning to admire a water fountain, which for some reason appears to her to be a mystical alien artifact. She is about to take a holo when the child restrains her.

"It's just a goddamned water bubbler, Ma," he says.

"But it's fascinating," she says. "Imagine what kind of beings used it in ages past."

"Thirsty ones," says the bored child.

She ignores him and turns back to me. "As I was saying, it must be criminal to rob the galaxy of such treasures."

"Yeah, well *somebody* destroyed some buildings around here," interjects the child, who seems intent on proving someone wrong about something. "Remember the hole in the ground we saw over that way?" He points in the direction of the Footprint. "Looks like a bomb crater to me."

"You are mistaken," I explain, leading them over to it. "It has always been there."

"It's just a big sinkhole," says the man, totally unimpressed.

"It is worshipped by my people as the Footprint of God," I explain.

"Once, many eons ago, Kalimetra was in the throes of a years-long drought. Finally Jorvash, our greatest priest, offered his own life if God would bring the rains. God replied that it would not rain until He wept again, and we had not yet suffered enough to bring forth His tears of compassion. But He promised that He would strike a bargain with Jorvash." I pause for effect, but the man is lighting another cigar and the child is concentrating on his pocket computer. "The next morning Jorvash was found dead inside his temple, while God had created this depression with His foot and filled it with water. It sustained us until He finally wept again."

The woman seems flustered. "Um…I hate to ask," she finally says, "but could you repeat that story? My recorder wasn't on."

The man looks uncomfortable. "She's always forgetting to turn the damned thing on," he explains, and flips me a coin. "For your trouble."

• • •

Lobilia was the greatest poet in the history of Antares III. Although he died during the 23rd Dynasty, most of his work survived him. But his masterpiece, "The Long Night of the Exile"—the epic of Bagata's Exile and his triumphant Return—was lost forever.

Though he was his race's most famous bard, Lobilia himself was illiterate, unable even to write his own name. He created his poetry extemporaneously, embellishing upon it with each retelling. He recited his epic just once, and was so satisfied with its form that he refused to repeat it for the scribes who were waiting for a final version and hadn't written it down.

• • •

"Thank you," says the woman, deactivating the recorder after I finish. She pauses. "Can I buy a book with some more of your quaint folk legends?"

I decide not to explain the difference between a folk legend and an article of belief. "They are for sale in the gift shop of your hotel," I reply.

"You don't have enough books?" mutters the man.

She glares at him, but says nothing, and I lead them to the Tomb, which always impresses visitors.

"This is the Tomb of Bedorian V, the greatest ruler of the 37th Dynasty," I say. "Bedorian was a commoner, a simple farmer who deposed the notorious Maelastri XII, himself a mighty warrior who was the last ruler of the 36th Dynasty. It was Bedorian who decreed universal education for all Antareans."

"What did you have before that?"

"Our females were not allowed the privilege of literacy until Bedorian's reign."

"How did this guy finally die?" asks the man, who doesn't really care but is unwilling to let the woman ask all the questions.

"Bedorian was assassinated by one of his followers," I reply.

"A male, no doubt," says the woman wryly.

"Before he died," I continue, "he united three warring states without fighting a single battle, decreed that all Antareans should use a common language, and outlawed the worship of *kreneks*."

"What are *kreneks?*"

"They are poisonous reptiles. They killed many worshippers in nameless, obscene ceremonies before Bedorian V came to power."

"Yeah?" says the child, alert again. "What were they like?"

"What is obscene to one being is simply boring to another," I say. "Terrans find them dull." Which is not true, but I have no desire to watch the child snicker as I describe the rituals.

"What a shame," says the woman, though her voice sounds relieved. "Still, you certainly seem to know your history."

I want to answer that I just make up the stories. But I am afraid if I say it, she will believe it.

"Where did you learn all this stuff?" she continues.

"To become a licensed guide," I reply, "an Antarean must undergo fourteen years of study, and must also speak a minimum of four alien languages fluently. Terran is always one of the four."

"That's some set of credentials," comments the man. "I made it through one year of dental school and quit."

And yet, it is you who are paying me.

"I'm surprised you don't work at one of the local universities," he continues.

"I did once."

Which is true. But I have my family to feed—and tourists' tips, however small and grudgingly given, are still greater than my salary as a teacher.

A *rapu*—an Antarean child—insinuates his way between myself and my clients. Scarcely more than an infant, he is dressed in rags, and his face is smudged with dirt. There are open sores on the reticulated plates of his skin, and his golden eyes water constantly. He begs plaintively for credits in his native tongue. When there is no response, he extends his hand in what has become a universal gesture that says: *You are rich. I am poor and hungry. Give me money.*

"Yours?" asks the man, frowning, as his wife takes half a dozen holos in quick succession.

"No, he is not mine."

"What is he doing here?"

"He lives in the street," I answer, my compassion for the *rapu* alternating with my humiliation at having to explain his presence and situation. "He is asking for coins so that he and his mother will not go hungry tonight."

I look at the *rapu* and think sadly: *Timing is everything. Once, long ago, we strode across our world like gods. You would not have gone hungry in any of the 43 Dynasties.*

The human child looks at his Antarean counterpart. I wonder if he realizes how fortunate he is. His face gives no reflection of his thoughts; perhaps he has none. Finally he picks his nose and goes back to manipulating his computer.

The man stares at the *rapu* for a moment, then flips him a two-credit coin. The *rapu* catches it, bows and blesses the man, and runs off. We watch him go. He raises the coin above his head, yelling happily—and a moment later, we are surrounded by twenty more street urchins, all filthy, all hungry, all begging for coins.

"Enough's enough!" says the man irritably. "Tell them to get the hell out of here and go home, Herman."

"They live here," I explain gently.

"Right here?" demands the man. He stomps the ground with his foot, and the nearest *rapus* jump back in fright. "On this spot? Okay, then tell them to stay here where they live and not follow us."

I explain to the *rapus* in our own tongue that these tourists will not give them coins.

"Then we will go to the ugly pink hotel where all the Men stay and rob their rooms."

"That is none of my concern," I say. "But if you are caught, it will go hard with you."

The oldest of the urchins smiles at my warning.

"If we are caught, they will lock us up, and because it is a jail they will have to feed us, and we will be protected from the rain and the cold—it is far better than being here."

I have no answer for *rapus* whose only ambition is to be warm and dry and well-fed, but merely shrug. They run off, laughing and singing, as if they are human children off to play some game.

"Damned aliens!" mutters the man.

"That is incorrect," I say.

"Oh?"

"A matter of semantics," I point out gently. "*They* are indigenous. *You* are the aliens."

"Well, they could do with some lessons in behavior from us aliens, then," he growls.

We walk up the long ramp to the Tomb and are about to enter it, when the woman stops.

"I'd like a holo of the three of you standing in the entrance," she announces. She smiles at me. "Just to prove to our friends we were here, and that we met a real Antarean."

The man walks over and stands on one side of me. The child reluctantly moves to my other side.

"Now put your arm around Herman," says the woman.

The child steps back, and I see a mixture of contempt and disgust on his face. "I'll pose with it, but I won't *touch* it!"

"You do what your mother says!" snaps the man.

"No way!" says the child, stalking sulkily back down the ramp. "You want to hug him, you go ahead!"

"You listen to me, young man!" says the man, but the child does not stop or give any indication that he has heard, and soon he disappears behind a temple.

•••

It was Tcharock, the founder of the 30th Dynasty, who decreed that the person of the Emperor was sacrosanct and could not be touched by any being other than his medics and his concubines, and then only with his consent.

His greatest advisor was Chaluba, who extended Tcharock's rule to more than 80% of the planet and halted the hyper-inflation that had been the 29th Dynasty's legacy to him.

One night, during a state function, Chaluba inadvertently brushed against Tcharock while introducing him to the Ambassador from far Domar.

The next morning Tcharock regretfully gave the signal to the executioner, and Chaluba was beheaded. Despite this unfortunate beginning, the 30th Dynasty survived for 1,062 Standard years.

• • •

The woman, embarrassed, begins apologizing to me. But I notice that she, too, avoids touching me. The man goes off after the child, and a few moments later the two of them return—which is just as well, for the woman has begun repeating herself.

The man pushes the child toward me, and he sullenly utters an apology. The man takes an ominous step toward him, and he reluctantly reaches out his hand. I take it briefly—the contact is no more pleasant for me than for him—and then we enter the Tomb. Two other groups are there, but they are hundreds of meters away, and we cannot hear what their guides are saying.

"How high is the ceiling?" asks the woman, training her camera on the exquisite carvings overhead.

"Thirty-eight meters," I say. "The Tomb itself is 203 meters long and 67 meters wide. The body of Bedorian V is in a large vault beneath the floor." I pause, thinking as always of past glories. "On the Day of Mourning, the day the Tomb was completed, a million Antareans stood patiently in line outside the Tomb to pay their last respects."

"I don't mean to ask a silly question," says the woman, "but why are all the buildings so *enormous?*"

"Ego," suggests the man, confident in his wisdom.

"The Maker Of All Things is huge," I explain. "So my people felt that any monuments to Him should be as large as possible, so that He might be comfortable inside them."

"You think your God can't find or fit into a small building?" asks the man with a condescending smile.

"He is everyone's God," I answer. "And while He can of course find a small temple, why should we force Him to live in one?"

"Did Bedorian have a wife?" asks the woman, her mind back to smaller considerations.

"He had five of them," I answer. "The tomb next to this one is known as the Place of Bedorian's Queens."

"He was a polygamist?"

I shake my head. "No. Bedorian simply outlived his first four queens."

"He must have died a very old man," says the woman.

"He did not," I answer. "There is a belief among my people that those who achieve public greatness are doomed to private misery. Such was Bedorian's fate." I turn to the child, who has been silent since returning, and ask him if he has any questions, but he merely glares at me without speaking.

"How long ago was this place built?" asks the man.

"Bedorian V died 6,302 Standard years ago. It took another seventeen years to build and prepare the Tomb."

"6,302 years," he muses. "That's a long time."

"We are an ancient race," I reply proudly. "A human anthropologist has suggested that our 3rd Dynasty commenced before your ancestors crossed over the evolutionary barrier into sentience."

"Maybe we spent a long time living in the trees," says the man, clearly unimpressed and just a bit defensive. "But look how quickly we passed you once we climbed down."

"If you say so," I answer noncommittally.

"In fact, everybody passed you," he persists. "Look at the record: How many times has Antares been conquered?"

"I am not sure," I lie, for I find it humiliating to speak of it.

•••

When the Antareans learned that Man's Republic wished to annex their world, they gathered their army in Zanthu and then marched out onto the battlefield, 300,000 strong. They were the cream of the planet's young warriors, gold of eye, the reticulated plates of their skin glistening in the morning sun, prepared to defend their homeworld.

The Republic sent a single ship that flew high overhead and dropped a single bomb, and in less than a second there was no longer an Antarean army, or a city of Zanthu, or a Great Library of Cthstoka.

Over the millennia Antares was conquered four times by Man, twice by the Canphor Twins, and once each by Lodin XI, Emra, Ramor, and the Sett Empire. It was said that the parched ground had finally quenched its thirst by drinking a lake of Antarean blood.

• • •

As we leave the Tomb, we come to a small, skinny *rapu*. He sits on a rock, staring at us with his large, golden eyes, his expression rapt in contemplation.

The human child pointedly ignores him and continues walking toward the next temple, but the adults stop.

"What a cute little thing!" enthuses the woman. "And he looks so hungry." She digs into her shoulder bag and withdraws a sweet that she has kept from breakfast. "Here," she says, holding it up. "Would you like it?"

The *rapu* never moves. This is unique not only in the woman's experience, but also in mine, for he is obviously undernourished.

"Maybe he can't metabolize it," suggests the man. He pulls a coin out, steps over to the *rapu,* and extends his hand. "Here you go, kid."

The *rapu,* his face frozen in contemplation, makes no attempt to grab the coin.

And suddenly I am thinking excitedly: *You disdain their food when you are hungry, and their money when you are poor. Could you possibly be the One we have awaited for so many millennia, the One who will give us back our former glory and initiate the 44th Dynasty?*

I study him intently, and my excitement fades just as quickly as it came upon me. The *rapu* does not disdain their food and their money. His golden eyes are clouded over. Life in the streets has so weakened him that he has become blind, and of course he does not understand what they are saying. His seeming arrogance comes not from pride or some inner light, but because he is not aware of their offerings.

"Please," I say, gently taking the sweet from the woman without coming into actual contact with her fingers. I walk over and place it in the *rapu*'s hand. He sniffs it, then gulps it down hungrily and extends his hand, blindly begging for more.

"It breaks your heart," says the woman.

"Oh, it's no worse than what we saw on Bareimus V," responds the man. "They were every bit as poor—and remember that awful skin disease that they all had?"

The woman considers, and her face reflects the unpleasantness of the memory. "I suppose you're right at that." She shrugs, and I can tell that even though the child is still in front of us, hand outstretched, she has already put him from her mind.

I lead them through the Garden of the Vanished Princes, with its tormented history of sacrifice and intrigue, and suddenly the man stops.

"What happened here?" he asks, pointing to a number of empty pedestals.

"History happened," I explain. "Or avarice, for sometimes they are the same thing." He seems confused, so I continue: "If any of our conquerors could find a way to transport a treasure back to his home planet, he did. Anything small enough to be plundered *was* plundered."

"And these statues that have been defaced?" he says, pointing to them. "Did you do it yourselves so they would be worthless to occupying armies?"

"No," I answer.

"Well, whoever did *that*"—he points to a headless statue—"ought to be strung up and whipped."

"What's the fuss?" asks the child in a bored voice. "They're just statues of aliens."

"Actually, the human who did that was rewarded with the governorship of Antares III," I inform them.

"What are you talking about?" says the man.

"The second human conquest of the Antares system was led by Commander Lois Kiboko," I begin. "She defaced or destroyed more than 3,000 statues. Many were physical representations of our deity, and since she and her crew were devout believers in one of your religions, she felt that these were false idols and must be destroyed."

"Well," the man replies with a shrug, "it's a small price to pay for her saving you from the Lodinites."

"Perhaps," I say. "The problem is that we had to pay a greater price for each successive savior."

He stares at me, and there is an awkward silence. Finally I suggest that we visit the Palace of the Supreme Tyrant.

"You seem such a docile race," she says awkwardly. "I mean, so civilized and unaggressive. How did your gene pool ever create a real, honest-to-goodness tyrant?"

The truth is that our gene pool was considerably more aggressive before a seemingly endless series of alien conquests decimated it. But I know that this answer would make them uncomfortable, and could affect the size of my tip, so I lie to them instead. (I am ashamed to admit that lying to aliens becomes easier with each passing day. Indeed, I am sometimes amazed at the facility with which I can create falsehoods.)

"Every now and then each race produces a genetic sport," I say, and I can see she believes it, "and we Antareans are so docile, to use your expression, that this particular one had no difficulty achieving power."

"What was his name?"

"I do not know."

"I thought you took fourteen years' worth of history courses," she says accusingly, and I can tell she thinks I am lying to her, whereas every time I have actually lied she has believed me.

"Our language has many dialects, and they have all evolved and changed over 36,000 years," I point out. "Some we have deciphered, but to this day many of them remain unsolved mysteries. In fact, right at this moment a team of human archaeologists is hard at work trying to uncover the Tyrant's name."

"If it's a dead language, how are they going to manage that?"

"In the days when your race was still planetbound, there was an artifact called the Rosetta Stone that helped you translate an ancient language. We have something similar—ours is known as the Bosperi Scroll—that comes from the Great Tyrant's era."

"Where is it?" asks the woman, looking around.

"I regret to inform you that both the archaeologists and the Bosperi Scroll are currently in a museum on Deluros VIII."

"Smart," says the man. "They can protect it better on Deluros."

"From who?" asks the woman.

"From anyone who wants to steal it, of course," he says, as if explaining it to a child.

"But I mean, who would want to steal the key to a dead language?"

"Do you know what it would be worth to a collector?" answers the man. "Or a thief who wanted to ransom it?"

They discuss it further, but the simple truth is that it is on Deluros because it was small enough to carry, and for no other reason. When they are through arguing I tell her that it is because they have devices on Deluros that will bring back the faded script, and she nods her head thoughtfully.

We walk another 400 meters and come to the immense Palace of the Kings. It is made entirely of gold, and becomes so hot from the rays of the sun that one can touch the outer surface only at night. This was the building in which all the rulers of the 7th through the 12th Dynasties resided. It was from here that my race received the Nine Proclamations of Ascendancy, and the Charter of Universal Rights, and our most revered document, the Mabelian Declaration.

It was a wondrous time to have lived, when we had never tasted defeat and all problems were capable of solution, when stately caravans plied their trade across secure boundaries and monarchs were just and wise, when each day brought new triumphs and the future held infinite promise.

I point to the broken and defaced stone chair. "Once there were 246 jewels and precious stones embedded in the throne."

The child walks over to the throne, then looks at me accusingly. "Where are they?" he demands.

"They were all stolen over the millennia," I reply.

"By conquerors, of course," offers the woman with absolute certainty.

"Yes," I say, but again I am lying. They were stolen by my own people, who traded them to various occupying armies for food or the release of captive loved ones.

We spend a few more minutes examining the vanished glory of the Palace of the Kings, then walk out the door and approach the next crumbling structure. It is the Hall of the Thinkers, revered to this day by all Antareans, but I know they will not understand why a race would create such an edifice to scholarship, and I haven't the energy to explain, so I tell them that it is the Palace of the Concubines, and of course they believe me. At one point the child, making no attempt to mask his disappointment, asks why there are no statues or carvings showing the concubines, and I think very quickly and explain that Lois Kiboko's religious beliefs were offended by the sexual frankness of the artifacts and she had them all destroyed.

I feel guilty about this lie, for it is against the Code of Just Behavior to suggest that a visitor's race may have offended in any way. Ironically, while the child voices his disappointment, I notice that none of the three seems to have a problem accepting that another human would destroy millennia-old artwork that upset his sensibilities. I decide that since they feel no guilt, this one time I shall feel none either. (But I still do. Tradition is a difficult thing to transcend.)

I see the man anxiously walking around, looking into corners and behind pedestals, and I ask him if something is wrong.

"Where's the can?" he says.

"I beg your pardon?"

"The can. The bathroom. The lavatory." He frowns. "Didn't any of these goddamned concubines ever have to take a crap?"

I finally discern what he wants and direct him to a human facility that has been constructed just beyond the Western Door.

He returns a few minutes later, and I lead them all outside, past the towering Onyx Obelisk that marked the beginning of the almost-forgotten 4th Dynasty. We stop briefly at the Temple of the River of Light, which was constructed *over* the river, so that the sacred waters flow through the temple itself.

We leave and turn a corner, and suddenly a single structure completely dominates the landscape.

"What's *that?*" asks the woman.

"That is the Spiral Ramp to Heaven," I answer.

"What a fabulous name!" she enthuses. "I just know a fabulous story goes with it!" She turns to me expectantly.

"There was a time, before our scientists knew better, that people thought you could reach heaven if you simply built a tall enough ramp."

The child guffaws.

"It is true," I continue. "Construction was begun during the 2nd Dynasty, and continued for more than 700 years until midway through the 3rd. It looks as if you can see the top from here, but you actually are looking only at the bottom half of it. The rest is obscured by clouds."

"How high does it go?" asked the woman.

"More than nine kilometers," I say. "Three kilometers higher than our tallest mountain."

"Amazing!" she exclaims.

"Perhaps you would like a closer look at it?" I suggest. "You might even wish to climb the first kilometer. It is a very gentle ascent until you reach the fifth kilometer."

"Yes," she replies happily. "I think I'd like that very much."

"I'm not climbing anything," says the man.

"Oh, come on," she urges him. "It'll be fun!"

"The air's too thin and the gravity's too heavy and it's too damned much like work. One of these days *I'm* going to choose our itinerary, and I promise you it won't involve so goddamned much walking."

"Can we go back and watch the game?" asks the child eagerly.

The man takes one more look at the Spiral Ramp to Heaven. "Yeah," he says. "I've seen enough. Let's go back."

"We really should finish the tour," says the woman. "We'll probably never be in this sector of the galaxy again."

"So what? It's just another backwater world," replies the man. "Don't tell your friends about the Stairway to the Stars or whatever the hell it's called and they'll never know you missed it."

Then the woman comes up with what she imagines will be the clinching argument. "But you've already agreed to pay for the tour."

"So we'll cut it short and pay him half as much," says the man. "Big deal."

The man pulls a wad of credits out of his pocket and peels off three ten-credit notes. Then he pauses, looks at me, pockets them, and presses a fifty-credit note into my hand instead.

"Ah, hell, you kept your end of the bargain, Herman," he says. Then he and the woman and child begin walking back to the hotel.

•••

The first aliens ever to visit Antares were rude and ill-mannered barbarians, but Perganian II, the greatest Emperor of the 31st Dynasty, decreed that they must be treated with the utmost courtesy. When the day of their departure finally arrived, the aliens exchanged farewells with Perganian, and one of them thrust a large, flawless blue diamond into the Emperor's hand in payment for his hospitality.

After the aliens left the courtyard, Perganian let the diamond drop to the ground, declaring that no Antarean could be purchased for any price.

The diamond lay where it had fallen for three generations, becoming a holy symbol of Antarean dignity and independence. It finally vanished during a dust storm and was never seen again.

THE GOLD BUG

ORSON SCOTT CARD

I t was all based on trust, wasn't it? You join the Fleet, you train until it's as natural to pilot your ship as to dance, as reflexive to fight with the ship's weapons as to use your fists. Then you go where they send you, leaving behind your family and friends, knowing that relativistic travel ensures you'll never see them again. To all intents and purposes, you've already given your life for your country—no, your species.

You can only trust that when you commit to battle near some far-off world, the commander they've assigned to you will actually win, will make it worth the sacrifice.

As to you, personally, does it matter whether you live or die? Sel Menach asked himself this question more than once during the two-year voyage to war. Sometimes he thought it really didn't matter at all. All he cared about was victory.

But when they got to the Formic world, forty lightyears from Earth, and he and his warship hurtled from the transport and faced the enemy formation, he discovered that no matter what his mind decided, his body was determined to live.

It was a child's voice he heard over his headset, giving commands to his squad. And another child giving commands to his commander. They had been warned; it had been explained to them. Mazer Rackham's voice came over the ansible, acquainting them with how these children had been screened, trained, tested, and now the finest military minds among the human race, the most relentlessly competitive, with the fastest reflexes, would give them their orders.

"They don't know the test they're taking is real," said Rackham. "To them, it's all about winning. I can assure you that the supreme commander, Ender Wiggin, does not waste his resources. He will be as careful of your lives as if he knew you were there."

We're trusting our lives to children?

But what choice did they have?

In some ways, the actual battle was not too different from what the children must be experiencing on their simulators. Inside Sel's fighter, there was no sound except the voices of commanders and fellow pilots, and the Dvorak and Smetana he always played to help keep him calm and focused. When a fellow pilot was killed, all Sel heard was the soft voice of the computer saying "Connection broken with" and the fighter's i.d. If the killed ship had been maneuvering fairly nearby, there would be a blink of light on the simulator.

An hour after they poured out of the transport it was over. Total victory. Not a Formic ship in the sky. And their losses had been, all else being equal, light.

Mazer's promise about the child commanders turned out to be true. When the surviving fighters returned to the transport and sat together to watch the replay of the battle on the large simulator, no one could find a single decision to criticize.

Each of the individual children had done well; but on the third viewing Sel began to grasp the genius of Ender Wiggin's overall strategy. He had maneuvered the enemy into an untenable position, forcing the enemy to expose himself, the enemy to be aggressive, the enemy to sustain the losses. Wiggin had been careful of lives that he didn't even know where involved.

But victory in this place was not complete victory. Who knew how many ships were under construction on the planet's surface? How long would it be before a new enemy arose?

They watched the succeeding battles, fought near different worlds, on their simulator, and Sel's awe at these children only grew. There were mistakes, but the overall design of the battles was always so deft that they were all in awe of Ender Wiggin.

As the Admiral of their expedition said, "No military force has ever been so well commanded or so wisely used."

Then came the final battle, when they were lost in despair. Vast swarms of enemy ships hopelessly outnumbered the human fleet.

"If he thinks it's a game," said Sel to his friend Ramon, "or even a test, what's to stop him from refusing to go on?"

"Refuse or not, we've lost the war right here."

And this time it seemed that Wiggin had met his match, as he broke with all his previous practice and simply sent his paltry fleet straight into the swarming enemy.

But there was a method to his madness, it seemed. As they listened to the chatter—the boy called Bean talking to Ender Wiggin—they began to get a glimmer of what Ender might have in mind.

And then the order came, the final mad assault on the planet's surface, the detonation of the M.D. device, the disintegration of the entire world. Victory.

They celebrated. They drank. They wept for joy. They remembered all the people back on Earth that once upon a time they knew and loved, and wept again in grief. For by now they were all forty years older, and before this fleet could return, eighty years would have gone by.

But they weren't going home. They had never planned to. Knowing what relativistic space travel would do to them, that they could never return to the lives they had once had, they set out on this expedition knowing that if they won, it would cease to be a military fleet and become, all at once, a colony.

They had expected to have to fight for control of the planet's surface, and it was to be a mission of extermination, like the one the Formics had launched against Earth. But after that last battle, it wasn't necessary. The queens of all the conquered worlds had been gathered together on the last planet. All their eggs in one basket, so to speak. When they died, the workers and larvae on all the worlds died with them. Not immediately, but within hours or days.

Sel Menach set foot on the Formic planet that the enemy had tried to protect from them, not as a soldier, but as a xenobiologist. It was his job to find some way to protect the alien life forms from the terrestrial ones, and vice versa. Could alien parasites pose a danger to them?

The answer was yes. Until Sel found a comprehensive drug treatment, more fighter pilots died from near-microscopic airborne burrowing worms than had died in their battle in space.

But he found the treatment, which, injected monthly, made human blood fatal to the worms. He found ways to keep maize and amaranth from succumbing to alien molds.

Within a few years, his expertise became less important, on a daily basis, and he was just another worker in the human colony. The Admiral was now the Governor. And Sel Menach was, to all intents and purposes, a peasant. He, like half the males, lost the lottery to have a fertile mate. The unchosen men had the option of taking drugs to control their libido, so they were not consumed with envy or frustration. Sel did not bother with the drug. Not that he felt no desire; he simply had better things to think about. He worked his turn as a farmer during the days, then returned to his lab at night to work on genetic solutions to the problems of yield and storage and pest resistance.

Others, with different areas of expertise, studied climate patterns and determined that this world was in a cycle of ice ages like those of Earth, though the hot phases would never be as intense or brief as the warm times on Earth. Earth would have another Ice Age long before this planet did; but the cold here would be deeper, and the terrestrial seeds and roots were not adapted. It was Sel's job to help them adapt to the extreme cold so that the plants that humans depended on for survival would outlast the thousands of years of winter, when at last they came.

It would be millennia from now. But that was the way Sel had learned to think. It was the only attitude that could make his losses bearable. I am not living in my own lifetime now, he told himself. I am living on a planetary scale. I am living for the survival of generations of children unrelated to me.

He was nearly fifty years old when the first generation of children reached a marriageable age. He went to the Governor then and told him that the first preference for mating should go to the older men who had not mated in the first generation. "These would be, in effect, exogamous marriages," Sel explained. "If this new generation marries only each other, then the gene pool will be too small; if they bring in the sperm of the older men who never mated, then the gene pool is vastly increased."

The Governor sighed. "This is not going to be a popular decision," he said. "These young people were not pilots or soldiers. They know the Formics only as legends and pictures and vids. They want to marry for love. They'll assume at once that your advice is that of an old man yearning for young flesh."

"Which is why I remove myself from consideration. I recommend as a scientist, not as a man; ten generations from now, we'll be far stronger for having followed my advice."

In the end, the Governor made it a voluntary and temporary thing. Young women who agreed would be married to older men, but only until one child was born. That child would be raised by the mother and her new, younger mate, with the biological father as godfather to the child. Some women refused. Most consented—and, as the Governor said to Sel, in private, "It was because of the great respect they have for you. They know they eat so bountifully because of your work with the plants and animals they use for food."

Sel refused to accept the praise. "I only happen to be our chief xeno-biologist. If another man of the same training had been in my place, he would have done the same things."

"The problem we have, my friend," said the Governor, "is that many of the women insist that it's your seed they want, and no other."

"But mine is not available," said Sel.

"Forgive my asking, my friend, but don't you like women?"

"Like them, love them—and children, too," said Sel. "But it will never be said that I benefited personally from this odd little experiment in exogamy."

"You disappoint many women."

"I would also disappoint them if I mated with them. My children would probably be as ugly as me, and as stubborn."

"You have a point," said the Governor, but his jest was a sad one. "Your sacrifice will make my job easier."

By then the Governor was old, and it was not his job much longer. He died, and the ship carrying the new governor, long ago dispatched from Earth, had not yet come.

So they held an election, and chose, for their acting governor, Sel Menach, father of none, uncle of all, or so it seemed. He governed for five years, continuing his scientific work, settling disputes, diversifying the colony and setting up smaller villages far enough away, and in different enough environments, that they could learn more about the life of this world.

Then the colony ship came from Earth. It had been sent only a few months after the great victory, but it was forty years in coming—though it seemed only two years to those aboard. It brought ten times as many people as were already in the colony. It also brought the new governor, appointed by the Ministry of Colonization and backed, should anyone choose to resist his authority, by forty well-armed young Marines among the new colonists.

The original colonists—the old settlers, they already called themselves—learned the new governor's name only a few weeks before the ship came into orbit. It was Ender Wiggin himself, the architect of victory, who would govern them, though he was still only a child of fourteen years.

The old settlers were angry and afraid. The generation that had fought and won the battle, that had first explored this planet's surface and cleared away and burned the bodies of the Formics who had died in this area, the ones who had first grown terrestrial crops here and lived in terror of the parasites that attacked the blood and lived for a time in the caves of the Formics until they developed the right tools to build with the right kinds of trees to make houses—that generation was old. The young ones, who were now in the strength of adulthood, in their twenties and thirties, knew nothing of Earth. This was their home, and someone in a far-off place had decided to dump so many new colonists on them that they would become a small minority. And to add insult to injury, a child would rule over them.

"He is not an ordinary child," Sel Menach said. "He's the reason the human race possesses this world, and the enemy does not. He's the reason human beings are spreading out through this corner of the galaxy, instead of struggling to survive in the back hills of our own world, hunted down by Formics."

"So they gave him a reward—our land! Us!"

"Do you think this is a reward?" said Sel. "I think his reward would have been to go home to Earth. To his mother and father. Instead he was sent here. They must have been afraid of him on Earth. In an earlier age, he would simply have been killed."

It was a sobering thought. But it didn't make the old settlers any more enthusiastic to have him rule over them.

"We who came with the original fleet, we knew that we would lose everything. If we had simply returned to Earth, all our friends would have been dead, our families as well. So before we ever left on this expedition, we were trained in the skills and sciences that would give us the best chance of survival on this planet. We thought we might have to fight for every inch of it; thanks to Ender Wiggin's complete victory, we did not. But we still struggled, and why? We're old now. We worked so hard in order to give this colony to other people, people we didn't know, people who hadn't even been born when we arrived. You."

"But that's different. We're your own children."

Sel smiled. "Not mine."

They had no answer for that.

"That's what civilization is," said Sel. "You labor all your life to create a gift, large or small, which you then hand to strangers to build on and improve for the generation after. Some of them might be genetically related to us; most of them will not. We've built something fine here, but with far larger numbers each of our little colonies can now become towns. We can begin to specialize, to trade, to spread farther across this planet's surface. We can make of this a world as diverse and rich and productive as Earth. Maybe even better. And we need their genes, these newcomers. We need a shot of fresh DNA to make our future generations competitive with the humans being born on Earth. We need them every bit as much as they needed us to prepare the ground for their arrival. We are allies in our species' war for survival. We are brothers and sisters on a planet where the indigenous life has no kinship with us at all."

Fine speeches were enough to quell the immediate rebellion. But once the new colonists arrived, there would be conflicts and misunderstandings—it was bound to be so. It would be a constant labor of explanation, of patience, of nudges here and accommodations there to keep the peace. Sel knew just how to do it, but it would be hard, and he was tired, and besides, it was someone else's job. Ender Wiggin's. Not his.

So Sel began quietly to prepare for an expedition southward. It would be on foot—there had been no beasts of burden in the original expedition, and he was not going to deprive the colony of any of its vehicles. And even though many of the new edible hybrids had spread widely, he meant to pass out of their optimum climate, which meant he would have to carry his food with him. Fortunately, he didn't eat much, and he would bring along six of the new dogs he had genetically altered to be able to metabolize the local proteins. The dogs would hunt, and then he would harvest two of them—and turn the other four loose, two breeding pairs that could live off the land.

New predators turned loose in the wild—Sel knew exactly how dangerous this could be to the local ecology. But they could not eat all the native species and could do nothing with the vegetation, and it would be important during later exploration and colonization to find edible and tamable creatures loose in the wild.

We aren't here to preserve the local ecology like a museum. We're here to colonize, to suit the world for ourselves.

Which is precisely what the Formics had started to do to Earth. Only their approach was much more drastic—burn all, and then plant vegetation from the Formics' native planet.

Was that what they had done here? Sel didn't think so. He had found none of the species the Formics had planted on Earth during the Scouring of China nearly a century ago. This was one of the Formics' oldest colonies, and its flora and fauna seemed to be too distant, genetically, to have shared common ancestors with the Formic varieties. It must have been settled before they developed the Formification strategy they had begun to use on Earth.

In all the years till now, Sel had had to devote himself entirely to the genetic research required to keep the colony viable, and then to governing the colony. Now that his replacement was here, he could go into hitherto unexplored lands and learn what he could.

He could not go any great distance—he supposed a few hundred kilometers would be his limit, for it would do no good to range so far that he could not return and report his findings.

With the help of the lead xenogeneticist, Ix Tolo, Sel prepared a kit of the sampling and testing equipment he'd need—well, not all that he'd need, but all that he could carry along with his supplies. It was a meager kit, but Ix didn't even argue with him about it, which was unusual. "Why aren't you telling me that there's no point in making this journey if I don't have the equipment I need?"

"Because," said Ix, "I know you're not really traveling as a scientist."

"I'm not?"

"Look at you—an old man, planning a hundred-klick journey."

"Farther than that."

"Like an old elephant, searching for a place to die."

"I don't plan on dying."

"Governor Menach," said Ix, "you're an old man who doesn't want to face his fourteen-year-old successor."

"I don't want to get in his way," said Sel.

"You know everybody and everything, and he knows very little."

"He saved the human race."

"He knows very little about governing this colony. He has authority without relationships or influence. You're making it far harder for him by going."

"I don't think so," said Sel. "It's going to be hard enough for him without everybody turning to me for answers all the time. And they will. You will. The new colonists have been in stasis throughout the voyage. They don't know him—so they'll tend to follow whomever the old settlers follow. And if I'm here, that'll be me. No matter what we do or say, Ender Wiggin will be treated like my grandson, not like the governor."

"Maybe Ender Wiggin needs a grandfather more than he needs a position as governor."

"Make no mistake," said Sel. "Wiggin will be governor. He'll be better than the Admiral and I ever were. But let's make it happen as quickly and smoothly as possible. You set the example—treat him as governor and help him as much as you can."

"I will."

"So you can unpack that other bag, because you're not going with me."

"Other bag?"

"I'm not an idiot. Half the equipment I decided not to take, you've put into another pack, along with more food and an extra bedroll."

"I never thought you were an idiot. But I'm not so stupid I'd endanger the colony by sending both our lead xenobiologists on the same journey."

"So who's the pack for?"

"My son Po."

"I've always been bothered that you named him for an insanely romantic Chinese poet. Why nobody from Mayan history?"

"All the characters in the Popol Vuh have numbers instead of names.

He's a sensible kid. Strong. If he had to, he could carry you back home."

"I'm not that old and wizened."

"He could do it," said Ix. "But only if you're alive. Otherwise, he'll watch and record the process of decomposition, and then sample the microbes and worms that manage to feed on your old Earthborn corpse."

"Glad to see you still think like a scientist and not a sentimental fool."

"Po is good company."

"And he'll allow me to carry enough equipment for the trip to be useful. While you stay here and play with the new stuff from the colony ship."

"And train the xenobiologists they've sent along. I'll have plenty of work to do without babysitting the new governor."

"And Po's mother is happy about his going with me?"

"No," said Ix. "But she knows he'd never speak to her again if she barred him from it. So we have her blessing. More or less."

"Then first thing in the morning, we're off."

"Unless the new governor forbids you."

"His authority doesn't begin until he sets foot on this planet. He isn't even in orbit yet."

"Haven't you looked at their manifest? They have four skimmers."

"If we need one, we'll radio back for it. Otherwise, don't tell them where we went."

"Good thing the Formics got rid of all the major predators on this planet."

"There's no self-respecting predator would eat an old wad of gristle like this."

"I was thinking of my son."

"I'll watch out for him."

That night, Sel went to bed early and then, as usual, got up to pee after only a few hours of sleep. He noticed that the ansible was blinking. Message. Not my problem.

Well, that wasn't true, was it? If Wiggin's authority didn't begin until he set foot on the planet, then Sel was still acting governor. So any messages from Earth, he had to receive.

He sat down and signaled that he was ready to receive.

There were two messages recorded. He played the first one. It consisted of the face of the Minister of Colonization, Graff, and his message was brief. "I know you're planning to skip town before Wiggin gets there.

Talk to Wiggin before you go. He won't try to stop you, so relax."

That was it.

The other message was from Wiggin. He really was fourteen, but his adult height was coming on him. He didn't look like an actual child now. In the colony, teenagers his size were expected to do a man's work. So maybe his work wouldn't be as hard as Sel expected.

"Please contact me by ansible as soon as you get this. We're in radio distance, but I don't want anyone else to be able to intercept the signal."

Sel toyed with the idea of turning the message over to Ix to answer, but decided against it. The point wasn't to hide from Wiggin, was it? Only to leave the field clear for him.

So he signaled his intention to make a connection. It took only a few minutes for Wiggin to appear. Now that the colony ship wasn't traveling at a relativistic speed, there was no time differential, and therefore the ansible transmitted instantly. Not even the time lag of radio.

"Governor Menach," said Ender Wiggin.

"Sir," Sel replied.

"When we got word that you were leaving, my first thought was to beg you to stay."

"I wonder who reported my plans?"

"Everyone with access to the ansible," said Wiggin. "They don't want you to go. And I thought at first that they were right. But the more I thought about it, the more I knew that if I've got any brains, I'll rely on the decision of the man who actually understands the situation on the ground."

"Good," said Sel.

"Your genetic work has been brilliant. The xenobiologists have been reviewing it ever since I woke them up. They were unanimous in praising the restrained way you adapted terrestrial plants and animals to the new environment. They are already working on following your example and using your techniques on the animals and plants we brought with us."

"On the manifest I saw a full range of beasts of burden as well as milk, wool, egg, and meat beasts."

"The Formics cleared out most of the larger indigenous animals. Within a few years we should be able to start filling those ecological niches."

"Ix Tolo has ongoing projects."

"Ix Tolo will remain the head xenobiologist, in your absence," said

Wiggin. "You have trained him to an exacting standard, and the xenos on this ship intend to learn from him. Though they're hoping you'll return soon. They want to meet you. You're something of a hero to them. This is the only world that has non-Formiform flora and fauna. The other colonies have been working with the same genetic groups—this is the only world that posed unique challenges, so you had to do, alone, what all the other colonies were able to do cooperatively."

"Me and Darwin."

"Darwin had more help than you," said Wiggin. "I hope you'll keep your radio dormant instead of off. Because I want to be able to ask for your counsel, if I need it."

"You won't."

"I'm fourteen, Governor Menach."

"You're Ender Wiggin, sir."

Wiggin said nothing.

"We soldiers who fought under you may be getting old, but we haven't forgotten what you did."

"I gave orders in a nice, safe room far from any danger, and without a clue what I was actually doing. You were the ones who fought the war."

"Who builds the house, the architect or the bricklayer? It's not an interesting question. You led us, sir. We destroyed the enemy. We lived to found this colony."

"And the human race will never again be tied to one world," said Wiggin. "We all did our part. The two of us will continue to do whatever we can."

"Yes, sir."

"Please. Call me Andrew. When you return, I want us to be friends. If I have any skill, it's knowing how to learn from the best teachers."

"If you call me Sel."

"I will."

"I'm going back to bed now. I have a lot of walking to do tomorrow."

"I can send a skimmer after you. So you don't have to carry your supplies. It would increase your range."

"But then the old settlers will expect me to come back soon. They'll be waiting for me instead of relying on you."

"I can't pretend that we're not able to track you and find you."

"But you can tell them that you're showing me the respect of not trying. At my request."

"Yes," said Ender. "I'll do that."

There was little more to say. They signed off and Sel went back to bed. He slept easily. And, as usual, woke just when he wanted to—an hour before dawn.

Po was waiting for him.

"I already said good-bye to Mom and Dad," he said.

"Good," said Sel.

"Thanks for letting me come."

"Could I have stopped you?"

"Yes," said Po. "I won't disobey you, Uncle Sel."

Sel nodded. "Good. Have you eaten?"

"Yes."

"Then let's go. I won't need to eat till noon."

•••

You take a step, then another. That's the journey. But to take a step with your eyes open is not a journey at all, it's a remaking of your own mind. You see things that you never saw before. Things never seen by the eyes of human beings. And you see with your particular eyes, which were trained to see not just a plant, but this plant, filling this ecological niche, but with this and that difference.

And when your eyes have been trained for forty years to be familiar with the patterns of a new world, then you are Antony van Leeuwenhoek, who first saw the world of animalcules through a microscope; you are Carl Linnaeus, first sorting creatures into families, genera, species; you are Darwin, sorting lines of evolutionary passage from one species to another.

So it was not a rapid journey. Sel had to force himself to move with any kind of haste.

"Don't let me linger so long over every new thing I see," he told Po. "It would be too humiliating for my great expedition to take me only ten kilometers south of the colony. I must cross the first range of mountains, at least."

"And how will I keep you from lingering, when you have me photo-graphing and sampling and storing and recording notes?"

"Refuse to do it. Tell me to get my bony knees up off the ground and start walking."

"All my life I'm taught to obey my elders and watch and learn. I'm your assistant. Your apprentice."

"You're just hoping we don't travel very far so when I die you don't have so long to carry the corpse."

"I thought my father told you—if you actually die, I'm supposed to call for help and observe your decomposition process."

"That's right. You only carry me if I'm breathing."

"Or do you want me to start now? Hoist you onto my shoulders so you can't discover another whole family of plants every fifty meters?"

"For a respectful, obedient young man, you can be very sarcastic."

"I was only slightly sarcastic. I can do better if you want."

"This is good. I've been so busy arguing with you, we've gone this far without my noticing anything."

"Except the dogs have found something."

It turned out to be a small family of the horned reptile that seemed to fill the bunny rabbit niche—a big-toothed leaf-eater that hopped, and would only fight if cornered. The horns did not seem to Sel to be weapons—too blunt—and when he imagined a mating ritual in which these creatures leapt into the air to butt their heads together, he could not see how it could help but scramble their brains, since their skulls were so light.

"Probably for a display of health," said Sel.

"The antlers?"

"Horns," said Sel.

"I think they're shed and then regrown. Don't these animals look like skin-shedders?"

"No."

"I'll look for a shed skin somewhere."

"You'll have a long look."

"Why, because they eat the skins?"

"Because they don't shed."

"How can you be sure?"

"I'm not sure," said Sel. "But this is not a Formic import, it's a native species, and we haven't seen any skin shedding from natives."

So the conversation went as they traveled—but they did cover the ground. They took pictures, yes. And now and then, when it was something really new, they stopped and took samples. But always they walked. Sel might be old and need to lean on his walking stick now and then, but he could still keep up a steady pace. Po was likely to move ahead of him more often than not, but it was Po who groaned when Sel said it was time to move on after a brief rest.

"I don't know why you have that stick," said Po.

"To lean on when I rest."

"But you have to carry it the whole time you're walking."

"It's not that heavy."

"It looks heavy."

"It's from the balsa tree—well, the one I call 'balsa,' since the wood is so light."

Po tried it. Only about a pound, though it was thick and gnarled and widened out at the top like a pitcher. "I'd still get tired of carrying it."

"Only because you put more weight in your backpack than I did." Po didn't bother arguing the point.

"The first human voyagers to the moon and the planets had an easy time of it," said Po, as they crested a high ridge. "Nothing but empty space between them and their destination. No temptation to stop and explore."

"Like the first sea voyagers. Going from land to land, ignoring the sea because they had no tools that would let them explore to any depth."

"We're the conquistadores," said Po. "Only we killed them all before we ever set foot on land."

"Is that a difference or a similarity? Smallpox and other diseases raced ahead of the conquistadores."

"If only we could have talked to them," said Po. "I read about the conquistadores—we Mayans have good reason to try to understand them. Columbus wrote that the natives he found 'had no language,' merely because they didn't understand any of the languages his interpreters knew."

"But the Formics had no language at all."

"Or so we think."

"No communication devices in their ships. Nothing to transmit voice or images. Because there was no need of them. Exchange of memory. Direct transfer of the senses. Whatever their mechanism was, it was better than language, but worse, because they had no way to talk to us."

"So who were the mutes?" asked Po. "Us, or them?"

"Both of us mutes," said Sel, "and all of us deaf."

"What I wouldn't give to have just one of them alive."

"But there couldn't be just one," said Sel. "They hived. They needed hundreds, perhaps thousands to reach the critical mass to achieve intelligence."

"Or not," said Po. "It could also be that only the queen was sentient. Why else would they all have died when the queens died?"

"Unless the queen was the nexus, the center of a neural network."

"As I said, I wish we had one alive, so we could know something instead of guessing from a few desiccated corpses."

"We have more of them preserved than any of the other worlds. Here, there are so few scavengers that can eat them, the corpses lasted long enough for us to get to the planet's surface and freeze some of them. We actually got to study structure."

"But no queens."

"The sorrow of my life," said Sel.

"Really? That's your greatest regret?"

Sel fell silent.

"Sorry," said Po.

"It's all right. I was just considering your question. My greatest regret. What a question. How can I regret leaving everything behind on Earth, when I left it in order to help save it? And coming here allowed me to do things that other scientists could only dream of. I have been able to name more than five thousand species already and come up with a rudimentary classification system for an entire native biota. More than on any of the other Formic worlds."

"Why?"

"Because they stripped those and then established only a limited subset of their own flora and fauna. This is the only world where most of the species evolved here. The only place that's messy. The Formics brought fewer than a thousand species to their colonies. And their home world, which might have had vastly more diversity, is gone."

"So you don't regret coming here?"

"Of course I do," said Sel. "And I also am glad to be here. I regret being an old wreck of a man. I'm glad I'm not dead. It seems to me that all my regrets are balanced by something I'm glad of. On average, then, I have no regrets at all. But I'm also not a bit happy. Perfect balance. On average, I don't actually exist."

"Father says that if you get absurd results, you're not a scientist, you're a philosopher."

"But my results are not absurd."

"You do exist. I can see you and hear you."

"Genetically speaking, Po, I do not exist. I am off the web of life."

"So you choose to measure by the only standard that allows your life to be meaningless?"

Sel laughed. "You are your mother's son."

"Not father's?"

"Both, of course. But it's your mother who won't put up with any bullshit."

"Speaking of which, I can hardly wait to see a bull."

By the time they had been a fortnight gone, with almost two hundred kilometers behind them, they had talked about every conceivable subject at least twice, and finally walked along in companionable silence most of the time, except when the exigencies of their journey forced them to speak.

"Don't grab that vine, it's not secure."

"I wonder if that bright-colored froglike thing is venomous?"

"I doubt it, considering that it's a rock."

"Oh. It was so vivid I thought—"

"A good guess. And you're not a geologist, so how could you be expected to recognize a rock?"

At two hundred klicks, though, it was time to stop. They had rationed carefully, but their food was half gone. They pitched a more permanent camp by a clear water source, chose a safe spot and dug a latrine, and pitched the tent with the stakes deeper and the ground more padded under the floor of it. They would be here for a week.

A week, because that's about how long they expected to be able to live on the meat of the two dogs they slaughtered that afternoon.

Sel was sorry that only two of the dogs were smart enough to extrapolate that their human masters were no longer reliable companions. Those two left—they had to drive the other pair away with stones.

By now, like everyone else in the colony, both Sel and Po knew how to preserve meat by smoking it; they cooked only a little of the meat fresh, but kept the fire going to smoke the rest as it hung from the bending limbs of a fernlike tree…or treelike fern.

They marked out a rough circle on the satellite map they carried with them and each morning they set out in a different direction to see what they might find. Now they collected samples in earnest, and took photographs that they bounced to the orbiting transport ship for storage on the big computers there. It was nothing but a big satellite now, its electronics running on a tiny amount of the fuel and its databases constantly being transmitted to Earth automatically by ansible. The pictures, the test results, those were secure—they would not be lost, no matter what happened to Sel and Po. The samples, though, were by far the most valuable items. Once they brought them back, they could be studied at great length using far more sophisticated equipment. The new equipment from the colony ship.

At night, Sel lay awake for long hours, thinking of what they had seen, classifying it in his mind, trying to make sense of the biology of this world.

But when he woke up, he could not remember having had any great insights the night before, and certainly had none by morning light. No great breakthroughs; just a continuation of the work he had already done.

I should have gone north, into the jungles.

But jungles are far more dangerous to explore. I'm an old man. Jungles could kill me. This temperate zone, colder than the colony because it's a little closer to the poles and higher in elevation, is also safer for an old man who needs open country to hike through and nothing unusually dangerous to snag or snap at him.

On the fifth day, they crossed a path.

There was no mistaking it. It was not a road, certainly not, but that was no surprise, the Formics had built few roads. What they made were paths, and those inadvertent, the natural result of thousands of feet treading the same route.

Those feet had trodden here, though it was forty years before. Trodden so long and often that after all these years, and overgrown as it was, the naked eye could trace the path of it through the pebbly soil of a narrow alluvial valley.

There was no question now of pursuing any more flora and fauna. The Formics had found something of value here, and archaeology took precedence, at least for a few hours, over xenobiology.

The path wound upward into the hills, but not terribly far before it led to a number of cave entrances.

"These aren't caves," said Po.

"Oh?"

"They're tunnels. These are too new, and the land hasn't shaped itself around them the way that it does with real caves. These were dug as doorways. All the same height, do you see?"

"That damnably inconvenient height that makes it such a pain for humans to go inside."

"It's not our purpose here, sir," said Po. "We've found the spot. Let's call for others to explore the tunnels. We're here for the living, not the dead."

"I have to know what they were doing here. Certainly not farming— there's no trace of their crops gone wild here. No orchards. No middens, either—this wasn't a great settlement. And yet there was so much traffic, along that single path."

"Mining?" asked Po.

"Can you think of any other purpose? There's something in those tunnels that the Formics thought was worth the trouble of digging out. In large quantities. For a long time."

"Not such large quantities," said Po.

"No?" said Sel.

"It's like steel-making back on Earth. Even though the purpose was smelting iron to make steel, and they mined coal only to fire their smelters and foundries, they didn't carry the coal to the iron, they carried the iron to the coal—because it took far more coal than iron to make steel."

"You must have gotten very good marks in geography."

"I never saw Earth," said Po. "Neither did my parents—all born here. But Earth is still my home."

"So you're saying that whatever they took out of these tunnels, it wasn't in such large quantities that it was worth building a city here."

"They put their cities where the food was, or the fuel. Whatever they got here, they took little enough of it that it was more economical to carry it to their cities, instead of building a city here to process it."

"You may grow up to amount to something, Po."

"I'm already grown up, sir," said Po. "And I already amount to something. Just not enough to get any girl to marry me."

"And knowing the principles of Earth's economic history will attract a mate?"

"As surely as that bunny-toad's antlers, sir."

"Horns," said Sel.

"So we're going in?"

Sel mounted one of the little oil lamps into the flared top of his walking stick.

"And here I thought that opening at the top of your stick was decoration," said Po.

"It was decorative," said Sel. "It was also the way the tree grew out of the ground."

Sel rolled up his blankets and put half the remaining food into his pack, along with their testing equipment.

"Are you planning to spend the night down there?"

"What if we find something wonderful, and then have to climb back out of the tunnels before we get a chance to explore?"

Dutifully, Po packed up. "I don't think we'll need the tent in there."

"I doubt there'll be much rain."

"Caves can be drippy."

"We'll pick a dry spot."

"What can live in there? It's not a natural cave, I don't think we'll find fish."

"There are birds and other creatures that like the dark. Or that find it safer and warmer indoors."

At the entrance, Po sighed. "If only the tunnels were higher."

"It's not my fault you grew so tall." Sel lit the lamp, fueled by the oils of fruit Sel had found in the wild. They grew it in orchards now, and pressed and filtered it in three harvests a year, though except for the oil the fruit was good for nothing except fertilizer. It was good to have clean-burning fuel for light, instead of wiring every building with electricity, especially in the outlying colonies. It was one of Sel's favorite discoveries—particularly since there was no sign the Formics had ever discovered its usefulness. Of course, the Formics were at home in the dark. Sel could imagine them scuttling along in these tunnels, content with smell and hearing to guide them.

Humans had evolved from creatures that took refuge in trees, not caves, thought Sel, and though humans had used caves many times in the past, they were always suspicious of them. Deep dark places were at once attractive and terrifying. There was no chance the Formics would have allowed any large predators to remain at large on this planet, particularly in caves, since the Formics themselves were tunnel makers and cave dwellers.

If only the Formic home world had not been obliterated in the war. What we could have learned, tracing an alien evolution that led to intelligence!

Then again, if Ender Wiggin had not blown the whole thing up, we would have lost the war. Then we wouldn't have even this world to study. Evolution here did not lead to intelligence—or if it did, the Formics already wiped it out, along with any traces the original sentient natives might have left behind.

Sel bent over and squat-walked into the tunnel. But it was hard to keep going that way—his back was too old. He couldn't even lean on his stick, because it was too tall for the space, and he had to drag it along, keeping it as close to vertical as possible so the oil didn't spill out of the canister that was holding it.

After a while he simply could not continue in that position. Sel sat down and so did Po.

"This is not working," said Sel.

"My back hurts," said Po.

"A little dynamite would be useful."

"As if you'd ever use it," said Po.

"I didn't say it would be morally defensible," said Sel. "Just convenient."

Sel handed his stick, with the lamp atop it, to Po. "You're young. You'll recover from this. I've got to try a new position."

Sel tried to crawl but instantly gave up on that—it hurt his knees too much to rest them directly on the rocky floor. He finally settled for sitting, leaning his arms forward, putting weight on them, and then scrabbling his legs and hips after him. It was slow going.

Po also tried crawling and soon gave up on it. But because he was holding the stick with the light, he was forced to return to walking bent over, knees in a squat. The boy would end up crippled, probably, but Sel would never have to hear his father and mother complain about it, because Sel himself would never get out of this tunnel alive.

And then, suddenly, the light went dim. For a moment Sel thought it had gone out, but no—Po had stood up and lifted the stick to a vertical position, so that the tunnel where Sel was creeping along was now in shadow.

It didn't matter. Sel could see the chamber ahead. It was a natural cavern, with stalactites and stalagmites forming columns that supported the ceiling.

But they weren't the normal straight-up-and-down columns that normally formed, when lime-laden water dripped straight down, leaving sediment behind. These columns twisted crazily. Writhed, really.

"Not natural deposits," said Po.

"No. These were made. But the twisting doesn't seem designed, either."

"Fractal randomness?" asked Po.

"I don't think so," said Sel. "Random, yes, but genuinely so, not fractal. Not mathematical."

"Like dog turds," said Po.

Sel stood looking at the columns. They did indeed have the kind of curling pattern that a long dog turd got as it was laid down from above. Solid yet flexible. Extrusions from above, only still connected to the ceiling. Sel looked up, then took the stick from Po and raised it.

The chamber seemed to go on forever, supported by the writhing stone pillars. Arches like an ancient temple, but half melted.

"It's composite rock," said Po.

Sel looked down at the boy and saw him with a self-lighting microscope, examining the rock of a column.

"Seems like the same mineral composition as the floor," said Po. "But grainy. As if it had been ground up and then glued back together."

"But not glued," said Sel. "Bonded? Cement?"

"I think it's been glued," said Po. "I think it's organic."

Po took the stick back and held the flame of the lamp under an elbow of one of the twistiest columns. The substance did not catch fire, but it did begin to sweat and drip.

"Stop," said Sel. "Let's not bring the thing down on us!"

Now that they could walk upright, they moved forward into the cavern. It was Po who thought of marking their path by cutting off bits of his blanket and dropping them. He looked back from time to time to make sure they were following a straight line. Sel looked back, too, and saw how impossible it would be ever to find the entrance they had come through, if the path were not marked.

"So tell me how this was made," said Sel. "No toolmarks on the ceiling or floor. These columns, made from ground-up stone with added glue.

A kind of paste that can hold up a chamber this size. But no grinding equipment left behind, no buckets to carry the glue."

"Giant rock-eating worms," said Po.

"That's what I was thinking, too," said Sel.

Po laughed. "I was joking."

"I wasn't," said Sel.

"How could worms eat rock?"

"Very sharp teeth that regrow quickly. Grinding their way through. The fine gravel bonds with some kind of gluey mucus and they extrude these columns, then bind them to the ceiling."

"But how could such a creature evolve?" said Po. "There's no nutrition in the rock. And it would take enormous energy to do all this. Not to mention whatever their teeth were made of."

"I don't think they evolved," said Sel. "Look—what's that?"

There was something shiny ahead. Reflecting the lamplight.

As they got closer, they saw spotty reflections from various spots on the columns, too. Even the ceiling.

But nothing else was as bright as the thing lying on the floor. "A glue bucket?" asked Po.

"No," said Sel. "It's a giant bug. Beetle. Ant. Something like—look at this, Po."

They were close enough now to see that it was six-legged, though the middle pair of limbs seemed more designed for clinging than walking or grasping. The front ones were for grasping and tearing. The hind ones, for digging and running.

"What do you think? Bipedal?" asked Sel.

"Both. Bipedal at need." Po nudged it with his foot. No response. The thing was definitely dead. He bent over and flexed and rotated the hind limbs. Then the front ones. "It could do both equally well, I think."

"Not a likely evolutionary path," said Sel. "Anatomy tends to commit one way or the other."

"Like you said. Not evolved, bred."

"For what?"

"For mining," said Po. He rolled the thing over onto its belly. It was very heavy; it took several tries. But now they could see much better what it was that caught the light. The thing's back was a solid sheet of gold. As smooth as a beetle's carapace, but so thick with gold that the thing must weigh ten kilos at least.

Twenty-five, maybe thirty centimeters long, thick and stubby. And its entire exoskeleton thinly gilt, with the back heavily armored in gold. "Do you think these things were mining for gold?" asked Po. "Not with that mouth," said Sel. "Not with those hands."

"But the gold got inside it somehow. To be deposited in the shell."

"I think you're right," said Sel. "But this is the adult. The harvest. I think the Formics carried these things out of the mine and took them off to be purified. Burn off the organics and leave the pure metal behind."

"So they ingested the gold as larvae…"

"Went into a cocoon…"

"And when they emerged, their bodies were encased in gold."

"And there they are," said Sel, holding up the light again. Only now he went closer to the columns, where they could now see that the glints of reflection were from the bodies of half-formed creatures, their backs embedded in the pillars, their foreheads and bellies shiny with a layer of thin gold.

"The columns are the cocoons," said Po.

"Organic mining," said Sel. "The Formics bred these things specifically to extract gold."

"But what for? It's not like the Formics used money. Gold is just a soft metal to them."

"A useful one. What's to say they didn't have bugs just like these, only bred to extract iron, platinum, aluminum, copper, whatever they wanted?"

"So they didn't need tools to mine."

"No, Po—these are the tools. The factories." Sel knelt down. "Let's see if we can get any kind of DNA sample from these.

"Dead all this time?"

"There's no way these are native to this planet. The Formics brought them here. So they're native to the Formic home world. Or bred from something native there."

"Not necessarily," said Po, "or other colonies would have found them long before now."

"It took us forty years, didn't it?"

"What if this is a hybrid?" asked Po. "So it exists only on this world?"

By now, Sel was sampling DNA and finding it far easier than he thought.

"Po, there's no way this has been dead for forty years."

Then it twitched reflexively under his hand.

"Or twenty minutes," said Sel. "It still has reflexes. It isn't dead."

"Then it's dying," said Po. "It has no strength."

"Starving to death, I bet," said Sel. "Maybe it just finished its meta-morphosis and was trying to get to the tunnel entrance and died here. Or stopped here to die."

Po took the samples from him and stowed them in Sel's pack.

"So these gold bugs are still alive, forty years after the Formics stopped bringing them food? How long is the metamorphosis?"

"Not forty years," said Sel. He stood up, then bent over again to look at the gold bug. "I think these cocooned-up bugs embedded in the columns are young. Fresh." He stood up and started striding deeper into the cavern.

There were more gold bugs now, many of them lying on the ground—but unlike the first one they found, these were often destroyed, hollowed out. Nothing but the thick golden shells of their backs, with legs discarded as if they had been…

"Spat out," said Sel. "These were eaten."

"By what?"

"Larvae," said Sel. "Cannibalizing the adults because otherwise there's nothing to eat here. Each generation getting smaller—look how large this one is? Each one smaller because they only eat the bodies of the adults."

"And they're working their way back toward the door," said Po. "To get outside where the nutrients are."

"When the Formics stopped coming…"

"Their shells are too heavy to make much progress," said Po. "So they get as far as they can, then the larvae feed on the corpse of the adult, then they crawl toward the light of the entrance as far as they can, cocoon up, and the next generation emerges, smaller than the last one."

Now they were among much larger shells. "These things are supposed to be more than a meter in length," said Sel. "The closer to the entrance, the smaller."

Po stopped, pointed at the lamp. "They're heading toward the light?"

"Maybe we'll be able to see one."

"Rock-devouring larvae that grind up solid rock and poop out bonded stone columns."

"I didn't say I wanted to see it up close."

"But you do."

"Well. Yes."

Now they were both looking around them, squinting to try to see movement somewhere in the cavern.

"What if there's something it likes much better than light?" asked Po.

"Soft-bodied food?" asked Sel. "Don't think I haven't thought of it. The Formics brought them food. Now maybe we have, too."

At that moment, Po suddenly rose straight up into the air.

Sel held up the stick. Directly above him, a huge sluglike larva clung to the ceiling. Its mouth end was tightly fastened on Po's back.

"Unstrap and drop down here!" called Sel.

"All our samples!"

"We can always get more samples! I don't want to have to extract bits of you from one of these pillars!"

Po got the straps open and dropped to the floor.

The pack disappeared into the larva's maw. They could hear hard metal squeaking and scraping as the larva's teeth tried to grind up the metal instruments. They didn't wait to watch. They started toward the entrance. Once they passed the first gold bug's body, they looked for the bits of blanket to mark the path.

"Take my pack," said Sel, shrugging it off as he walked. "It's got the radio and the DNA samples in it—get out the entrance and radio for help."

"I'm not leaving you," said Po. But he was obeying.

"You're the only one who can get out the entrance faster than that thing can crawl."

"We haven't seen how fast it can go."

"Yes we have," said Sel. He walked backward for a moment, holding up the lamp.

The larva was about thirty meters behind them and coming on faster than they had been walking.

"Is it following the light or our body heat?" asked Po as they turned again and began to jog.

"Or the carbon dioxide of our breath? Or the vibrations of our footfalls? Or our heartbeats?" Sel held out the stick toward him. "Take it and run."

"What are you going to do?" said Po, not taking the stick.

"If it's following the light, you can stay ahead of it by running."

"And if it's not?"

"Then you can get out and call for help."

"While it has you for lunch."

"I'm tough and gristly."

"The thing eats stone."

"Take the light," said Sel, "and get out of here."

Po hesitated a moment longer, then took it. Sel was relieved that the boy would keep his promise of obedience.

Either that, or Po was convinced the larva would follow the light.

It was the right guess—as Sel slowed down and watched the larva approach, he could see that it was not heading directly toward him, but rather listed off to the side, heading for Po. And as Po ran, the larva began speeding up.

It went right past Sel. It was more than a half-meter thick. It moved like a snake, with a back-and-forth movement, writhing along the floor, shaping itself exactly like the columns, only horizontally and, of course, moving.

It was going to reach Po before he could get out of the tunnel.

"Leave the light!" shouted Sel. "Leave it!"

In a few moments, Sel could see the light leaning against the wall of the cavern, beside where the low tunnel began, leading toward the outside world. Po must already be through the tunnel.

But the larva was ignoring the light and heading into the tunnel behind him. With Po struggling to move through the low tunnel, the larva would catch him easily.

"No. No, stop!" But then he thought: What if Po hears me? "Keep going, Po! Run!"

And then, wordlessly, Sel shouted inside his mind: Stop and come back here! Come back to the cavern! Come back to your children!

Sel knew it was insane, but it was all he could think of to do. The Formics communicated mind to mind. This was also a large insectoid life form from the Formics' home world. Maybe he could speak to it the way the Hive Queens spoke to the individual worker and soldier Formics.

Speak? That was asinine. They had no language. They wouldn't speak.

Sel stopped and formed in his mind a clear picture of the gold bug lying on the cavern floor. Only the legs were writhing. And as he pictured it, Sel tried to feel hungry, or at least remember how it felt to be hungry. Or to find hunger within himself—after all, he hadn't eaten for a few hours.

Then he pictured the larva coming to the gold bug. Circling it.

The larva reemerged from the tunnel. There had been no screaming from Po—it hadn't caught him. Maybe it got too near the sunlight and it blinded the larva and it couldn't go on. Or maybe it had responded to the images and feelings in Sel's mind. Either way, Po was safely outside.

Of course, maybe the larva had simply decided not to bother with the prey that was running, and had come back for the prey that was standing very still, pressing himself against a column.

"Nice larva," whispered Sel. "How about some nice dried dog?"

When he reached for his pack, to extract the food, it wasn't there. Po had his pack.

But he had the little bag at his waist where he carried the food for each day's hike. He opened it, took out the dried dog meat and the vegetables that he carried there, and tossed them toward the larva.

It stopped. It nudged the food lying on the ground. Then it rose up and plunged its gaping mouth down on the food like a remora attaching itself to a shark.

Sel could imagine a smaller version of the larva being exactly that—a remora, attaching itself to larger creatures to suck the blood out of them. Or to burrow into them?

He remembered the tiny parasites that had killed people when the colony was first formed. The ones Sel had invented blood additives to repel.

This creature is a hybrid. Half native to this world. Half formed from something from the Formic world.

No, not "something." Formics themselves. This thing was a hybrid between Formic and parasite. It would take very expert gene-splicing to construct a viable creature that combined attributes of two species growing out of such disparate genetic heritages. The result would be a species that was half Formic, so that perhaps the Hive Queens could communicate with them mentally, control them like any other Formics. Only they were still different enough that they didn't completely bond with the queen—so when this world's Hive Queen died, the gold bugs didn't.

Maybe not. Maybe they already had a species they used for menial tasks, one that had a weak mental bond with the Hive Queens, and that's what they interbred with the parasitic worms. Those incredible teeth that could burrow right through leather, cloth, skin, and bone. But sentient, or nearly so. It could be ruled by the Hive Queens' minds.

And mine? Or did it come back for the easy food?

By now the larva had plunged down onto each of the bits of food and devoured them—along with a thin layer of the stone floor at each spot. The thing was hungry.

Hungry enough to override Sel's commands?

He formed a picture in his mind—a complicated one now. A picture of Sel and Po bringing food into the tunnel. Feeding the larva. He pictured himself and Po going in and out of the cave, bringing food. Lots of food. Leaves. Grain. Fruit. Small animals.

The larva came toward him, but then circled around him. Writhed around his legs. Like a constrictor? Did it have that snakelike pattern, too? No. It didn't get tighter. It was more like a cat.

Then it pushed from behind. Nudging him toward the tunnel. Sel obeyed. The thing understood. There was rudimentary communication going on.

Sel hurried to the tunnel, then knelt and sat and started to try to slide along as he had coming in.

The larva slid past him in the tunnel and then stopped.

Sel took hold of the creature's dry, articulated surface, and it began moving forward again. It was carefully not thrashing him against the wall, though he scraped now and then. It hurt and probably drew blood, but it didn't break anything. It wouldn't even have bothered a Formic. Maybe the Formics rode the larvae in and out of the tunnel just like this.

The larva stopped. But now Sel could see the light of day. So could the larva. It didn't go out there; it shied from the light and backed down the tunnel past Sel.

When Sel emerged into the daylight and stood up, Po ran to him and hugged him. "It didn't eat you!"

"No, it gave me a ride," he said.

Po wasn't sure how to make sense of this.

"All our food," said Sel. "I promised we'd feed it."

Po didn't argue. He ran to the pack and started handing food to Sel, who gathered it into a basket made by holding his shirt out in front of him.

"Enough for the moment," said Sel.

In a few moments, he had his shirt off and stuffed with food. Then he started laboriously down the tunnel again. In moments the larva was there again, coiling around him. Sel opened the shirt and dropped the food. The larva began eating ravenously. Sel was still close enough to the entrance that he could squat-walk out again.

"We'll need more food," said Sel.

"What's food to the larva?" asked Po. "Grass? Bushes?"

"It ate the vegetables from my lunch pack."

"There's not going to be anything edible growing around here."

"Not edible to us," said Sel. "But if I'm right, this thing is half native to this world, and it can probably metabolize the local vegetation."

If there was one thing they knew how to do, it was identify the local flora.

Soon they were shuttling shirtfuls of tuberous vegetables down the tunnel.

They took turns carrying food to the larva.

It was still eating when two skimmers arrived. It was new technology, obviously developed long after Sel's transport had left Fleet Command on the long voyage to war. The pilots were strong young soldiers, with potent-looking side arms. One skimmer held supplies in bags and boxes. The other had a passenger. A fourteen-year-old boy in civilian clothes.

"Ender Wiggin," said Sel.

"Sel Menach," said Wiggin. "Po said you had a giant worm situation going on here."

"No weapons needed," Sel said to the soldiers, who already had their weapons at the ready. "We're not exactly talking with the thing, but it understands rudimentary images." And he explained about his theory of crossbreeding.

"So these aren't actually Formics," said Wiggin. He looked disappointed.

"None of the Formics could have survived," said Sel. "But they're somewhat like Formics. When we get back, we can do the gene comparison and see just how these things were made. And also, we can get all the gold we'll ever want. There might be iron bugs and silver bugs and copper bugs elsewhere. We need to do a search for the likely sites—forty years of surviving by cannibalizing each other is a long time, and they might all be on their last legs, so to speak."

"Count on it, we'll do it at once," said Wiggin.

They stayed long enough to make sure the soldiers could project images of food to the larva—at least enough not to get eaten when they carried food down the tunnel. Then a training course in which plants had nutrient-rich roots. Then, leaving Po behind to supervise, Sel climbed into one of the skimmers with Wiggin and the DNA samples and headed back to the colony.

•••

Over the next few weeks, as Po organized the search for more Formic mines that might contain similar bugs and Sel learned how to use the new, improved equipment so he and the new xenobiologists could decode what the Formics had done to create these creatures, a few of the old settlers did come to him, just as he had feared, trying to enlist him in some kind of resistance to whatever it was the new colonists were doing.

Sel's answer was always the same. "I've got real work to do here! Get out of my lab! Go take your complaints to the Governor. That's his job now, not mine."

Something of the Formics had survived on this world after all. Only a biological remnant, but it was something. It was so irritating that he was probably going to die before they had learned everything this world could teach them. How have other scientists put up with this death thing? It would be such a tedious interruption to his career, just when it was getting really interesting.

KIN

Bruce McAllister

The alien and the boy, who was twelve, sat in the windowless room high above the city that afternoon. The boy talked and the alien listened.

The boy was ordinary—the genes of three continents in his features, his clothes cut in the style of all boys in the vast housing project called LAX. The alien was something else, awful to behold; and though the boy knew it was rude, he did not look up as he talked.

He wanted the alien to kill a man, he said. It was that simple.

As the boy spoke, the alien sat upright and still on the one piece of furniture that could hold him. Eyes averted, the boy sat on the stool, the one by the terminal where he did his schoolwork each day. It made him uneasy that the alien was on his bed, though he understood why. It made him uneasy that the creature's strange knee was so near his in the tiny room, and he was glad when the creature, as if aware, too, shifted its leg away.

He did not have to look up to see the Antalou's features. That one glance in the doorway had been enough, and it came back to him whether he wanted it to or not. It was not that he was scared, the boy told himself. It was just the idea—that such a thing could stand in a doorway built for humans, in a human housing project where generations had been born and died, and probably would forever. It did not seem possible.

He wondered how it seemed to the Antalou.

Closing his eyes, the boy could see the black synthetic skin the alien wore as protection against alien atmospheres. Under that suit, ropes of muscles and tendons coiled and uncoiled, rippling even when the alien was still. In the doorway the long neck had not been extended, but he knew what it could do. When it telescoped forward—as it could instantly—the head tipped up in reflex and the jaws opened.

Nor had the long talons—which the boy knew sat in the claws and even along the elbows and toes—been unsheathed. But he imagined them sheathing and unsheathing as he explained what he wanted, his eyes on the floor.

When the alien finally spoke, the voice was inhuman—filtered through the translating mesh that covered half its face. The face came back: The tremendous skull, the immense eyes that could see so many kinds of light and make their way in nearly every kind of darkness. The heavy welts—the auxiliary gills—inside the breathing globe. The dripping ducts below them, ready to release their jets of acid.

"Who is it...that you wish to have killed?" the voice asked, and the boy almost looked up. It was only a voice—mechanical, snakelike, halting—he reminded himself. By itself it could not kill him.

"A man named James Ortega-Mambay," the boy answered.

"Why?" The word hissed in the stale apartment air.

"He is going to kill my sister."

"You know this...how?"

"I just do."

The alien said nothing, and the boy heard the long whispering pull of its lungs.

"Why," it said at last, "did you think...I would agree to it?"

The boy was slow to answer.

"Because you're a killer."

The alien was again silent.

"So all Antalou," the voice grated, "are professional killers?"

"Oh, no," the boy said, looking up and trying not to look away. "I mean...."

"If not...then how...did you choose me?"

The boy had walked up to the creature at the great fountain by the Cliffs of Monica—a landmark any visitor to Earth would take in, if only because it appeared on the sanctioned itineraries—and had handed him a written message in crude Antalouan. *I know what you are and what you do,* the message read. *I need your services. LAX cell 873-2345-2657 at 1100 tomorrow morning. I am Kim.*

"Antalou are well known for their skills, Sir," the boy said respectfully. "We've read about the Noh campaign, and what happened on Hoggun II when your people were betrayed, and what one company of your mercenaries were able to do against the Gar-Betties." The boy paused. "I had to give out ninety-eight notes, Sir, before I found you. You were the only one who answered...."

The hideous head tilted while the long arms remained perfectly still, and the boy found he could not take his eyes from them.

"I see," the alien said.

It was translator's idiom only. "Seeing" was not the same as "understanding." The young human had done what the military and civilian intelligence services of five worlds had been unable to do—identify him as a professional—and it made the alien reflect: Why had he answered the message? Why had he taken it seriously? A human child had delivered it, after all. Was it that he had sensed no danger and simply followed professional reflex, or something else? Somehow the boy had known he would. How?

"How much..." the alien said, curious, "are you able to pay?"

"I've got two hundred dollars, Sir."

"How...did you acquire them?"

"I sold things," the boy said quickly.

The rooms here were bare. Clearly the boy had nothing to sell. He had stolen the money, the alien was sure.

"I can get more. I can—"

The alien made a sound that did not translate. The boy jumped.

The alien was thinking of the 200,000 inters for the vengeance assassination on Hoggun's third moon, the one hundred kilobucks for the renegade contract on the asteroid called Wolfe, and the mineral shares, pharmaceuticals, and spacelock craft—worth twice that—which he had in the end received for the three corporate kills on Alama Poy. What could two hundred *dollars* buy? Could it even buy a city rail ticket?

"That is not enough," the alien said. "Of course," it added, one arm twitching, then still again, "you may have thought to record…our discussion…and you may threaten to release the recording…to Earth authorities…if I do not do what you ask of me…."

The boy's pupils dilated then—like those of the human province official on Diedor, the one he had removed for the Gray Infra there.

"Oh, no—" the boy stammered. "I wouldn't do that—" The skin of his face had turned red, the alien saw. "I didn't even think of it."

"Perhaps…you should have," the alien said. The arm twitched again, and the boy saw that it was smaller than the others, crooked but strong.

The boy nodded. Yes, he should have thought of that. "Why…" the alien asked then, "does a man named…James Ortega-Mambay…wish to kill your sister?"

When the boy was finished explaining, the alien stared at him again and the boy grew uncomfortable. Then the creature rose, joints falling into place with popping and sucking sounds, legs locking to lift the heavy torso and head, the long arms snaking out as if with a life of their own.

The boy was up and stepping back.

"Two hundred…is not enough for a kill," the alien said, and was gone, taking the same subterranean path out of the building which the boy had worked out for him.

•••

When the man named Ortega-Mambay stepped from the bullet elevator to the roof of the federal building, it was sunset and the end of another long but productive day at BuPopCon. In the sun's final rays the helipad glowed like a perfect little pond—not the chaos of the Pacific Ocean in the distance—and even the mugginess couldn't ruin the scene. It was the kind of weather one conventionally took one's jacket off in; but there was only one place to remove one's jacket with at least a modicum of dignity, and that was, of course, in the privacy of one's own FabHome-by-the-Sea. To thwart convention, he was wearing his new triple-weave "gauze" jacket in the pattern called "Summer Shimmer"—handsome, odorless, waterproof, and cool. He would not remove it until he wished to.

He was the last, as always, to leave the Bureau, and as always he felt the pride. There was nothing sweeter than being the last—than lifting off from the empty pad with the rotor blades singing over him and the setting sun below as he made his way in his earned solitude away from the city up the coast to another, smaller helipad and his FabHome near Oxnard. He had worked hard for such sweetness, he reminded himself.

His heli sat glowing in the sun's last light—part of the perfect scene— and he took his time walking to it. It was worth a paintbrush painting, or a digital one, or a multimedia poem. Perhaps he would make something to memorialize it this weekend, after the other members of his triad visited for their intimacy session.

As he reached the pilot's side and the little door there, a shadow separated itself from the greater shadow cast by the craft, and he nearly screamed.

The figure was tall and at first he thought it was a costume, a joke played by a colleague, nothing worse.

But as the figure stepped into the fading light, he saw what it was and nearly screamed again. He had seen such creatures in newscasts, of course, and even at a distance at the shuttleport or at major tourist landmarks in the city, but never like this. *So close.*

When it spoke, the voice was low and mechanical—the work of an Ipoor mesh.

"You are," the alien said, "James Ortega-Mambay...Seventh District Supervisor...BuPopCon?"

Ortega-Mambay considered denying it, but did not. He knew the reputation of the Antalou as well as anyone did. He knew the uses to which his own race, not to mention the other four races mankind had met among the stars, had put them. The Antalou did not strike him as creatures one lied to without risk.

"Yes.... I am. I am Ortega-Mambay."

"My own name," the Antalou said, "does not matter, Ortega-Mambay. You know what I am.... What matters...is that you have decreed...the pregnancy of Linda Tuckey-Yatsen illegal.... You have ordered the unborn female sibling...of the boy Kim Tuckey-Yatsen...aborted. Is this true?"

The alien waited.

"It may be," the man said, fumbling. "I certainly do not have all of our cases memorized. We do not process them by family name—"

He stopped as he saw the absurdity of it. It was outrageous.

"I really do not see what business this is of yours," he began. "This is a Terran city, and an overpopulated one—in an overpopulated nation on an overpopulated planet that cannot afford to pay to move its burden offworld. We are faced with a problem and one we are quite happy solving by ourselves. None of this can possibly be any of your affair, Visitor. Do you have standing with your delegation in this city?"

"I do not," the mesh answered, "and it is indeed...my affair if...the unborn female child of Family Tuckey-Yatsen dies."

"I do not know what you mean."

"She is to live, Ortega-Mambay... Her brother wishes a sibling.... He lives and schools...in three small rooms while his parents work... somewhere in the city.... To him...the female child his mother carries... is already born. He has great feeling for her...in the way of your kind, Ortega-Mambay."

This could not be happening, Ortega-Mambay told himself. It was insane, and he could feel rising within him a rage he hadn't felt since his first job with the government. "How dare you!" he heard himself say. "You are standing on the home planet of another race and ordering me, a federal official, to obey not only a child's wishes, but your own—you, a Visitor and one without official standing among your own kind—"

"The child," the alien broke in, "will not die. If she dies, I will...do what I have been...retained to do."

The alien stepped then to the heli and the man's side, so close they were almost touching. The man did not back up. He would not be intimidated. *He would not.*

The alien raised two of its four arms, and the man heard a snickering sound, then a pop, then another, and something caught in his throat as he watched talons longer and straighter than anything he had ever dreamed of slip one by one through the creature's black syntheskin.

Then, using these talons, the creature removed the door from his heli.

One moment the alloy door was on its hinges; the next it was impaled on the talons, which were, Ortega-Mambay saw now, so much stronger than any nail, bone, or other integument of Terran fauna. Giddily he wondered what the creature possibly ate to make them so strong.

"Get into your vehicle, Ortega-Mambay," the alien said. "Proceed home. Sleep and think...about what you must do...to keep the female sibling alive."

Ortega-Mambay could barely work his legs. He was trying to get into the heli, but couldn't, and for a terrible moment it occurred to him that the alien might try to help him in. But then he was in at last, hands flailing at the dashboard as he tried to do what he'd been asked to do: *Think.*

•••

The alien did not sit on the bed, but remained in the doorway. The boy did not have trouble looking at him this time.

"You know more about us," the alien said suddenly, severely, "than you wished me to understand.... Is this not true?"

The boy did not answer. The creature's eyes—huge and catlike—held his.

"Answer me," the alien said.

When the boy finally spoke, he said only, "Did you do it?"

The alien ignored him.

"Did you kill him?" the boy said.

"Answer me," the alien repeated, perfectly still.

"Yes..." the boy said, looking away at last.

"How?" the alien asked.

The boy did not answer. There was, the alien could see, defeat in the way the boy sat on the stool.

"You will answer me...or I will...damage this room."

The boy did nothing for a moment, then got up and moved slowly to the terminal where he studied each day.

"I've done a lot of work on your star," the boy said. There was little energy in his voice now.

"It is more than that," the alien said.

"Yes. I've studied Antalouan history." The boy paused and the alien felt the energy rise a little. "For school, I mean." There was feeling again—a little—to the boy's voice.

The boy hit the keyboard once, then twice, and the screen flickered to life. The alien saw a map of the northern hemisphere of Antalou, the trade routes of the ancient Seventh Empire, the fragmented continent, and the deadly seas that had doomed it.

"More than this...I think," the alien said.

"Yes," the boy said. "I did a report last year—on my own, not for school—about the fossil record on Antalou. There were a lot of animals that wanted the same food you wanted—that your kind wanted. On Antalou, I mean."

Yes, the alien thought.

"I ran across others things, too," the boy went on, and the alien heard the energy die again, heard in the boy's voice the suppressive feeling his kind called "despair." The boy believed that the man named Ortega-Mambay would still kill his sister, and so the boy "despaired."

Again the boy hit the keyboard. A new diagram appeared. It was familiar, though the alien had not seen one like it—so clinical, detailed, and ornate—in half a lifetime.

It was the Antalouan family cluster, and though the alien could not read them, he knew what the labels described: The "kinship obligation bonds" and their respective "motivational weights," the "defense-need parameters" and "bond-loss consequences" for identity and group membership. There was an inset, too, which gave—in animated three-dimensional display—the survival model human exopsychologists believed could explain all Antalouan behavior.

The boy hit the keyboard and an iconographic list of the "totemic bequeaths" and "kinships inheritances" from ancient burial sites near Toloa and Mantok appeared.

"You thought you knew," the alien said, "what an Antalou feels."

The boy kept his eyes on the floor. "Yes."

The alien did not speak for a moment, but when he did, it was to say: "You were not wrong...Tuckey-Yatsen."

The boy looked up, not understanding.

"Your sister will live," the Antalou said.

The boy blinked, but did not believe it.

"What I say is true," the alien said.

The alien watched as the boy's body began to straighten, as energy, no longer suppressed in "despair," moved through it.

"It was done," the alien explained, "without the killing...which neither you nor I...could afford."

"They will let her live?"

"Yes."

"You are sure?"

"I do not lie…about the work I do."

The boy was staring at the alien.

"I will give you the money," he said.

"No," the alien said. "That will not…be necessary."

The boy stared for another moment, and then, strangely, began to move.

The alien watched, curious. The boy was making himself step toward him, though why he would do this the alien did not know. It was a human custom perhaps, a "sentimentality," and the boy, though afraid, thought he must offer it.

When the boy reached the alien, he put out an unsteady hand, touched the Antalou's shoulder lightly—once, twice—and then, remarkably, drew his hand down the alien's damaged arm.

The alien was astonished. It was an Antalouan gesture, this touch.

This is no ordinary boy, the alien thought. It was not simply the boy's intelligence—however one might measure it—or his understanding of the Antalou. It was something else—something the alien recognized.

Something any killer needs….

The Antalouan gesture the boy had used meant "obligation to blood," though it lacked the slow unsheathing of the *demoor*. The boy had chosen well.

"Thank you," the boy was saying, and the alien knew he had rehearsed both the touch and the words. It had filled the boy with great fear, the thought of it, but he had rehearsed until fear no longer ruled him.

As the boy stepped back, shaking now and unable to stop it, he said, "Do you have a family-cluster still?"

"I do not," the alien answered, not surprised by the question. The boy no longer surprised him. "It was a decision…made without regrets. Many Antalou have made it. My work…prevents it. You understand…."

The boy nodded, a gesture which meant that he did.

And then the boy said it:

"What is it like to kill?"

It was, the alien knew, the question the boy had most wanted to ask. There was excitement in the voice, but still no fear.

When the alien answered, it was to say simply:

"It is both…more and less…than what one…imagines it will be."

•••

The boy named Kim Tuckey-Yatsen stood in the doorway of the small room where he slept and schooled, and listened as the man spoke to his mother and father. The man never looked at his mother's swollen belly. He said simply, "You have been granted an exception, Family Tuckey-Yatsen. You have permission to proceed with the delivery of the unborn female. You will be receiving confirmation of a Four-Member Family Waiver within three workweeks. All questions should be referred to BuPopCon, Seventh District, at the netnumber on this card."

When the man was gone, his mother cried in happiness and his father held her. When the boy stepped up to them, they embraced him, too. There were three of them now, hugging, and soon there would be four. That was what mattered. His parents were good people. They had taken a chance for him, and he loved them. That mattered, too, he knew.

That night he dreamed of her again. Her name would be Kiara. In the dream she looked a little like Siddo's sister two floors down, but also like his mother. Daughters should look like their mothers, shouldn't they? In his dream the four of them were hugging and there were more rooms, and the rooms were bigger.

•••

When the boy was seventeen and his sister five, sharing a single room as well as siblings can, the trunk arrived from Romah, one of the war-scarred worlds of the Pleiades. Pressurized and dented, the small alloy container bore the customs stamps of four spacelocks, had been opened at least seven times in its passage, and smelled. It had been disinfected, the USPUS carrier who delivered it explained. It had been kept in quarantine for a year and had nearly not gotten through, given the circumstances.

The boy did not know what the carrier meant.

The trunk held many things, the woman explained. The small polished skull of a carnivore not from Earth. A piece of space metal fused like the blossom of a flower. Two rings of polished stone which tingled to the touch. An ancient device which the boy would later discover was a third-generation airless communicator used by the Gar-Betties. A coil made of animal hair and pitch, which he would learn was a rare musical instrument from Hoggun VI. And many smaller things, among them the postcard of the Pacific Fountain the boy had given the alien.

Only later did the family receive official word of the 300,000 inters deposited in the boy's name in the neutral banking station of HiVerks; of the cache of specialized weapons few would understand that had been placed in perpetual care on Titan, also in his name; and of the offworld travel voucher purchased for the boy to use when he was old enough to use it.

Though it read like no will ever written on Earth, it was indeed a will, one that the Antalou called a "bequeathing cantation." That it had been recorded in a spacelock lobby shortly before the alien's violent death on a world called Glory did not diminish its legal authority.

Although the boy tried to explain it to them, his parents did not understand; and before long it did not matter. The money bought them five rooms in the northeast sector of the city, a better job for his mother, better care for his father's autoimmunities, more technical education for the boy, and all the food and clothes they needed; and for the time being (though only that) these things mattered more to him than Saturn's great moon and the marvelous weapons waiting patiently for him there.

GUERRILLA MURAL OF A SIREN'S SONG

ERNEST HOGAN

L ike a miniature Jupiter gone insane, the paint-blob hangs in the middle of the room—a Jupiter whose tides and weather and powerful gravity snapped on the strain of the secret of its monstrous microscopic inhabitants so its regular bands are broken up into gaily swirling asymmetrical patterns of mingling paint with color almost computer-exaggerated—like the glorious unholy mother of all cat's eye marbles, it glares at me.

I try not to see her.

There's no gravity here, but that floating blob has a pull just the same. I orbit in freefall, make 'em let me paint in the center of these cans where the spinning doesn't suck you to the floor—and like the irresistible pull of Jupiter, so big, so bad, so goddam awesome that you feel yourself fall into those convulsive, frenzied clouds, like you're being sucked *up*, not pulled down (Jupiter is too big, too gigantic for you to ever be on top of it)—and *it* still pulls me.

And she pulls me.

I take the stick like an Aztec priest wielding a flint knife, or that cop swinging his baton on that cool, starless night years ago in L.A.—crushing the buckle from my gas mask into my skull, leaving a cute little scar on my scalp that I shaved my head for months to show off.

It exploded—like an amphetamine-choked blob. Amorphous little monsters sailed through the air, some colliding with me and sticking to my naked flesh. One sought my eyes in order to blind me. Lucky I have goggles like Tlaloc, the Rain, Water, and Thunder God…and a breathing mask—that's all the covering I need! I wipe away the paint, my vision is smeared with color.

The entire little canvas-lined room is exploding with color. Beautiful. Like her.

Still, the paint has this sickening tendency to settle into little jiggling globes that just sit there like mini-Jupiters, mocking me. I refuse to allow entropy to happen in my presence, so, like a samurai Jackson Pollock, I scream through my mask and thrash the disgusting little buggers into tinier flying sky-serpents that merrily decorate me, and the canvas on the walls.

And the canvas is raw, unprimed and the paint is mixed with a base that gives it the consistency of water. Splatter marks don't just sit there looking pretty—no, they grow fur as the canvas absorbs it, thirstily. My work is always wild and woolly.

Soon the colorful swordplay is over and I am victorious. All (except for a few little stubborn, but insignificant BB's) the paint is slapped down to the canvas. I shed my goggles for a while and the furious splatters change into visions.

André Masson, eat your heart out!

Bizarre hieroglyphs materialize in the Jovian storm clouds: *Demonic cartoon characters exhaling balloons full of obscenity—hordes of baby godzilloids crawling through vacuum and eating rocks—endless three-D labyrinths of orbital castles complete with living gargoyles and tapestries you can walk into—large, luxuriant cars encrusted with jewels and tailfins that race the crowded, tangled spaghetti of freeways with off-ramps all over the galaxy—the vegetal love poetry that an intelligent network of vines sings to the jungle it intricately embraces—the ecstatic rush of falling into an ocean of warm mud that tastes delicious and makes you feel so good—pornographic geometries that can only be imagined on a scale more than intergalactic—the Byzantine plots of surrealistic soap operas that take place outside of spacetime, in Omeyocan, the highest heaven—the ballet of subatomic particles smaller than any yet discovered!*

Letting the stick fly, I attack the canvas with paint-covered fingers—desperately trying to record the visions before they fade, but never finishing before they do, so I have to fill many gaps with memory and imagination.

Then I see her face again.

That beautiful, perfect Zulu face, with impossibly intense eyes—beauty that puts the cold, marble-white classicism of dead and buried ancient Greece to shame, causing arrogant statues to crack and crumble to dust—making you see how right the barbarians were in knocking their heads off. A presence that is soft, yet extremely powerful, like the fearful sound of the soft, swishing skirt that reveals that an umkhovu—like a bad memory of apartheid—is roaming the midnight streets of Soweto, making its way past the sleepy suburbs, to the shiny new university to the Center of Parapsychology...

I find myself drawing that magnificent face. The face of Willa Shembe, a pampered little (she was taller than me, but still, somehow, *little*) psychic from Zululand, from whom I'll never be free. The sorcery that caused her "death" has contaminated me, enslaved me. I will see, draw, and paint her forever.

I should have known the first time I saw her—who knows how long after my surprisingly non-fatal encounter with the Sirens...

Whatever made Calvino send her to me? I guess a little inspiration flickers under that pale, bald head, behind those thick, old-fashioned glasses and fat, gray eyebrows on occasion.

I suddenly saw her—clearly and distinctly out of my feverish delirium and telepathic hangover—dancing galaxies and soft, squishy, organic cities faded to let her power through.

Calvino must have been desperate. I, of all people, survived a mind-to-whatever encounter with the Sirens!

Me, Pablo Cortez, infamous guerrilla muralist from the wild, crumbling concrete and stucco overgrowth of L.A.—who refused to be absorbed into the decaying society I satirized in my work long after my fellow wall-defacers were caught, arrested, and offered a chance to become honest artists who paint on neat, clean canvases that are displayed in sterile galleries, and bought by the affluent to show everybody how sensitive they are by what they choose to decorate their expensive, prestigious apartments with. I, who tattooed the Picasso quote, "PAINTING IS NOT DONE TO DECORATE APARTMENTS. IT IS AN INSTRUMENT OF WAR FOR ATTACK AND DEFENSE AGAINST THE ENEMY," on my own left arm with a felt-tip pen and a safety-pin. The guy who *really* meant it when he helped paint—fast, so we could get it done 'and get the hell out of there before getting our heads busted—Quetzalcoatl choking on smog, Uncle Sam holding up the heart of a draftee for the "disturbance" in South Africa (soon to be Zululand—again) to the gaping jaws of a Biomechanoid War God, mutilated/spacesuited corpses and countless mass portraits of the ever-growing throngs of the homeless to decorate the featureless, empty walls of the blank architecture where Mr. and Ms. Los Angeles could see as they did the freeway boogie to work. Siquerios and Orozco and every spray-can wielding vato would've been proud!

That fast, slashing, hit-and-run style of the Guerrilla Muralists of L.A. was mine—a direct outgrowth of my rushed, rabid scribblings of monsters from my id that I leave on any available surface. Moe, Desiree, Johnny, Maria, LeRoy, Buck, and Estela were all really quiet *artistes* at heart. They preferred to work quietly, in air-conditioned, sound-proof studios with neat, meticulously laid-out materials. Just a bunch of nice kids pushed to the edge of a demented society—but I had fallen off that edge long ago. I *really* believed in our rebellion, and wouldn't be satisfied with becoming a darling of rich liberals. If any one of them was lowered down into the Great Red Spot, their sensitive, humane, artistic minds would have blown out so fast they'd have sprayed out of the exoskeleton and coated the entire inside of the dirgiscaphe with their gooey remains.

No, it took a maniac like me.

They could be comfortable lapping up the regurgitated wealth in the center of the Hollywood Empire, or fly out to the colonies to help create the new official art of the Space Culture Project, while I created splatter-painting, my Freefall Abstract Expressionism, and got my ass kicked out.

It didn't bother me. Not me. I had to keep going. Keep wandering. Volunteered to go to Ithaca Base and get lowered through the dangerous radioactive magnetosphere of the Big Planet, down to the Great Red Spot, into the heart of the Sirens' sphere of influence, let their alien thoughts flow through my skull *and* survive!

But I did need her to bring me out of it. Willa Shembe, the pride of the scientific community of Zululand. A girl used to experiencing the universe through other peoples' minds.

She keeps showing up in the images, in the paint. Unexpectedly. Automatically.

Just like the first time she showed up in my life. When I was still lost in the influence of the Sirens. After they locked me into the exoskeleton, into the dirigiscaphe, and lowered me by remote control down into evil, heavy gravity and big, beautiful stormclouds out of Turner's wetdreams, or Chalchiuhtlicue's most passionate rituals of whirlpools, violence, growth, and young love.

"Do you feel anything yet?" Dr. Calvino buzzed into my earphone on that day.

"If only those bastards could go through this," I said into the throat-mike. "They should all come here and see this planet up close before they call me undisciplined!"

"What are you talking about?" The doc never understood me.

"This sight! Jupiter up close! Wagstaff and the rest of those tight-assed idiots at the Space Culture Project should see *this*. That is what space art should be about. This energy! This power! This freedom! This is what I had in mind when I created splatterpainting."

"What about the Sirens? Are you feeling any effects?"

"In my mind? No. This gravity is a bitch, though. If only I could see these clouds while weightless! If only I could come here and paint! Can't they build one of these exoskeletons with more freedom of movement?"

"The one you have on is the state of the art. The instruments show a high concentration of Sirens in the clouds around you. Do you feel anything yet?"

"Yeah, now that you mention it. The gravity. It's getting hard to move, breathe…"

"Should we abort?"

"No! I'm feeling better now. Lighter. The gravity seems to be going away. I almost feel weightless. It's really great! Feels like I could peel this exoskeleton right off…"

"Don't!"

"I'm not stupid, Calvino! This is probably an illusion, like what happened to the others. I do plan on surviving this!"

"Any change in sensations?"

"It's like one long rush. Ecstasy—like I'm weightless, painting away like crazy, making a big, juicy mess. I'm getting an erection. The exoskeleton seems to be holding me down."

Then I got a strong rotten-eggs whiff of methane. Could the dirgiscaphe be leaking? I was about to say something, but couldn't move—first I was paralyzed, every muscle locked tight, then it all turned to mush—flesh, bones, exoskeleton, dirgiscaphe, Jupiter, space...

"Cortez, are you all right?" said Calvino.

I was getting softer—like a Salvador Dalí watch. Everything was getting softer. Putty. Liquid. Gas. Like those colorful, flowing clouds that were all around.

"Cortez, are you there?"

I was a twisting, bubbling cloud—dancing among the gorgeous clouds of Jupiter. Among microscopic creatures I couldn't see, but could feel—like spirits, like ghosts.

"Abort! Abort!"

I felt that I was dissolving. Being absorbed. I panicked.

Then they had me. *Me.* Who has never given in to anybody!

I passed from the realm of Xiuhtecuhtli—the supreme being within space and time, the power of life and fire, the center of all things and spindle of the universe—to Omeyocan, realm of Ometecuhtli, the male/female supreme being, the dual lord, source of all existence, the essential unity in difference. Spacetime was flushed down the toilet—a cute cartoon Einstein offered himself as a blood sacrifice.

Somewhere I was aware of the dirgiscaphe's engines burning and the Gs building up so that even the exoskeleton couldn't save me from harm. Also: *I was being born—I was alive and well millions of years ago on Mars—I was back in Hightown having an argument with Wagstaff of the Space Culture Project.*

"You should really be more cooperative, Mr. Cortez," he said from inside his tight, crisp facade, more acrylic than flesh.

"Where have I heard that before?" I said, going into a rant. "What you want isn't art. It's municipal garbage, state-sponsored bullshit, committee-conceived caca!"

I heard the big beat of whales and dolphins in perfect sync with songs of sentient stars and the Sirens, that toy robots and nude bettyboopoids joyously danced to in endless halls that were covered with animated hieroglyphs that joined in the Futuro-Afro-PreColumbian-TransSpacetime-

Zen-Quantum Musical Comedy!

"The space hieroglyphics you started out with were interesting, but everything you've done since has become more and more unacceptable. Too messy. Dripping all over the place…"

"All I did was what you asked me to do—come into this new environment and create a new art for it. It developed into splatterpainting, not the middle-class kitsch you lust after!"

I was thirteen years old and enticing an eleven-year-old girl into letting me pop her cherry in sacrifice to Tlazolteotl—Aztec goddess of filth and depravity—past midnight in an empty high school campus on a hot, Southern California night! I saw the programmed dreams of hibernating seeds traveling near the speed of light through gulfs of interstellar space! I shot bold, colorful graffiti on the walls of gravity-less artificial worlds, asteroids, moons, planets to the timeless tune of a symphony of countless Big Bangs!

"I'm afraid we can't waste money on you any longer. We'll have to send you back to Earth!"

"No! You don't understand me, and I'm human—from your world! How do you expect to face the rest of the universe if you can't deal with me?"

But I showed them. I volunteered for the Odysseus Project. They didn't care what kind of pictures I painted, just that I realized that *everybody* who contacted the Sirens so far had died.

But I didn't die. I survived, because I'm mad enough to see it all without going mad. Because my imagination is powerful enough to face what most people find unthinkable.

I wallowed in it, dreamed of painting eye-frying pictures of it that would prove my genius to everyone—later, when it was over—but it didn't end. Just went on and on. Image after goddam image. I was totally delighted. Flow an endless stream of bizarre imagery before my eyes and I'm in paradise. It was like—no, better than that weightless fuck with a sculptress who was disgusted when I got cum all over her work—like when I first discovered the Aztecs as a wee tot, delighted that these bloodthirsty, cannibalistic, colorful monsters were *mine,* not the property of the light-skinned aliens from "back East"—they were *my* heritage, it was *my* blood that stained those pyramids, *my* art that survived the campaign of another Cortez centuries ago, so powerful that it took Western art until the Twentieth Century to catch up—like all this was something I dreamed up and was damn proud to have such a fantastic imagination!

Sure, I was vaguely aware that just outside Jupiter's magnetosphere, in the hospital section of Ithaca Base, my body was lying there with tubes and wires stuck into it, with a concussion, a ruptured spleen, and assorted broken bones. But somehow it didn't seem important. Sure, it was Pablo Cortez, but I was so many other places. My body and its suffering were just part of the Sirens' show: *Like pentasexual orgies in sparkling caverns, or sonic wars in oceans that flowed through endless, gigantic tubes, or electronic epic chants of a silicon-crystal disc-jockey!*

"He may not have survived after all," Calvino said.

I heard that, in the distance—*beyond the parade of idols hewn out of the hearts of neutron stars, hungrily marching through the cosmos to galaxies where entire civilizations were offered as sacrifices, and herds of armored, winged worms devoured planets and shit art and technology!*

Then, like the soft sound of a swishing skirt, the trademark of the um-khovu, the living dead—she trickled into my mind that the Sirens had scattered all over the universe. Willa Shembe, shy and curious, bored with all the human minds she had plugged into, eager to wrap her telepathic tendrils around something different, something alien—the Sirens.

I was jolted. It was being outside of space and time with Ometecuhtli—then suddenly feeling the presence of Nkulunkulu, the Zulus' maker of all things. I was being manipulated by an unseen sangoma, a Zulu diviner with cattle gall bladder crown and necklace of herbs—no, rather an abathakathi, an evil wizard whose most important product is misery, killing, illness, and drought—making a diabolical potion out of pieces of a human body—me! I felt a phantom kiss where she bit off the tip of my tongue, and left me animal-eyed, and forever spooked—her umkhovu, a slave to her magic, locked in her spell.

What was even more shocking was that I didn't know shit about the Zulus, their mythology, or superstitions—like all the rest of the Sirens' song, it just flooded my skull, only more intense—the taste of roast chicken and uputhu drowned out that of hot, greasy tacos and the bitter blood of long crunchy caterpillars in my mouth! It was a presence closer to my body than my mind. None of the Sirens' spacetime short-circuitry. This was here, now. There, then. Before I came out of the Sirens' spell, lying there with a broken body stuck with tubes and wires with a beautiful Zulu telepath sucking my blown-out mind.

She relished it. Devoured greedily.

My memories. The Sirens' maelstrom of imagery. My fantasies. Alien realities.

"You're crazy, Pablo! You got talent, but you're more a criminal than an artist!" echoed back from an argument I had with the rest of the Guerrilla Muralists at our trial.

Rainbow-filled skies over effervescent seas—me shedding my own blood so I could have something to paint with at age eight—the joy I felt the first time I was weightless, and decided that gravity was the enemy of true freedom, and decided to splash my paint, and created splatterpainting—a war of radioactive cloud-beings that goes on for millennia across billions of light-years—cartoons I'd draw on my clothes when I got bored—invisible beasts that flex gravity at will and eat black holes!

She smiled. Then moaned with delight.

And I received input from her mind—she was strange, like the humanoids who rode see-through ships to the end of time to observe the aesthetic qualities of the heat death of the universe—other people's experiences and thoughts were what she lived for. She rarely ate, or moved—was more interested in reading more and more minds than the university's experiments—she wasted away. They thought she would die.

Then she found out about the Sirens, and said some of her few words: "Take me to them!"

Soon I could see her clearly through my own eyes, and see me through her eyes, *and* watch the song of the Sirens with no eyes at all.

She said a few more words. "Beautiful. I love it!"

Crack! Something snapped. The deadly intensity in those big, brown eyes clicked off. She dropped on top of me.

The orderlies grabbed her and after a few skilled, strategic feels, one said, "She's dead."

I laughed. A lovely demonic laugh that took my entire aching body and all my strength. It hurt like hell and was worth it. They all, even Calvino, looked into my crazed eyes.

"Idiots! Fools! Assholes! She's…" I screamed.

"You're alive!"

"What happened?"

"Are you all right?"

"How do you feel?" some of them asked. The rest just looked scared and perplexed.

"Shut up!" I said. "There's so much… I can't… Let me out of this!"

"No!" Calvino said. You have several broken bones and internal injuries!"

It hurt like a bitch, but I didn't care, gritted my teeth, and slid myself off the bunk. They tried to stop me, but a few throat-rupturing banshee-screams kept them at bay. The floor hit me like a macrocosm of pain. Damn gravity—even the centrifugal force, fake kind!

After a while they watched me with awe and dread as if I was a rotting corpse that suddenly sprang back to life. Luckily, my right arm was working in a cast, but I could move it at the shoulder, where it counts. I reached under my gown and tore off the hospital diaper.

I needed something to paint with. Something that would smear and leave a mark. It had been years since I'd painted with my own shit. It'd have to do.

And it did nicely.

Before they shot a sedative into my veins, I managed to smear one vision onto the floor.

When I woke up, I was strapped down, re-tubed and wired, watching that vision in caca come to focus before my face.

Calvino was holding it. He'd had that section of floor torn out and sealed in acrylic. My work mummified for posterity.

"What is it?" he asked.

"Shit on laminated metal," I smartassed.

"No," he said, being unusually patient. "The subject matter. What is it?"

"It looks like some kind of soft, lovely tree that is rooted to the ground while it grows, but breaks free and flies around when it's full-grown."

"Where did it come from?"

"The Sirens. They made me see it. Made me *be* it."

"Was that all?"

"Hell no! It was a constant flow of images, all at once and all jumbled together. I could see, hear, feel, and taste it all. I wanted to paint it. I could spend my entire life on it!"

"Notice anything strange about it?"

"Doc, it was *all* strange!"

"Surely your artist's eyes can see it. Mr. Cortez, you always have been a mystery to me, almost as if *you* were from another planet, but I did learn to recognize your style."

I was stunned. "Yeah. The style! It's different! Not my usual high-power scribble, it looks…"

"More detailed, and more alien."

"But I couldn't help it, it just happened…"

"Like Willa's death," a nurse said, cool as a sip of liquid nitrogen.

"She's not dead," I said.

"All vital functions stopped. No brain activity," Calvino said, bringing those fuzzy gray eyebrows together. "She's dead."

"She's alive," I insisted. "Maybe not in that cute body, but I can still feel the presence of that insatiable suction-pump of a mind."

Calvino smiled, with some effort. "I didn't suspect you of having *any* religious beliefs, Mr. Cortez."

"Damn right I don't," I snapped. "Even the Aztec gods I'm always babbling about are basically a joke to me—I like the way it bothers the hell out of the believers… I guess the only thing I really believe in is myself."

"And that Willa Shembe is alive," he shot at me.

"I can feel her. She's the source of the images that still parade through the back of my mind. She went through me to get them. Her mindtracks are permanently etched into my nervous system. I'm always going to receive her signals.

"…She had this fantasy that she never told anybody. She probably didn't even want me to know about it, but to get to the Sirens she gave me a grand tour of her mind. She wanted to be invisible and fly through the entire universe, faster than the speed of light, and see and *be* it all. And that's what she's doing.

"…I couldn't have done it… I'm an egomaniac. I'm too much in love with being the great Pablo Cortez to ever let go the way she did. I could never give myself totally. I'm hanging on too tight."

They all just looked confused.

"In the name of Tlazolteotl, give me something to paint—or at least draw—with! These images are driving me crazy! If you don't let me paint, my skull will swell up, pop, and leave you covered with a sticky-slimy masterpiece! These images will open up the cosmos! Transform our way of life!"

"You're too weak," Calvino said, real sincere.

"Bullshit!" I screamed. "I could paint with the bloody stumps right after my arms and legs were hacked off! The pain is nothing compared to my need! If I were decapitated, I could roll my head around and leave a blood-trail that the world will cherish!"

They brought me a pad and a marker. Nothing like a little hyperbole to get your point across.

The scientists were fascinated. They'd see things I didn't notice. Soon they were anxiously waiting for my next piece. As soon as I could move around, they let me paint, sloshing colors on whatever I could for a canvas. Some high-decibel hyperbole got me my zero-G studio at the center of Ithaca Base.

Grumblings of prosecuting me for the murder of Willa Shembe eventually petered out.

And the work came effortlessly, rapidly, ecstatically—I'd revel in it for hours, and hate myself for not being able to keep up with it, for getting tired, and needing sleep. I'd beg Calvino for drugs so I could work for weeks at a time (he refused, of course—hyperbole won't get you everything).

I'm now the most important artist of the Solar System. Scientists analyze my work for clues about the nature of other worlds. The art world hails me as the new master. Calvino hung that first shit-smear painting in his office. The Space Culture Project began making policy changes—the murals on future space colonies and starships will show my influence.

And Willa—a Siren in her own right, perhaps my most important Siren—keeps showing up through it all. Her face. Her body. Dancing through the universe. Dancing with the universe. Dancing the universe. Showing everybody that I'm not the only one responsible for all this great art. It embarrasses me—but I must acknowledge that Willa and the Sirens are my collaborators. I'd like to ignore it all and hog all the glory for myself, but she keeps showing up in the patterns of the flying paint.

In a way I enjoy painting her, as much as the rest. She's so beautiful. Her classic Zulu features. Her bold, quiet, unending curiosity. The way she sacrificed herself, willingly and without hesitation, when others simply were torn apart and I hung onto my ego with a death-grip. She alone had the courage to truly hear the song of the Sirens, and join them in their cosmic dance.

Maybe she was the only human being I could love more than I love myself. Maybe...

I'll never know. I'll never be able to touch her. I can only paint her.

And the cosmos she's rapturously exploring.

ANGEL

PAT CADIGAN

S tand with me awhile, Angel, I said and Angel said he'd do that. Angel was good to me that way, good to have with you on a cold night and nowhere to go. We stood on the street corner together and watched the cars going by and people and all. The streets were lit up like Christmas, streetlights, store lights, marquees over the all-night movie houses and bookstores blinking and flashing; shank of the evening in east midtown. Angel was getting used to things here and getting used to how I did, nights. Standing outside, because what else are you going to do. He was my Angel now, had been since that other cold night when I'd been going home, because where are you going to go, and I'd found him and took him with me. It's good to have someone to take with you, someone to look after. Angel knew that. He started looking after me, too.

Like now. We were standing there awhile and I was looking around at nothing and everything, the cars cruising past, some of them stopping now and again for the hookers posing by the curb, and then I saw it, out of the corner of my eye. Stuff coming out of the Angel, shiny like sparks but flowing like liquid. Silver fireworks. I turned and looked all the way at him and it was gone. And he turned and gave a little grin like he was embarrassed I'd seen. Nobody else saw it, though; not the short guy who paused next to the Angel before crossing the street against the light, not the skinny hype looking to sell the boom-box he was carrying on his shoulder, not the homeboy strutting past us with both his girlfriends on his arms, nobody but me.

The Angel said, Hungry?

Sure, I said. I'm hungry.

Angel looked past me. Okay, he said. I looked, too, and here they came, three leather boys, visor caps, belts, boots, keyrings. On the cruise together. Scary stuff, even though you know it's not looking for you.

I said, Them? *Them?*

Angel didn't answer. One went by, then the second, and the Angel stopped the third by taking hold of his arm.

Hi.

The guy nodded. His head was shaved. I could see a little grey-black stubble under his cap. No eyebrows, disinterested eyes. The eyes were because of the Angel.

I could use a little money, the Angel said. My friend and I are hungry.

The guy put his hand in his pocket and wiggled out some bills, offering them to the Angel. The Angel selected a twenty and closed the guy's hand around the rest.

This will be enough, thank you.

The guy put his money away and waited.

I hope you have a good night, said the Angel.

The guy nodded and walked on, going across the street to where his two friends were waiting on the next corner. Nobody found anything weird about it.

Angel was grinning at me. Sometimes he was the Angel, when he was doing something, sometimes he was Angel, when he was just with me. Now he was Angel again. We went up the street to the luncheonette and got a seat by the front window so we could still watch the street while we ate.

Cheeseburger and fries, I said without bothering to look at the plastic-covered menus lying on top of the napkin holder. The Angel nodded.

Thought so, he said. I'll have the same, then.

The waitress came over with a little tiny pad to take our order. I cleared my throat. It seemed like I hadn't used my voice in a hundred years. "Two cheeseburgers and two fries," I said, "and two cups of—" I looked up at her and froze. She had no face. Like, nothing, blank from hairline to chin, soft little dents where the eyes and nose and mouth would have been. Under the table, the Angel kicked me, but gentle.

"And two cups of coffee," I said.

She didn't say anything—how could she?—as she wrote down the order and then walked away again. All shaken up, I looked at the Angel but he was calm like always.

She's a new arrival, Angel told me and leaned back in his chair. Not enough time to grow a face.

But how can she breathe? I said.

Through her pores. She doesn't need much air yet.

Yah, but what about—like, I mean, don't other people notice that she's got nothing there?

No. It's not such an extraordinary condition. The only reason you notice is because you're with me. Certain things have rubbed off on you. But no one else notices. When they look at her, they see whatever face they expect someone like her to have. And eventually, she'll have it.

But you have a face, I said. You've always had a face.

I'm different, said the Angel.

You sure are, I thought, looking at him. Angel had a beautiful face. That wasn't why I took him home that night, just because he had a beautiful face—I left all that behind a long time ago—but it was there, his beauty. The way you think of a man being beautiful, good clean lines, deep-set eyes, ageless. About the only way you could describe him—look away and you'd forget everything except that he was beautiful. But he did have a face. He did.

Angel shifted in the chair—these were like somebody's old kitchen chairs, you couldn't get too comfortable in them—and shook his head, because he knew I was thinking troubled thoughts. Sometimes you could think something and it wouldn't be troubled and later you'd think the same thing and it would be troubled. The Angel didn't like me to be troubled about him.

Do you have a cigarette? he asked.

I think so.

I patted my jacket and came up with most of a pack that I handed over to him. The Angel lit up and amused us both by having the smoke come out his ears and trickle out of his eyes like ghostly tears. I felt my own eyes watering for his; I wiped them and there was that stuff again, but from me now. I was crying silver fireworks. I flicked them on the table and watched them puff out and vanish.

Does this mean I'm getting to be you, now? I asked.

Angel shook his head. Smoke wafted out of his hair. Just things rubbing off on you. Because we've been together and you're—susceptible. But they're different for you.

Then the waitress brought our food and we went on to another sequence, as the Angel would say. She still had no face but I guess she could see well enough because she put all the plates down just where you'd think they were supposed to go and left the tiny little check in the middle of the table.

Is she—I mean, did you know her, from where you—

Angel gave his head a brief little shake. No. She's from somewhere else. Not one of my—people. He pushed the cheeseburger and fries in front of him over to my side of the table. That was the way it was done; I did all the eating and somehow it worked out.

I picked up my cheeseburger and I was bringing it up to my mouth when my eyes got all funny and I saw it coming up like a whole series of cheeseburgers, whoom-whoom-whoom, trick photography, only for real. I closed my eyes and jammed the cheeseburger into my mouth, holding it there, waiting for all the other cheeseburgers to catch up with it.

You'll be okay, said the Angel. Steady, now.

I said with my mouth full, That was—that was weird. Will I ever get used to this?

I doubt it. But I'll do what I can to help you.

Yah, well, the Angel *would* know. Stuff rubbing off on me, he could feel it better than I could. He was the one it was rubbing off from.

I had put away my cheeseburger and half of Angel's and was working on the french fries for both of us when I noticed he was looking out the window with this hard, tight expression on his face.

Something? I asked him.

Keep eating, he said.

I kept eating but I kept watching, too. The Angel was staring at a big blue car parked at the curb right outside the diner. It was silvery blue, one of those lots-of-money models and there was a woman kind of leaning across from the driver's side to look out the passenger window. She was beautiful in that lots-of-money way, tawny hair swept back from her face and even from here I could see she had turquoise eyes. Really beautiful woman. I almost felt like crying. I mean, jeez, how did people get that way and me too harmless to live.

But the Angel wasn't one bit glad to see her. I knew he didn't want me to say anything, but I couldn't help it.

Who is she?

Keep eating, Angel said. We need the protein, what little there is. I ate and watched the woman and the Angel watch each other and it was getting very—I don't know, very *something* between them, even through the glass. Then a cop car pulled up next to her and I knew they were telling her to move it along. She moved it along.

Angel sagged against the back of his chair and lit another cigarette, smoking it in the regular, unremarkable way.

• • •

What are we going to do tonight? I asked the Angel as we left the restaurant.

Keep out of harm's way, Angel said, which was a new answer. Most nights we spent just kind of going around soaking everything up. The Angel soaked it up, mostly. I got some of it along with him, but not the same way he did. It was different for him. Sometimes he would use me like a kind of filter. Other times he took it direct. There'd been the big car accident one night, right at my usual corner, a big old Buick running a red light smack into somebody's nice Lincoln. The Angel had had to take it direct because I couldn't handle that kind of stuff. I didn't know how the Angel could take it but he could. It carried him for days afterwards, too. I only had to eat for myself.

It's the intensity, little friend, he'd told me, as though that were supposed to explain it.

It's the intensity, not whether it's good or bad. The universe doesn't know good or bad, only less or more. Most of you have a bad time reconciling this. *You* have a bad time with it, little friend, but you get through better than other people. Maybe because of the way you are. You got squeezed out of a lot, you haven't had much of a chance at life. You're as much an exile as I am, only in your own land.

That may have been true, but at least I belonged here, so that part was easier for me. But I didn't say that to the Angel. I think he liked to think he could do as well or better than me at living—I mean, I couldn't just look at some leather boy and get him to cough up a twenty dollar bill. Cough up a fist in the face or worse, was more like it.

Tonight, though, he wasn't doing so good and it was that woman in the car. She'd thrown him out of step, kind of.

Don't think about her, the Angel said, just out of nowhere. Don't think about her any more.

Okay, I said, feeling creepy because it was creepy when the Angel got a glimpse of my head. And then, of course, I couldn't think about anything else hardly.

Do you want to go home? I asked him.

No. I can't stay in now. We'll do the best we can tonight but I'll have to be very careful about the tricks. They take so much out of me and if we're keeping out of harm's way, I might not be able to make up for a lot of it.

It's okay, I said. I ate. I don't need anything else tonight, you don't have to do any more.

Angel got that look on his face, the one where I knew he wanted to give me things, like feelings I couldn't have any more. Generous, the Angel was. But I didn't need those feelings, not like other people seem to. For a while, it was like the Angel didn't understand that but he let me be.

Little friend, he said, and almost touched me. The Angel didn't touch a lot. I could touch him and that would be okay but if he touched somebody, he couldn't help doing something to them, like the trade that had given us the money. That had been deliberate. If the trade had touched the Angel first, it would have been different, nothing would have happened unless the Angel touched him back. All touch meant something to the Angel that I didn't understand. There was touching without touching, too. Like things rubbing off on me. And sometimes, when I did touch the Angel, I'd get the feeling that it was maybe more his idea than mine, but I didn't mind that. How many people were going their whole lives never being able to touch an Angel?

We walked together and all around us the street was really coming to life. It was getting colder, too. I tried to make my jacket cover more. The Angel wasn't feeling it. Most of the time hot and cold didn't mean much to him. We saw the three rough trade guys again. The one Angel had gotten the money from was getting into a car. The other two watched it drive away and then walked on. I looked over at the Angel.

Because we took his twenty, I said.

Even if we hadn't, Angel said.

So we went along, the Angel and me, and I could feel how different it was tonight than it was all the other nights we'd walked or stood together. The Angel was kind of pulled back into himself and it seemed to be keeping a check on me, pushing us closer together. I was getting more of those fireworks out of the corners of my eyes but when I'd turn my head to look, they'd vanish. It reminded me of the night I'd found the Angel standing on my corner all by himself in pain. The Angel told me later that was real talent, knowing he was in pain. I never thought of myself as any too talented but the way everyone else had been just ignoring him, I guess I must have had something to see him after all.

The Angel stopped us several feet down from an all-night bookstore. Don't look, he said. Watch the traffic or stare at your feet, but don't look or it won't happen.

There wasn't anything to see right then but I didn't look anyway. That was the way it was sometimes, the Angel telling me it made a difference whether I was watching something or not, something about the other people being conscious of me being conscious of them. I didn't understand but I knew Angel was usually right. So I was watching traffic when the guy came out of the bookstore and got his head punched.

I could almost see it out of the corner of my eye. A lot of movement, arms and legs flying and grunty noises. Other people stopped to look but I kept my eyes on the traffic, some of which was slowing up so they could check out the fight. Next to me, the Angel was stiff all over. Taking it in, what he called the expenditure of emotional kinetic energy. No right, no wrong, little friend, he'd told me. Just energy, like the rest of the universe.

So he took it in and I felt him taking it in and while I was feeling it, a kind of silver fog started creeping around my eyeballs and I was in two places at once. I was watching the traffic and I was in the Angel watching the fight and feeling him charge up like a big battery.

It felt like nothing I'd ever felt before. These two guys slugging it out—well, one guy doing all the slugging and the other skittering around trying to get out from under the fists and having his head punched but good and the Angel drinking it like he was sipping at an empty cup and somehow getting it to have something in it after all. Deep inside him, whatever made the Angel go was getting a little stronger.

I kind of swung back and forth between him and me, or swayed might be more like it was. I wondered about it, because the Angel wasn't touching me. I really was getting to be him, I thought; Angel picked that up and put the thought away to answer later. It was like I was traveling by the fog, being one of us and then the other, for a long time, it seemed, and then after a while I was more me than him again and some of the fog cleared away.

And there was that car, pointed the other way this time and the woman was climbing out of it with this big weird smile on her face, as though she'd won something. She waved at the Angel to come to her.

Bang went the connection between us dead and the Angel shot past me, running away from the car. I went after him. I caught a glimpse of her jumping back into the car and yanking at the gear shift.

Angel wasn't much of a runner. Something funny about his knees. We'd gone maybe a hundred feet when he started wobbling and I could hear him pant. He cut across a Park & Lock that was dark and mostly empty. It was back-to-back with some kind of private parking lot and the fences for each one tried to mark off the same narrow strip of lumpy pavement. They were easy to climb but Angel was too panicked. He just *went* through them before he even thought about it; I knew that because if he'd been thinking, he'd have wanted to save what he'd just charged up for when he really needed out bad enough.

I had to haul myself over the fences in the usual way and when he heard me rattling on the saggy chainlink, he stopped and looked back.

Go, I told him. Don't wait on me!

He shook his head sadly. Little friend, I'm a fool. I could stand to learn from you a little more.

Don't stand, run! I got over the fences and caught up with him. Let's go! I yanked his sleeve as I slogged past and he followed at a clumsy trot.

Have to hide somewhere, he said, camouflage ourselves with people.

I shook my head, thinking we could just run maybe four more blocks and we'd be at the freeway overpass. Below it were the butt-ends of old roads closed off when the freeway had been built. You could hide there the rest of your life and no one would find you. But Angel made me turn right and go down a block to this rundown crack-in-the-wall called Stan's Jigger. I'd never been in there—I'd never made it a practice to go into bars—but the Angel was pushing too hard to argue.

Inside it was smelly and dark and not too happy. The Angel and I went down to the end of the bar and stood under a blood-red light while he searched his pockets for money.

Enough for one drink apiece, he said.

I don't want anything.

You can have soda or something.

The Angel ordered from the bartender, who was suspicious. This was a place for regulars and nobody else, and certainly nobody else like me or the Angel. The Angel knew that even stronger than I did but he just stood and pretended to sip his drink without looking at me. He was all pulled into himself and I was hovering around the edges. I knew he was still pretty panicked and trying to figure out what he could do next. As close as I was, if he had to get real far away, he was going to have a problem and so was I. He'd have to tow me along with him and that wasn't the most practical thing to do.

Maybe he was sorry now he'd let me take him home. He'd been so weak then and now what with all the filtering and stuff I'd done, he couldn't just cut me off without a lot of pain.

I was trying to figure out what I could do for him when the bartender came back and gave us a look that meant order or get out and he'd have liked it better if we got out. So would everyone else there. The few other people standing at the bar weren't looking at us but they knew right where we were, like a sore spot. It wasn't hard to figure out what they thought about us, either, maybe because of me or because of the Angel's beautiful face.

We got to leave, I said to the Angel but he had it in his head this was good camouflage. There wasn't enough money for two more drinks so he smiled at the bartender and slid his hand across the bar and put it on top of the bartender's. It was tricky doing it this way; bartenders and waitresses took more persuading because it wasn't normal for them just to give you something.

The bartender looked at the Angel with his eyes half-closed. He seemed to be thinking it over. But the Angel had just blown a lot going through the fence instead of climbing over it and the fear was scuttling his concentration and I just knew that it wouldn't work. And maybe my knowing that didn't help, either.

The bartender's free hand dipped down below the bar and came up with a small club. "Faggot!" he roared and caught Angel just over the ear. Angel slammed into me and we both crashed to the floor. Plenty of emotional kinetic energy in here, I thought dimly as the guys standing at the bar fell on us and I didn't think anything more as I curled up into a ball under their fists and boots.

We were lucky they didn't much feel like killing anyone. Angel went out the door first and they tossed me out on top of him. As soon as I landed on him, I knew we were both in trouble; something was broken inside him. So much for keeping out of harm's way. I rolled off him and lay on the pavement, staring at the sky and trying to catch my breath. There was blood in my mouth and my nose and my back was on fire.

Angel? I said, after a bit.

He didn't answer. I felt my mind get kind of all loose and runny, like my brains were leaking out my ears. I thought about the trade we'd taken the money from and how I'd been scared of him and his friends and how silly that had been. But then, I was too harmless to live.

The stars were raining silver fireworks down on me. It didn't help.

Angel? I said again.

I rolled over onto my side to reach for him and there she was. The car was parked at the curb and she had Angel under the armpits, dragging him toward the open passenger door. I couldn't tell if he was conscious or not and that scared me. I sat up.

She paused, still holding the Angel. We looked into each other's eyes and I started to understand.

"Help me get him into the car," she said at last. Her voice sounded hard and flat and unnatural. "Then you can get in, too. In the *back* seat."

I was in no shape to take her out. It couldn't have been better for her than if she'd set it up herself. I got up, the pain flaring in me so bad that I almost fell down again and sort of took the Angel's ankles. His ankles were so delicate, almost like a woman's, like hers. I didn't really help much except to guide his feet in as she sat him on the seat and strapped him in with the shoulder harness. I got in the back as she ran around to the other side of the car, her steps real light and peppy, like she'd found a million dollars lying there on the sidewalk.

• • •

We were out on the freeway before the Angel stirred in the shoulder harness. His head lolled from side to side on the back of the seat. I reached up and touched his hair lightly, hoping she couldn't see me do it.

Where are you taking me? the Angel said.

"For a ride," said the woman. "For the moment."

Why does she talk out loud like that? I asked the Angel.

Because she knows it bothers me.

"You know I can focus my thoughts better if I say things out loud," she said. "I'm not like one of your little pushovers." She glanced at me in the rear view mirror. "Just what have you gotten yourself into since you left, darling? Is that a boy or a girl?"

I pretended I didn't care about what she said or that I was too harmless to live or any of that stuff but the way she said it, she meant it to sting.

Friends can be either, Angel said. It doesn't matter which. Where are you taking us?

Now it was *us*. In spite of everything, I almost could have smiled.

"Us? You mean, you and me? Or are you really referring to your little pet back there?"

My friend and I are together. You and I are *not*.

The way the Angel said it made me think he meant more than not together; like he'd been with her once the way he was with me now. The Angel let me know I was right. Silver fireworks started flowing slowly off his head down the back of the seat and I knew there was something wrong about it. There was too much all at once.

"Why can't you talk out loud to me, darling?" the woman said with fakey-sounding petulance. "Just say a few words and make me happy. You have a lovely voice when you use it."

That was true, but the Angel never spoke out loud unless he couldn't get out of it, like when he'd ordered from the bartender. Which had probably helped the bartender decide about what he thought we were, but it was useless to think about that.

"All right," said Angel, and I knew the strain was awful for him. "I've said a few words. Are you happy?" He sagged in the shoulder harness.

"Ecstatic. But it won't make me let you go. I'll drop your pet at the nearest hospital and then we'll go home." She glanced at the Angel as she drove. "I've missed you so much. I can't stand it without you, without you making things happen. Doing your little miracles. You knew I'd get addicted to it, all the things you could do to people. And then you just took off, I didn't know what had happened to you. And it *hurt*." Her voice turned kind of pitiful, like a little kid's. "I was in *real* pain. You must have been, too. Weren't you? Well, *weren't* you?"

Yes, the Angel said. I was in pain, too.

I remembered him standing on my corner where I'd hung out all that time by myself until he came. Standing there in pain. I didn't know why or from what then, I just took him home and after a little while, the pain went away. When he decided we were together, I guess.

The silvery flow over the back of the car seat thickened. I cupped my hands under it and it was like my brain was lighting up with pictures. I saw the Angel before he was my Angel in this really nice house, the woman's house, and how she'd take him places, restaurants or stores or parties, thinking at him real hard so that he was all filled up with her and had to do what she wanted him to. Steal sometimes; other times, weird stuff, make people do silly things like suddenly start singing or taking their clothes off. That was mostly at the parties, though she made a waiter she didn't like burn himself with a pot of coffee. She'd get men, too, through the Angel, and they'd think it was the greatest idea in the world to go to bed with her. Then she'd make the Angel show her the others, the ones that had been sent here the way he had for crimes nobody could have understood, like the waitress with no face. She'd look at them, sometimes try to do things to them to make them uncomfortable or unhappy. But mostly she'd just stare.

It wasn't like that in the very beginning, the Angel said weakly and I knew he was ashamed.

It's okay, I told him. People can be nice at first, I know that. Then they find out about you.

The woman laughed. "You two are so sweet and pathetic. Like a couple of little children. I guess that's what you were looking for, wasn't it, darling? Except children can be cruel, too, can't they? So you got this— creature for yourself." She looked at me in the rear view mirror again as she slowed down a little and for a moment I was afraid she'd seen what I was doing with the silvery stuff still pouring out of the Angel. It was starting to slow now. There wasn't much time left. I wanted to scream but the Angel was calming me for what was coming next. "What happened to you, anyway?"

Tell her, said the Angel. To stall for time, I knew, keep her occupied.

I was born funny, I said. I had both sexes.

"A hermaphrodite!" she exclaimed with real delight.

She loves freaks, the Angel said but she didn't pay any attention.

There was an operation but things went wrong. They kept trying to fix it as I got older but my body didn't have the right kind of chemistry or something. My parents were ashamed. I left after a while.

"You poor thing," she said, not meaning anything like that. "You were just what darling, here, needed, weren't you? Just a little nothing, no demands, no desires. For anything." Her voice got all hard. "They could probably fix you up now, you know."

I don't want it. I left all that behind a long time ago, I don't need it.

"Just the sort of little pet that would be perfect for you," she said to the Angel. "Sorry I have to tear you away. But I can't get along without you now. Life is so boring. And empty. And—" She sounded puzzled. "And like there's nothing more to live for since you left me."

That's not me, said the Angel. That's you.

"No, it's a lot of you, too, and you know it. You know you're addictive to human beings, you knew that when you came here—when they *sent* you here. Hey, you, pet, do you know what his crime was, why they sent him to this little backwater penal colony of a planet?"

Yeah, I know, I said. I really didn't, but I wasn't going to tell her that.

"What do you think about that, little pet neuter?" she said gleefully, hitting the accelerator pedal and speeding up. "What do you think of the crime of refusing to mate?"

The Angel made a sort of an out loud groan and lunged at the steering wheel. The car swerved wildly and I fell backwards, the silvery stuff from the Angel going all over me. I tried to keep scooping it into my mouth the way I'd been doing but it was flying all over the place now. I heard the crunch as the tires left the road and went onto the shoulder. Something struck the side of the car, probably the guard rail, and made it fishtail, throwing me down on the floor. Up front the woman was screaming and cursing and the Angel wasn't making a sound but in my head, I could hear him sort of keening. Whatever happened, this would be it. The Angel had told me all that time ago after I'd taken him home that they didn't last long after they got here, the exiles from his world and other worlds. Things tended to happen to them, even if they latched on to someone like me or the woman. They'd be in accidents or the people here would kill them. Like antibodies in a human rejecting something or fighting a disease. At least I belonged here, but it looked like I was going to die in a car accident with the Angel and the woman both. I didn't care.

The car swerved back onto the highway for a few seconds and then pitched to the right again. Suddenly there was nothing under us and then we thumped down on something, not road but dirt or grass or something, bombing madly up and down. I pulled myself up on the back of the seat just in time to see the sign coming at us at an angle. The corner of it started to go through the windshield on the woman's side and then all I saw for a long time was the biggest display of silver fireworks ever.

• • •

It was hard to be gentle with him. Every move hurt but I didn't want to leave him sitting in the car next to her, even if she was dead. Being in the back seat had kept most of the glass from flying into me but I was still shaking some out of my hair and the impact hadn't done much for my back.

I laid the Angel out on the lumpy grass a little ways from the car and looked around. We were maybe a hundred yards from the highway, near a road that ran parallel to it. It was dark but I could still read the sign that had come through the windshield and split the woman's head in half. It said, CONSTRUCTION AHEAD, REDUCE SPEED. Far off on the other road, I could see a flashing yellow light and at first I was afraid it was the police or something but it stayed where it was and I realized that must be the construction.

"Friend," whispered the Angel, startling me. He'd never spoken aloud to me, not directly.

Don't talk, I said, bending over him, trying to figure out some way I could touch him, just for comfort. There wasn't anything else I could do now.

"I have to," he said, still whispering. "It's almost all gone. Did you get it?"

Mostly, I said. Not all.

"I meant for you to have it."

I know.

"I don't know that it will really do you any good." His breath kind of bubbled in his throat. I could see something wet and shiny on his mouth but it wasn't silver fireworks. "But it's yours. You can do as you like with it. Live on it the way I did. Get what you need when you need it. But you can live as a human, too. Eat. Work. However, whatever."

I'm not human, I said. I'm not any more human than you, even if I do belong here.

"Yes you are, little friend. I haven't made you any less human," he said, and coughed some. "I'm not sorry I wouldn't mate. I couldn't mate with my own. It was too, I don't know, too little of me, too much of them, something. I couldn't bond, it would have been nothing but emptiness. The Great Sin, to be unable to give, because the universe knows only less or more and I insisted that it would be good or bad. So they sent me here. But in the end, you know, they got their way, little friend." I felt his hand on me for a moment before it fell away. "I did it after all. Even if it wasn't with my own."

The bubbling in his throat stopped. I sat next to him for a while in the dark. Finally I felt it, the Angel stuff. It was kind of fluttery-churny, like too much coffee on an empty stomach. I closed my eyes and lay down on the grass, shivering. Maybe some of it was shock but I don't think so. The silver fireworks started, in my head this time, and with them came a lot of pictures I couldn't understand. Stuff about the Angel and where he'd come from and the way they mated. It was a lot like how we'd been together, the Angel and me. They looked a lot like us but there were a lot of differences, too, things I couldn't make out. I couldn't make out how they'd sent him here, either—by light, in, like, little bundles or something. It didn't make any sense to me but I guessed an Angel could be light. Silver fireworks.

I must have passed out or something because when I opened my eyes, it felt like I'd been lying there a long time. It was still dark, though. I sat up and reached for the Angel, thinking I ought to hide his body.

He was gone. There was just a sort of wet sandy stuff where he'd been.

I looked at the car and her. All that was still there. Somebody was going to see it soon. I didn't want to be around for that.

Everything still hurt but I managed to get to the other road and start walking back toward the city. It was like I could feel it now, the way the Angel must have, as though it were vibrating like a drum or ringing like a bell with all kinds of stuff, people laughing and crying and loving and hating and being afraid and everything else that happens to people. The stuff that the Angel took in, energy, that I could take in now if I wanted.

And I knew that taking it in that way, it would be bigger than anything all those people had, bigger than anything I could have had if things hadn't gone wrong with me all those years ago.

I wasn't so sure I wanted it. Like the Angel, refusing to mate back where he'd come from. He wouldn't, there, and I couldn't, here. Except now I could do something else.

I wasn't so sure I wanted it. But I didn't think I'd be able to stop it, either, any more than I could stop my heart from beating. Maybe it wasn't really such a good thing or a right thing. But it was like the Angel said: the universe doesn't know good or bad, only less or more.

Yeah. I heard *that*.

I thought about the waitress with no face. I could find them all now, all the ones from the other places, other worlds that sent them away for some kind of alien crimes nobody would have understood. I could find them all. They threw away their outcasts, I'd tell them, but here, we kept ours. And here's how. Here's how you live in a universe that only knows less or more.

I kept walking toward the city.

THE FIRST CONTACT
WITH THE GORGONIDS

Ursula K. Le Guin

Mrs. Jerry Debree, the heroine of Grong Crossing, liked to look pretty. It was important to Jerry in his business contacts, of course, and also it made her feel more confident and kind of happy to know that her cellophane was recent and her eyelashes really well glued on and that the highlighter blush was bringing out her cheekbones like the nice girl at the counter had said. But it was beginning to be hard to feel fresh and look pretty as this desert kept getting hotter and hotter and redder and redder until it looked, really, almost like what she had always thought the Bad Place would look like, only not so many people. In fact none.

"Could we have passed it, do you think?" she ventured at last, and received without surprise the exasperation she had safety-valved from him: "How the fuck could we have *passed* it when we haven't *passed* one fucking *thing* except those fucking *bushes* for ninety miles? *Christ* you're dumb."

Jerry's language was a pity. And sometimes it made it so hard to talk to him. She had had the least little tiny sort of feeling, woman's intuition maybe, that the men that had told him how to get to Grong Crossing were teasing him, having a little joke. He had been talking so loud in the hotel bar about how disappointed he had been with the Corroboree after flying all the way out from Adelaide to see it. He kept comparing it to the Indian dance they had seen at Taos. Actually he had been very bored and restless at Taos and they had had to leave in the middle so he could have a drink and she never had got to see the people with the masks come, but now he talked about how they really knew how to put on a native show in the U.S.A. He said a few scruffy abos jumping around weren't going to give tourists from the real world anything to write home about. The Aussies ought to visit Disney World and find out how to do the real thing, he said.

She agreed with that; she loved Disney World. It was the only thing in Florida, where they had to live now that Jerry was ACEO, that she liked much. One of the Australian men at the bar had seen Disneyland and agreed that it was amazing, or maybe he meant amusing; what he said was amizing. He seemed to be a nice man. Bruce, he said his name was, and his friend's name was Bruce too. "Common sort of name here," he said, only he said nime, but he meant name, she was quite sure. When Jerry went on complaining about the Corroboree, the first Bruce said, "Well, mite, you might go out to Grong Crossing, if you really want to see the real thing—right, Bruce?"

At first the other Bruce didn't seem to know what he meant, and that was when her woman's intuition woke up. But pretty soon both Bruces were talking away about this place, Grong Crossing, way out in "the bush," where they were certain to meet real abos really living in the desert. "Near Alice Springs," Jerry said knowledgeably, but it wasn't, they said; it was still farther west from here. They gave directions so precisely that it was clear they knew what they were talking about. "Few hours' drive, that's all," Bruce said, "but y'see most tourists want to keep on the beaten path. This is a bit more on the inside track."

"Bang-up shows," said Bruce. "Nightly Corroborees."

"Hotel any better than this dump?" Jerry asked, and they laughed. No hotel, they explained. "It's like a safari, see—tents under the stars. Never rines," said Bruce.

"Marvelous food, though," Bruce said. "Fresh kangaroo chops.

Kangaroo hunts daily, see. Witchetty grubs along with the drinks before dinner. Roughing it in luxury, I'd call it; right, Bruce?"

"Absolutely," said Bruce.

"Friendly, are they, these abos?" Jerry asked.

"Oh, salt of the earth. Treat you like kings. Think white men are sort of gods, y'know," Bruce said. Jerry nodded.

So Jerry wrote down all the directions, and here they were driving and driving in the old station wagon that was all there was to rent in the small town they'd been at for the Corroboree, and by now you only knew the road was a road because it was perfectly straight forever. Jerry had been in a good humor at first. "This'll be something to shove up that bastard Thiel's ass," he said. His friend Thiel was always going to places like Tibet and having wonderful adventures and showing videos of himself with yaks. Jerry had bought a very expensive camcorder for this trip, and now he said, "Going to shoot me some abos. Show that fucking Thiel and his musk-oxes!" But as the morning went on and the road went on and the desert went on—did they call it "the bush" because there was one little thorny bush once a mile or so?—he got hotter and hotter and redder and redder, just like the desert. And she began to feel depressed and like her mascara was caking.

She was wondering if after another forty miles (four was her lucky number) she could say, "Maybe we ought to turn back?" for the first time, when he said, "There!"

There was something ahead, all right.

"There hasn't been any sign," she said, dubious. "They didn't say anything about a hill, did they?"

"Hell, that's no hill, that's a rock—what do they call it—some big fucking red rock—"

"Ayers Rock?" She had read the Welcome to Down Under flyer in the hotel in Adelaide while Jerry was at the plastics conference. "But that's in the middle of Australia, isn't it?"

"So where the fuck do you think we are? In the middle of Australia! What do you think this is, fucking East Germany?" He was shouting, and he speeded up. The terribly straight road shot them straight at the hill, or rock, or whatever it was. It *wasn't* Ayers Rock, she *knew* that, but there wasn't any use irritating Jerry, especially when he started shouting.

It was reddish, and shaped kind of like a huge VW bug, only lumpier;

and there were certainly people all around it, and at first she was very glad to see them. Their utter isolation—they hadn't seen another car or farm or anything for two hours—had scared her. Then as they got closer she thought the people looked rather funny. Funnier than the ones at the Corroboree even. "I guess they're natives," she said aloud.

"What the shit did you expect, Frenchmen?" Jerry said, but he said it like a joke, and she laughed. But—"Oh! Goodness!" she said involuntarily, getting her first clear sight of one of the natives.

"Big fellows, huh," he said. "Bushmen, they call 'em."

That didn't seem right, but she was still getting over the shock of seeing that tall, thin, black-and-white, weird person. It had been just standing looking at the car, only she couldn't see its eyes. Heavy brows and thick, hairy eyebrows hid them. Black, ropy hair hung over half its face and stuck out from behind its ears.

"Are they—are they painted?" she asked weakly.

"They always paint 'emselves up like that." His contempt for her ignorance was reassuring.

"They almost don't look human," she said, very softly so as not to hurt their feelings, if they spoke English, since Jerry had stopped the car and flung the doors open and was rummaging out the video camera.

"Hold this!"

She held it. Five or six of the tall black-and-white people had sort of turned their way, but they all seemed to be busy with something at the foot of the hill or rock or whatever it was. There were some things that might be tents. Nobody came to welcome them or anything, but she was actually just as glad they didn't.

"Hold this! Oh for Chrissake what did you do with the—All right, just give it here."

"Jerry, I wonder if we should ask them," she said.

"Ask who what?" he growled, having trouble with the cassette thing.

"The people here—if it's all right to photograph. Remember at Taos they said that when the—"

"For fuck sake you don't need fucking *permission* to photograph a bunch of *natives!* God! Did you ever *look* at the fucking *National Geographic*? Shit! *Permission!*"

It really wasn't any use when he started shouting. And the people didn't seem to be interested in what he was doing. Although it was quite hard to be sure what direction they were actually looking.

"Aren't you going to get out of the fucking *car?*"

"It's so hot," she said.

He didn't really mind it when she was afraid of getting too hot or sun-burned or anything, because he liked being stronger and tougher. She probably could even have said that she was afraid of the natives, because he liked to be braver than her, too; but sometimes he got angry when she was afraid, like the time he made her eat that poisonous fish, or a fish that might or might not be poisonous, in Japan, because she said she was afraid to, and she threw up and embarrassed everybody. So she just sat in the car and kept the engine on and the air-conditioning on, although the window on her side was open.

Jerry had his camera up on his shoulder now and was panning the scene—the faraway hot red horizon, the queer rock-hill-thing with shiny places in it like glass, the black, burned-looking ground around it, and the people swarming all over. There were forty or fifty of them at least. It only dawned on her now that if they were wearing any clothes at all, she didn't know which was clothes and which was skin, because they were so strange-shaped, and painted or colored all in stripes and spots of white on black, not like zebras but more complicated, more like skeleton suits but not exactly. And they must be eight feet tall, but their arms were short, almost like kangaroos'. And their hair was like black ropes standing up all over their heads. It was embarrassing to look at people without clothes on, but you couldn't really see anything like *that*. In fact she couldn't tell, actually, if they were men or women.

They were all busy with their work or ceremony or whatever it was. Some of them were handling some things like big, thin, golden leaves, others were doing something with cords or wires. They didn't seem to be talking, but there was all the time in the air a soft, drumming, dron-ing, rising and falling, deep sound, like cats purring or voices far away.

Jerry started walking towards them.

"Be careful," she said faintly. He paid no attention, of course.

They paid no attention to him either, as far as she could see, and he kept filming, swinging the camera around. When he got right up close to a couple of them, they turned towards him. She couldn't see their eyes at all, but what happened was their *hair* sort of stood up and bent towards Jerry—each thick, black rope about a foot long moving around and bending down exactly as if it were peering at him. At that, her own hair tried to stand up, and the blast of the air conditioner ran like ice down her sweaty arms. She got out of the car and called his name.

He kept filming.

She went towards him as fast as she could on the cindery, stony soil in her high-heeled sandals.

"Jerry, come back. I think—"

"Shut up!" he yelled so savagely that she stopped short for a moment. But she could see the hair better now, and she could see that it did have eyes, and mouths too, with little red tongues darting out.

"Jerry, come back," she said. "They're not natives, they're Space Aliens. That's their saucer." She knew from the *Sun* that there had been sightings down here in Australia.

"Shut the fuck up," he said. "Hey, big fella, give me a little action, huh? Don't just stand there. Dancee-dancee, OK?" His eye was glued to the camera.

"Jerry," she said, her voice sticking in her throat, as one of the Space Aliens pointed with its little weak-looking arm and hand at the car. Jerry shoved the camera right up close to its head, and at that it put its hand over the lens. That made Jerry mad, of course, and he yelled, "Get the fuck off that!" And he actually looked at the Space Alien, not through the camera but face to face. "Oh, gee," he said.

And his hand went to his hip. He always carried a gun, because it was an American's right to bear arms and there were so many drug addicts these days. He had smuggled it through the airport inspection the way he knew how. Nobody was going to disarm *him*.

She saw perfectly clearly what happened. The Space Alien opened its eyes.

There were eyes under the dark, shaggy brows; they had been kept closed till now. Now they were open and looked once straight at Jerry, and he turned to stone. He just stood there, one hand on the camera and one reaching for his gun, motionless.

Several more Space Aliens had gathered round. They all had their eyes shut, except for the ones at the ends of their hair. Those glittered and shone, and the little red tongues flickered in and out, and the humming, droning sound was much louder. Many of the hair-snakes writhed to look at her. Her knees buckled and her heart thudded in her throat, but she had to get to Jerry.

She passed right between two huge Space Aliens and reached him and became large enough to be called the first cities; before the first city held a parade in honor of its first confirmed mugging; before Independence and the Corporate Communities and the opening of Lunar Disney on the Sea of Tranquility. These days, the Moon itself is no big deal except for rubes and old-timers. Nobody looks out the windows; they're far too interested in their sims, or their virts, or their newspads or (for a vanishingly literate few) their paperback novels, to care about the sight of the airless world waxing large in the darkness outside.

I wanted to shout at them. I wanted to make a great big eloquent speech about what they were missing by taking it all for granted, and about their total failure to appreciate what others had gone through to pave the way. But that wouldn't have moved anybody. It just would have established me as just another boring old fart.

So I stayed quiet until we landed, and then I rolled my overnighter down the aisle, and I made my way through the vast carpeted terminal at Armstrong Interplanetary (thinking all the while *carpet, carpet, why is there carpet, dammit, there shouldn't be carpeting on the moon*). Then I hopped a tram to my hotel, and I confirmed that the front desk had followed instructions and provided me one of their few hideously expensive rooms with an Outside View. Then I went upstairs and thought it all again when I saw that the view was just an alien distortion of the moon I had known. Though it was night, and the landscape was as dark as the constellations of manmade illumination peppered across its cratered surface would now ever allow it to be, I still saw marquee-sized advertisements for soy houses, strip clubs, rotating restaurants, golden arches, miniature golf courses, and the one-sixth-g Biggest Rollercoaster In The Solar System. The Earth, with Europe and Africa centered, hung silently above the blight.

I tried to imagine two gentle old people, and a golden retriever dog, wandering around somewhere in the garish paradise framed by that window.

I failed.

I wondered whether it felt good or bad to be here. I wasn't tired, which I supposed I could attribute to the sensation of renewed strength and vigor that older people are supposed to feel after making the transition to lower gravities. Certainly, my knees, which had been bothering me for more than a decade now, weren't giving me a single twinge here. But

patted him—"Jerry, wake up!" she said. He was just like stone, paralyzed. "Oh," she said, and tears ran down her face. "Oh, what should I do, what can I do?" She looked around in despair at the tall, thin, black-and-white faces looming above her, white teeth showing, eyes tight shut, hairs staring and stirring and murmuring. The murmur was soft, almost like music, not angry, soothing. She watched two tall Space Aliens pick up Jerry quite gently, as if he were a tiny little boy—a stiff one—and carry him carefully to the car.

They poked him into the back seat lengthwise, but he didn't fit. She ran to help. She let down the back seat so there was room for him in the back. The Space Aliens arranged him and tucked the video camera in beside him, then straightened up, their hairs looking down at her with little twinkly eyes. They hummed softly, and pointed with their childish arms back down the road.

"Yes," she said. "Thank you. Good-bye!"

They hummed.

She got in and closed the window and turned the car around there on a wide place in the road—and there *was* a signpost, Grong Crossing, although she didn't see any crossroad.

She drove back, carefully at first because she was shaky, then faster and faster because she should get Jerry to the doctor, of course, but also because she loved driving on long straight roads very fast, like this. Jerry never let her drive except in town.

The paralysis was total and permanent, which would have been terrible, except that she could afford full-time, round-the-clock, first-class care for poor Jerry, because of the really good deals she made with the TV people and then with the rights people for the video. First it was shown all over the world as "Space Aliens Land in Australian Outback," but then it became part of real science and history as "Grong Crossing, South Australia: The First Contact With the Gorgonids." In the voice-over they told how it was her, Annie Laurie Debree, who had been the first human to talk with our friends from Outer Space, even before they sent the ambassadors to Canberra and Reykjavik. There was only one good shot of her on the film, and Jerry had been sort of shaking, and her highlighter was kind of streaked, but that was all right. She was the heroine.

SUNDAY NIGHT YAMS AT MINNIE AND EARL'S

ADAM-TROY CASTRO

Frontiers never die. They just become theme parks.

I spent most of my shuttle ride to Nearside mulling sour though[ts] about that. It's the kind of thing that only bothers lonely an[d] nostalgic old men, especially when we're old enough to remember th[e] days when a trip to Luna was not a routine commuter run, but instea[d] a never-ending series of course corrections, systems checks, best-and[-] worst-case simulations, and random unexpected crises ranging fron[m] ominous burning smells to the surreal balls of floating upchuck tha[t] got into everywhere if we didn't get over our nausea fast enough t[o] clean them up. Folks of my vintage remember what it was to spend hal[f] their lives in passionate competition with dozens of other frighteningl[y] qualified people just to earn themselves seats on cramped rigs outfitte[d] by the lowest corporate bidders—and then to look down at the ragge[d] landscape of Sister Moon and know that the sight itself was a privileg[e] well worth the effort. But that's old news now: before the first develop- ment crews gave way to the first settlements; before the first settlements patted him—"Jerry, wake up!" she said. He was just like stone, paralyzed. "Oh," she said, and tears ran down her face. "Oh, what should I do, what can I do?" She looked around in despair at the tall, thin, black-and-white faces looming above her, white teeth showing, eyes tight shut, hairs staring and stirring and murmuring. The murmur was soft, almost like music, not angry, soothing. She watched two tall Space Aliens pick up Jerry quite gently, as if he were a tiny little boy—a stiff one—and carry him carefully to the car.

They poked him into the back seat lengthwise, but he didn't fit. She ran to help. She let down the back seat so there was room for him in the back. The Space Aliens arranged him and tucked the video camera in beside him, then straightened up, their hairs looking down at her with little twinkly eyes. They hummed softly, and pointed with their childish arms back down the road.

"Yes," she said. "Thank you. Good-bye!"

They hummed.

She got in and closed the window and turned the car around there on a wide place in the road—and there *was* a signpost, Grong Crossing, although she didn't see any crossroad.

She drove back, carefully at first because she was shaky, then faster and faster because she should get Jerry to the doctor, of course, but also because she loved driving on long straight roads very fast, like this. Jerry never let her drive except in town.

The paralysis was total and permanent, which would have been terrible, except that she could afford full-time, round-the-clock, first-class care for poor Jerry, because of the really good deals she made with the TV people and then with the rights people for the video. First it was shown all over the world as "Space Aliens Land in Australian Outback," but then it became part of real science and history as "Grong Crossing, South Australia: The First Contact With the Gorgonids." In the voice-over they told how it was her, Annie Laurie Debree, who had been the first human to talk with our friends from Outer Space, even before they sent the ambassadors to Canberra and Reykjavik. There was only one good shot of her on the film, and Jerry had been sort of shaking, and her highlighter was kind of streaked, but that was all right. She was the heroine.

SUNDAY NIGHT YAMS AT MINNIE AND EARL'S

ADAM-TROY CASTRO

Frontiers never die. They just become theme parks.

I spent most of my shuttle ride to Nearside mulling sour thoughts about that. It's the kind of thing that only bothers lonely and nostalgic old men, especially when we're old enough to remember the days when a trip to Luna was not a routine commuter run, but instead a never-ending series of course corrections, systems checks, best-and-worst-case simulations, and random unexpected crises ranging from ominous burning smells to the surreal balls of floating upchuck that got into everywhere if we didn't get over our nausea fast enough to clean them up. Folks of my vintage remember what it was to spend half their lives in passionate competition with dozens of other frighteningly qualified people just to earn themselves seats on cramped rigs outfitted by the lowest corporate bidders—and then to look down at the ragged landscape of Sister Moon and know that the sight itself was a privilege well worth the effort. But that's old news now: before the first development crews gave way to the first settlements; before the first settlements became large enough to be called the first cities; before the first city held a parade in honor of its first confirmed mugging; before Independence and the Corporate Communities and the opening of Lunar Disney on the Sea of Tranquility. These days, the Moon itself is no big deal except for rubes and old-timers. Nobody looks out the windows; they're far too interested in their sims, or their virts, or their newspads or (for a vanishingly literate few) their paperback novels, to care about the sight of the airless world waxing large in the darkness outside.

I wanted to shout at them. I wanted to make a great big eloquent speech about what they were missing by taking it all for granted, and about their total failure to appreciate what others had gone through to pave the way. But that wouldn't have moved anybody. It just would have established me as just another boring old fart.

So I stayed quiet until we landed, and then I rolled my overnighter down the aisle, and I made my way through the vast carpeted terminal at Armstrong Interplanetary (thinking all the while *carpet, carpet, why is there carpet, dammit, there shouldn't be carpeting on the moon*). Then I hopped a tram to my hotel, and I confirmed that the front desk had followed instructions and provided me one of their few hideously expensive rooms with an Outside View. Then I went upstairs and thought it all again when I saw that the view was just an alien distortion of the moon I had known. Though it was night, and the landscape was as dark as the constellations of manmade illumination peppered across its cratered surface would now ever allow it to be, I still saw marquee-sized advertisements for soy houses, strip clubs, rotating restaurants, golden arches, miniature golf courses, and the one-sixth-g Biggest Rollercoaster In The Solar System. The Earth, with Europe and Africa centered, hung silently above the blight.

I tried to imagine two gentle old people, and a golden retriever dog, wandering around somewhere in the garish paradise framed by that window.

I failed.

I wondered whether it felt good or bad to be here. I wasn't tired, which I supposed I could attribute to the sensation of renewed strength and vigor that older people are supposed to feel after making the transition to lower gravities. Certainly, my knees, which had been bothering me for more than a decade now, weren't giving me a single twinge here. But